Changeling Press LLC

ChangelingPress.com

Rocky/Bull Duet

Harley Wylde

Rocky/Bull Duet
Harley Wylde

All rights reserved.
Copyright ©2018 Harley Wylde

ISBN: 9781730894503

Publisher:
Changeling Press LLC
315 N. Centre St.
Martinsburg, WV 25404
ChangelingPress.com

Printed in the U.S.A.

Editor: Crystal Esau
Cover Artist: Bryan Keller

The individual stories in this anthology have been previously released in E-Book format.

No part of this publication may be reproduced or shared by any electronic or mechanical means, including but not limited to reprinting, photocopying, or digital reproduction, without prior written permission from Changeling Press LLC.

This book contains sexually explicit scenes and adult language which some may find offensive and which is not appropriate for a young audience. Changeling Press books are for sale to adults, only, as defined by the laws of the country in which you made your purchase.

Table of Contents

Rocky (Dixie Reapers MC 3) 4
   Chapter One 5
   Chapter Two..17
   Chapter Three 28
   Chapter Four 44
   Chapter Five 55
   Chapter Six 72
   Chapter Seven 82
   Chapter Eight 94
   Chapter Nine 106
   Chapter Ten 122
Bull (Dixie Reapers MC 4) 140
   Prologue 141
   Chapter One 143
   Chapter Two..155
   Chapter Three 165
   Chapter Four 183
   Chapter Five 198
   Chapter Six 222
   Chapter Seven 240
   Chapter Eight 254
   Chapter Nine 265
   Epilogue 273
Harley Wylde 277
Changeling Press E-Books....................................278

Rocky (Dixie Reapers MC 3)
Harley Wylde

Mara: I was daddy's little girl, until he didn't come home one day. Mom moved on, married a rich guy I can't stand, and his son, Sebastian Rossi, wants what he can't have -- me. I didn't realize when I chose to run that I would crash down a mountain, or that the man who pulled me from the wreckage would rescue me in every way that counts. Rocky is the biggest, sexiest badass I've ever seen. And the more time I spend with him, the more I want to feel his lips on mine, his hands holding me, his body claiming me. I want him so bad I can taste it, but the stubborn man says I'm too young. I'll just have to prove him wrong.

Rocky: All I wanted was to brood in peace and quiet on my mountaintop while I tried to outrun my demons. I never expected that past to show up in the form of a sexy-as-fuck woman -- a woman I shouldn't touch. I'm not only twenty years older than her, I'm part of the reason her dad never came home. I'll do anything it takes to keep her safe, even go home to Alabama. My brothers, the Dixie Reapers, will help protect her. I'm just not sure who's going to protect her from me, because if I ever get my hands on all those curves, I'm not ever going to let her go.

Chapter One

Mara

My hands clenched the wheel tighter as my small car careened around another curve on the icy mountain road. How the weather could be this bad in early fall, I didn't know. My heart raced in my chest, and my gaze shot to the rearview mirror. Still alone. If they were following me, I didn't see them. Even Sebastian's men wouldn't be dumb enough to drive these roads as fast as I was taking them, would they? They were New Yorkers, though, and would be used to bad driving conditions. I, however, was a California girl and hadn't had much experience driving on icy and snow-covered roads.

Something darted across the road, and I reflexively hit the brakes. My car fishtailed, then started to slide. A scream tore from my throat as the small compact crashed through the railing and down the side of the mountain. The crunch of metal made my heart beat faster, and I wondered if I was about to die. Glass exploded into the car as it bounced against the mountainside. My head slammed into the steering wheel more than once, and black dots swam across my vision.

The car landed upside down at the bottom of the craggy cliff. My harsh breathing filled the air as I tried to focus. I was dazed and hung limply from the seat belt, my hands brushing the roof of the car. Blood trickled into my hair and more ran down my arm. I groaned, feeling battered and bruised, but thankful to be alive. I didn't know how long I hung there… minutes… hours… but the crunch of snow alerted me to another presence. I hoped like hell it wasn't Sebastian or his men. I'd rather die than see them.

A gruff voice cursed, one I didn't recognize.

"Hello?" I called out, my voice weaker than usual. "Help. Please, help me."

For a moment, I wondered if I should have kept quiet. Just because I didn't recognize the man outside my car didn't mean he wouldn't hurt me. I didn't know everyone in Sebastian's employ, and there were monsters out in the world other than the man who wanted to claim me. As if I'd ever let him touch me!

Denim-clad legs came into view with massive feet encased in brown boots. The man dropped to one knee, his gloved hand braced in the snow as he peered into what was left of my car. Blue eyes met mine, and my breath stilled. Fine lines fanned from the corners, and his nose looked like it had been broken at some point. But that was all I could see of the man. His face was covered in a beard, and the parts of his hair not covered by a hat spilled around his face, looking as if it hadn't seen a brush today.

"Don't move," he said.

Something about that voice, dark and commanding, sent a chill down my spine. Not in a bad way, though. Something about that voice made me want to obey. The man rose to his feet, and his hands closed around the door of my car, or what was left of it. The metal groaned as he ripped the door off and flung it away. My mouth dropped at the brute strength on display. How strong exactly did you have to be to rip off a car door? I'd never seen anything like it.

His hands, now bare, reached for me. The seat belt wouldn't release, and he reached into his pocket, withdrawing a knife. He easily sliced through the belt. I fell to the top of the car, and hands far gentler than I'd have expected pulled me from the wreckage. As the man stood, lifting me as if I were no more than a child,

I realized that the hunk of man who had helped me was way taller than my first impression. And much, much broader.

"My bag," I said softly.

He grunted and eased me down. I wobbled a moment, my hand braced on his wide chest. When I got my footing, he released me long enough to pull my bag from the front seat. It didn't have much in it, but wherever I was going, I would need the things inside. The man slung the bag over his shoulder before lifting me once more, then we were off, striding through the knee-deep snow. Or rather, he was walking through knee-deep snow.

"I'm Mara," I said. "Mara O'Malley."

His gaze flicked down to mine. "Rocky."

I waited, but no last name was forthcoming, and I wasn't going to press him for it. He didn't have to pull me from that car. He could have left me for the wildlife to find, or to freeze to death and not be found until spring when everything thawed out.

Snow began to fall in thick gusts, and soon I couldn't see in front of my face. The man holding me trudged forward through the ever-thickening snow, not stopping, not even slowing down. I didn't know how long we walked, but soon I saw a structure come into view. No. A cabin. There was a wide porch across the front and a large stack of wood near the door. Another pile of wood peeked around the corner of the house with a tarp over the top.

Rocky clomped up the steps and pushed open the front door. The crackle of a fire welcomed us, and I moaned as the warmth from inside the house licked at my skin. I was frozen everywhere. He eased me down onto the bearskin rug in front of the fireplace and pulled a blanket from the couch, wrapping it around my shoulders.

My teeth chattered with such force I thought they might break, and I trembled from head to toe. I watched the mesmerizing flames as Rocky stepped away. I heard him trudging upstairs, only to return a few minutes later with two thick pairs of wool socks, some sweatpants, and a flannel shirt clutched in his massive hands. He crouched in front of me and slowly removed my shoes and socks.

I let out a squeak when he reached for the top of my jeggings and began sliding them down my legs. Too stunned to do much but stare, I didn't protest as he pulled the blanket from my shoulders and removed my coat and sweater. Even though his gaze didn't stray anywhere for too long, I felt exposed. No one had ever seen me in my underwear before, and I knew I should say something. Then again, he probably didn't like women with as much meat on their bones as I had. My thighs were thick and jiggled when I walked, and my ass should probably have been assigned its own zip code. And while my breasts were large and sometimes drew male attention, they weren't big enough to make my rounded stomach look any smaller.

His gaze roamed my body before he rose to his feet and disappeared again, leaving me mostly naked in front of the fire. When he returned, there was a wet rag clutched in one hand and a tube of ointment in the other. Rocky crouched in front of me again, gently wiping the blood from my body. I winced as he applied the ointment to my cuts. There was one on my forehead and another near my collarbone, and my arm was dotted with smaller cuts from the broken glass. He sat back on his heels and studied me again, his gaze caressing every inch of my body. Did he like what he saw?

Rocky grunted, then rose to his feet, carrying the ointment and rag with him. He came back a moment later, kneeling in front of me again. My mouth opened and no words came out as the gruff man in front of me slid the flannel shirt up my arms and quickly began fastening it. When he was finished, he pulled the sweats up my legs, rolling the waist and ankles a few times, then put both pairs of socks on my feet. His gaze met my startled one. I hadn't had someone dress me since I was a small child, but the feel of his hands against my skin felt anything but parental. Warmth suffused me, and I began to tingle for a reason other than being cold.

"I'll wash and dry your clothes," he said, rising to his feet and leaving me in front of the toasty fire once more, my discarded clothes clutched in his hands.

I didn't know what to think of my rescuer. He was a man of few words, but despite his size, I didn't feel afraid of him. I should. I was alone, in the middle of nowhere, with a huge man I knew nothing about. But his eyes… the way he looked at me made me feel small and precious, as if he would keep me safe always. It was crazy. Maybe I was crazy.

But whatever the mountain man wanted from me, whatever he tried to take, wouldn't be any worse than what I faced if Sebastian got his hands on me. I'd rather go through anything other than that. Rocky might not be the type of man I was used to being around, but at least he didn't have the eyes of a killer. His gaze was warm, and for the first time in my life, I wasn't worried about what tomorrow would bring.

Rocky returned a short while later, a steaming mug in his hands.

"Coffee," he said, although it came out more like a grunt.

I accepted the cup, the warmth of it seeping into my chilled fingers, and took a sip. Despite the bitter taste, I didn't wince. I'd always been more of a caramel skinny latte kind of girl, but the hot coffee slid down my throat and began to warm me from the inside out. Rocky watched me a few minutes before walking off again, his boots thudding against the wood floors.

When the coffee was gone, I set the cup aside and tried to push myself to my feet. I groaned, and the room spun as I staggered upright. As everything began to tilt and I felt myself falling back to the floor, strong arms wrapped around me, drawing my body tight against my rescuer. Rocky's hands splayed across my back, and I couldn't remember ever feeling so delicate. I was small in stature at just a hair over five feet, but I had more curves than most. Men had called me chunky most of my life. But with Rocky, I felt… feminine. Womanly. I felt…

The warmth that began to spread through me made me gasp and jerk my gaze to his face. Something hard and thick pressed against my belly. I might not be experienced, but even I couldn't deny that Rocky seemed attracted to me. Or maybe he hadn't had a woman in so long that just anyone would do. I saw his eyes flare a moment before he lifted me into his arms and began striding for the stairs.

I clung to him, not knowing where we were going, but suspecting it was his bedroom. I should tell him to return me to the fire, tell him I didn't want this.

But you do, a voice whispered in my ear.

And I did. I've never found a man attractive before, not like this. But with Rocky's arms holding me, I wanted to know what it would feel like to be

- 10 -

pressed against him, skin to skin. I wanted to feel him slide inside me, claim me, and make me his. I wanted to feel that beard rub against my skin. I wanted... him. I briefly wondered what kind of woman that made me since I'd crashed down a damn mountain and now wanted to have sex with my hunky rescuer. Maybe I'd suffered head trauma.

The stairs ended at a large room with no door. The bed against the wall looked far bigger than a regular king-size, the covers rumpled. Rocky carried me across the room and eased me down onto the soft mattress, then pulled the covers up to my chin. He paused a moment before turning to the fireplace across the room. Wood was stacked nearby, and he began building a fire. Watching his muscular back and shoulders move was starting another kind of fire too. One I had never felt before. I pressed my thighs together to ease the ache.

When the blaze was glowing brightly, Rocky rose to his feet and studied me. There was heat in his gaze, and I wondered if I was finally going to find out what it was like to have a man claim me. I'd held onto my virginity for so long, never had been tempted to lose it. Until now.

"Dinner will be ready in an hour. You should rest," he said gruffly before turning and leaving me alone.

My jaw dropped at his retreating back, and when I heard the last of his steps carrying him down the stairs, I slumped against his pillows and drew in a deep breath. My eyes closed as his scent surrounded me. Something woodsy and full of spice. Curling onto my side, I buried my face in his pillow and just breathed him in. Whoever the strange man was who had pulled me from the car, it was obvious he wasn't going to take advantage. And for some reason, that disappointed me.

"Stupid woman," I muttered. I felt the tingle between my legs and moaned. "And stupid hormones."

Of all times to finally get turned on by a guy, it was now. With a man who didn't seem to want to touch me, despite the fact he was obviously hard. I bit my lip as my hands skimmed over my breasts. My nipples were hard, and my body was more than ready for him to come back up here and take me. I slid a hand down my belly and under the waistband of the sweatpants he'd put on me. My hand dipped inside my panties, over my mound, until I felt the slickness.

My eyes shut, and I moaned softly as I stroked my clit. I spread my legs a little farther, pretending that Rocky was here, watching me, wanting me. I squeezed my nipple while I toyed with my pussy. It didn't take long before I was coming, grinding my teeth to keep from crying out. The room spun for a moment as I breathed heavily. As my heart slowed, I pulled my hand from my panties and huffed out an aggravated breath. Even after finding that quick release, I drifted but never really fell asleep. I eventually heard him coming back up the stairs, and my eyes opened as he drew near.

"Dinner's ready," he said.

Before I could move, the covers were yanked from my body, and he was reaching for me. Rocky drew me tight against his chest, his arms braced under my back and legs, and carried me downstairs. I didn't know if he didn't trust me not to fall, or if this was more of a caveman thing. We crossed through the living room and into the kitchen. There was a square table with four chairs, and he nudged one out from the table with his foot before settling me on the seat.

Rocky turned to the counter and grabbed two plates steaming with meat and veggies. He set them down, then turned again to retrieve the silverware and two glasses of water. His chair groaned as he sank onto it.

"Thank you," I said softly.

My cheeks flushed as I stood up and went to the sink to wash my hands, remembering just what I'd been doing upstairs. When I sat back down, I picked up my fork and took a bite.

I didn't know what the meat was, and I wasn't about to ask. A man living alone in the mountains? It was likely something he'd hunted and killed himself. If I was eating Bambi, I didn't want to know, but it was well-flavored, the seasonings bursting on my tongue. The veggies were covered in butter and were the best I'd ever tasted.

"It's really good," I said, a small smile tugging at my lips.

He watched me as he ate but didn't say anything. The amount of food he'd given me was insane, but somehow, I managed to finish all of it. When I was done, I picked up my plate and went to stand. His hand shot out, curling around my wrist and keeping me seated.

"I'll wash them," he said. "Sit."

I nodded and released the plate.

Rocky didn't remove his hand until he seemed certain I wouldn't move, then he finished his food and stood. Grabbing both plates, he carried them to the sink and ran some water. I didn't know if I should try talking to him or let him work in peace. He seemed to be a man of few words. But then, living up here, I doubted he had company all that often.

"How far are we from my car?" I asked.

"Few hours walk."

It hadn't seemed that far at the time.

"And by car?" I asked.

He glanced at me over his shoulder, his brows lowered. I heard the clank of a dish in the sink, then he was drying his hands and turning to face me. His hands braced on either side of him on the counter, and he waited.

"If someone sees my car, can they find me here?" I asked. If there was even a chance that Sebastian would come here, I needed to know. The last thing I wanted was for that man to find me.

"Not easily, and with all this snow it would be a while before they could reach us."

My shoulders sagged with relief. "Then I'm safe," I said in a near whisper.

"Safe from what?" he asked.

"Not what." I licked my lips. "Who."

He didn't move, didn't blink, and I knew he wanted me to say more. I supposed I owed him that. He had saved me, after all, and was taking care of me.

"My mother married Carl Rossi three years ago. I was only sixteen and still in high school, and no matter how much I tried to talk her out of it, she was adamant."

"Why?" he asked.

"Because we were poor," I said. "And my mother wanted a better life. The Rossis are rich, far richer than anything we've ever known. She didn't care about the rumors, she only saw dollar signs. They'd been dating for a long time, and I guess he finally popped the question."

"And your dad?"

Pain pierced my heart. "Killed in action. He was a Marine. My parents were never married, so my mom didn't receive any benefits from the military when he died. We had to move out of the apartment he'd rented for us."

"When?" he asked, his voice tight.

"Ten years ago," I said softly. "He was part of an elite team. He wouldn't say more than that about it, but I know he was sent on special missions. One of them didn't go according to plan."

Something flashed across his face, but it was gone so fast I thought I'd imagined it. Guilt. I couldn't imagine what Rocky would have to feel guilty about. My dad had died so long ago, and there was no way this hunk of mountain man had anything to do with it.

"Why are you running from the Rossis?" he asked.

"Because my stepbrother, Sebastian, has never made it a secret that he wants me. And now he's decided he's going to have me, whether I'm willing or not. He broke into my room and..." My lip trembled.

"Did he hurt you?" Rocky asked gruffly.

"He tried." My gaze met his. "I had an old knife that had belonged to my dad and I started sleeping with it at night, the more persistent Sebastian became. I didn't feel safe in that house. When he started tearing my nightgown from my body, I grabbed the knife and stabbed him with it."

He grunted, but I thought it was in approval of my actions.

"I'd been thinking about running and had packed a bag the previous week. I snatched some clothes and shoes, grabbed my bag, and ran. I hid in the house long enough to dress and see if they were looking for me, then I snuck out to my car."

"And ended up crashing on my mountain," he said.

"Yes."

Rocky watched me a few minutes, then turned to finish the dishes.

"You should go get warm by the fire," he said.

Knowing I'd been dismissed, I stood on shaky legs and left the kitchen. I collapsed onto the couch near the fire in the living room and stared into the flames. I didn't know what had happened, but I knew my mountain man was thinking hard. Probably wondering if I was worth having under his roof if the Rossi family was looking for me. No one wanted to make an enemy of them. I had my suspicions they were involved in criminal activity, but I'd never seen proof.

With a sigh, I curled into the arm of the couch and wondered what I'd do if he threw me out. With no car, there was only so far I could go. And I knew that I'd be caught, and then there would be hell to pay. Sebastian might have wanted to claim my body before, but now he'd be after so much more. I knew the price for stabbing him and running would be steep, far steeper than I ever wanted to pay.

Chapter Two

Rocky

Christ! I'd come to this mountain to hide, to forget the past. Not that I could ever forget, but the quiet made things more bearable. I'd tried going back to civilization, had tried to stick it out, but sometimes the voices in my head couldn't be drowned out until I came to the mountains. I'd been up here almost a year this time, and hadn't had any plans of returning anytime soon.

Then Thomas O'Malley's daughter had to crash on my damn mountain. I'd thought her eyes looked familiar, and when she'd said her last name, I'd thought it merely a coincidence. But the fact she said her daddy was a Marine who died ten years ago, that cinched it.

I had thought I was safe here, that the tragedies of the past wouldn't touch me. I'd been safe the other times I'd taken refuge up here. Whenever I couldn't take it anymore, when the guilt weighed me down too much, I came here. I'd been coming here off and on since I left the service. But I'd been wrong this time. It had come crashing down my mountain and was now lounging on my couch.

As much as I wanted to run, or send her packing, I knew I couldn't. She was in danger, and I owed it to her old man to take care of her. I'd known Thomas had a kid, but since the man had never married Mara's mom, the military hadn't been able to help me track down the family. Fuck, no one had even known her name, or her mother's. I couldn't remember a single time Thomas had flashed a picture of either of them.

I didn't understand why Mara hadn't received benefits, though. As Thomas' kid, she was entitled to them, even if her parents hadn't tied the knot. While he hadn't shared a lot about his daughter with his team, the military had to have known about her. It was a puzzle I'd have to figure out later. Right now, I had to figure out what the hell I was going to do with the woman invading my home. Despite her battered condition, I'd gotten hard looking at all those soft curves of hers, and then felt like an asshole for noticing. Now I felt even worse. I'd known she was young, but she was only nineteen. At thirty-nine, I shouldn't even think of her as anything other than a kid. But she damn sure didn't have the body of one.

Not that it mattered. Once she knew about my past, who I was, what I'd done... she'd never want anything to do with me. Her father's blood, as well as those of the entire team, was on my hands. If I'd reacted faster, had gone with my gut and gotten us the hell out of there, then she'd still have her dad and would have never ended up on Sebastian Rossi's radar. So, no matter how much I wanted to run, I wouldn't. I'd help her. Protect her. I just had to get the message to my dick that we weren't going to fuck her.

I stayed in the kitchen as long as I could, but knew I had to face her sometime. We were safe in this cabin for now, but if Sebastian Rossi was after her, it was only a matter of time before he came knocking. My cabin was the only one within fifty miles, which meant when they found her car, they would come here sooner or later. While my cabin was hidden by the trees, the smoke from the fireplaces would alert someone that a house was here. For the most part, people left me alone. But a guy like Rossi wasn't going to back down, not without good reason.

I knew what I needed to do, but fuck if I wanted to. I'd come here to hide and lick my wounds. But whether I liked it or not, it was time to face the world once more. While I could protect Mara, she would be a lot safer if I got her out of here. Far from here. Back to my brothers. This cabin had been my refuge, and I'd come here often over the years, but I knew I couldn't stay forever. Especially now. I might have hidden out here a few more years, if the assholes at my club didn't bug the shit out of me about coming home, but Mara needed me. And knowing I was her only hope was enough to get me down off the mountain.

Gusts of snow slammed against the windows, and I wondered how long we'd be snowed in. They were predicting at least three feet, but the way the storm was blowing out there, I was expecting more. Even if I wanted to get her as far from the fucking Rossi family as I could, it wasn't going to happen right away. It would take at least a few days before I'd be able to get down the mountain, maybe a week if the snow didn't let up by morning.

I made my way into the living room and found her curled in the corner of the couch, staring at the flames. She looked so damn small, and completely helpless. I had no doubt if Sebastian Rossi got his hands on her, he would completely destroy her. The man was a complete monster and he'd beat her down, physically and emotionally, until there was nothing left. What the hell had her mother been thinking? Everyone knew that the Rossi family were criminals. Maybe not your basic criminal, but Carl Rossi was part of the Italian mob, just like his father before him, and he was training Sebastian to take over the family business one day.

It made me ill to think of those people raising Mara. She should have been with her father's family, and I wondered why she wasn't. I knew that Thomas

O'Malley's mom would have taken in her granddaughter without any question. When I'd asked Wilma O'Malley where her granddaughter was, she hadn't seemed to know what I was talking about. It hadn't taken a genius to figure out that Thomas never introduced his family to Mara, but I couldn't understand why. He'd had a loving and supportive mother, and it seemed unusual that he would have kept Mara from her. All of my digging had never produced any answers, and since I'd never known Mara's mother's name, or Mara's for that matter, the trail had run cold pretty fast.

"Mara, do you remember a man in uniform coming to your home when your dad died? Someone who would have given your mother the bad news?" I asked, knowing damn well no one had. Or rather, they had, but someone else had moved into the apartment by then. The military had only had two addresses on file for Thomas O'Malley. The apartment we'd assumed he shared with Mara and her mom, and his mother's house.

Her brow furrowed. "No. Mom woke me up one night and said we had to leave. She packed a bag for each of us and left everything else behind. It was the dead of night when she said we had to go."

So, they'd been on the run, but from what or who? I had a feeling we might never know, not unless Mara's mother volunteered the information, and since she was deep in Carl Rossi's pocket, that wasn't likely to happen. I didn't know what type of relationship Mara had with her mom and didn't want to press. Something didn't feel right, though. That sixth sense that had never steered me wrong said there was way more to the story. Mara's mother must have had a reason to run out in the middle of the night.

"You think she's been hiding something, don't you?" Mara asked.

"I think there's a lot she hasn't told you," I said. "It doesn't make any sense that you would have had to leave in the middle of the night and leave all your things behind. And how did she know your father was dead if the military hadn't shown up yet to tell her?"

Mara opened and shut her mouth a few times before shrugging. "I was too little to really understand what was going on. I just know she told me that my daddy wasn't coming back ever again. I cried that night and every night after. A few months later, she told me that my daddy had died."

Months later?

"Mara, do you remember what month it was when you moved out of the apartment?"

"It was still summer because school hadn't started yet. I had to start a new school after we left because we moved to the other side of town. The bad part."

Summer. They'd fucking left during summer and her mom had said Thomas wasn't coming back? We'd reported for duty in May, and Thomas had died in the fall. So, what had made her mom think Thomas wasn't returning? Why would she vanish in the middle of the night? Mara's mom knew something. I'd always thought our mission was fucked to hell, and now I had to wonder if we'd been set up. But by whom and for what reason? And had Mara's mother had something to do with it? I didn't think she could have, but the fact she'd moved so fast -- and months before Thomas died -- left me suspicious.

My stomach soured, and rage filled me. All those lives lost. What if it could have been avoided? If we'd been set up, I wasn't going to rest until I knew the truth and brought the people responsible to justice. Thomas wasn't the only one who'd lost his life that day. Other families had been broken apart, and while I'd always blamed myself, maybe it really hadn't been my fault. Yes, I'd thought something felt off about the entire thing, but my commanding officer had forced us to go in. I hated to think he might have been in on it too.

Mara's hand reached over and lightly touched my arm. There was concern in her eyes, and something else. I wasn't doing a very good job of hiding my emotions. I'd thought I needed to keep my past a secret from her, at least, for a while longer. But if I truly wasn't responsible for the death of Thomas and all the others, then I no longer had a reason to hide.

I pulled up the sleeve of my shirt and showed her the tattoo on the inside of my forearm. She gasped and reached over to trace it with her fingers.

"My daddy had one of these."

I nodded. "Devil dog. I was with him when he got his."

Her eyes widened, and she looked at me. "You knew my dad?"

"Yeah, sweetheart. I knew Thomas O'Malley. We served together. I tried to find you when I came back stateside, but you were gone. I never knew your mom's name, or yours, and couldn't find you no matter how hard I tried. The last name O'Malley isn't exactly rare."

"Why did you ask when we moved if you already knew?" she asked.

"Because I didn't know. Not for certain. But I can tell you right now, your mom knows something. Your daddy wasn't dead when you moved. So why did she tell you he was never coming back?" I asked.

Mara paled. "Did my mom have something to do with daddy dying?"

"I don't know, but I intend to find out. How long after you left did she hook up with Carl Rossi?"

"Maybe a month or two, but they seemed really close from the start. It's possible she knew him longer. They didn't get married that fast, though. At first, they were just dating. I couldn't understand how she could move on so quickly. My heart was still broken, but she acted like she hadn't a care in the world. We were living in the slums, the worst part of that area, but she carried on as if nothing was wrong. Even when I was starving, she was still going out at night with a smile on her face, leaving me alone in the rat-infested apartment."

The more she told me about her mother, the more I wanted to kill the bitch. Even if she hadn't had a hand in Thomas' death, the way she'd treated her daughter was enough reason for me to take her out. Killing women had never been something I enjoyed, but this time, I'd make an exception.

"I need any information you can give me on your mother, sweetheart. I'm going to have someone do a bit of digging to see what we can find. And once this snow lets up, we're out of here. I'm taking you far from Colorado." I frowned. "What the hell are the Rossis doing here anyway?"

"Ski trip," she said. "They come every year. Carl Rossi has homes all over the place. Colorado, California, New York, the Hamptons, Florida. He even has some outside the US, but I've never been to them. My daddy was from a small town just outside Los Angeles, but I guess you already know that. I think my mom met Carl Rossi during one of his trips out that way."

I grabbed a pad and pen off the table, where I'd left them earlier when I was making a supply list. Handing them over to Mara, I waited while she wrote down her mother's information, or what little she knew. When she was finished, I pulled out my phone, took a photo of the pad, and sent it to Wire. If anyone could track down information on Sara Rossi, it would be Wire. The man was a genius when it came to computers, and he could hack into anything.

"Now what?" she asked.

"Now we wait. Wire will get something to me as soon as he finds it, and we're stuck until the storm passes. It will likely take a few days for the drifts to melt a bit so we can get out. I have four-wheel drive, but even I can't get through over three feet of snow. Not unless we took a snowmobile."

She nodded and settled back into the corner of the couch.

"What was my dad like?" she asked softly. "I remember him tickling me until I cried. Remember him tucking me in at night, the times he was home. He was gone more often than not, though. His smile... it always made me feel special when he smiled at me, probably because he didn't smile a lot. And I remember his scent. Fresh pine, like he'd just been out in the woods chopping down trees."

"He was a good man," I said. "An honorable one. And he talked about you, Mara. Everyone knew he had a kid he wanted to get home to. Some of us thought it a little odd he never called you by name, but he talked about his little angel waiting at home. He never talked about your mom much, but you... you were the light of his life. His face would light up every time he told someone about his awesome kid. He never said much, but there was pride in his eyes when he spoke of you.

He was a dedicated Marine, and one hell of a man. He was my friend. My brother-in-arms. And I will do whatever it takes to avenge him. If he died for no fucking reason, you'd better believe I'm going to make someone pay."

"Good," she said softly. "I want them all to die. They took away the only person who ever loved me."

"I will make them pay. Every last one of them. I won't stop until they're dead or behind bars."

She nodded her acceptance and went back to watching the fire. The more I looked at her, the more I could see Thomas. A more delicate, feminine version, but his features were there just the same. And it seemed she'd inherited his bloodthirsty sense of justice. He'd be proud of her.

"You have a grandmother," I said. "Her name is Wilma O'Malley. Your dad's mom. She didn't know anything about you. When I asked about Thomas' daughter, she said the only granddaughter she'd had died as an infant. I knew that couldn't be you, but I didn't know why she hadn't met you before."

"No one ever mentioned a grandmother to me," Mara said. "I thought maybe I just didn't have grandparents. The only family I ever had was my mom and dad. And like I said, Daddy wasn't around that much. Is my grandmother nice?"

"She's the best. When all this is over, when I know you're safe, I'll take you to meet her. I think she'd like to know that a piece of her son lives on through you."

"Why would my dad have kept me a secret? I was nine when he died. That seems like a long time to keep your daughter hidden from your mom. You said he seemed proud of me, but... maybe he was ashamed?"

"I don't know what he was thinking, sweetheart. Maybe when we find out what happened to your dad, we'll find answers to that question too. I can't imagine him keeping you from your family, and there was no way that man was ever ashamed of you."

"Did he suffer?" she asked after a few minutes of silence. "Or was it quick?"

The mission was classified, which meant that I couldn't really tell her anything. Even Wilma didn't know the truth behind her son's death. But if my hunch was correct, it was about to make nationwide news. I didn't like the haunted look in Mara's eyes. While I couldn't give her specifics, maybe I could at least give her peace of mind.

"It happened quick," I told her. "I don't think he even saw it coming."

She nodded.

"You should get some sleep," I told her. "I'll stay down here on the couch. You can have the bed."

She eyed the couch, then me. "I don't think you'll fit."

"Trust me, I've slept in worse places. I'll be fine."

"I don't feel right claiming your bed."

"Mara," I said softly. "Take the fucking bed. I'm not asking you. I'm telling you to get your tiny ass up the stairs."

She looked like she wanted to argue, but I narrowed my eyes at her. She huffed at me and then went upstairs like I'd demanded. I heard her rustling around, and finally the cabin became still and quiet, except for the crackling of the fire. My phone dinged, and I pulled it out.

Wire: Holy shit! No word for months and now you drop this mess on me?

Me: How big of a mess?

Wire: Dude, this is some seriously fucked up shit. You need to come home.

I sighed. Yeah, I had planned to head that way as soon as the weather permitted. But knowing that Wire had found something so fast, it meant this shit was way worse than I'd thought. And I knew he wasn't going to tell me a damn thing over the phone.

Me: As soon as the snow clears. I'm bringing someone with me.

Wire: You're alone on a fucking mountain. Who are you bringing? A bear?

Me: Funny, asshole.

Wire: You know I have to tell Torch.

Fuck me sideways. Just what the Pres needed, more shit coming down on the club. Torch was not going to be happy with me, but I knew I'd have his support just the same. He knew what I went through, what I battled every day, and I knew he'd want justice too. The man had served his country and would understand how important it was to clear up this mess.

Me: Do it. I'll let you know when I'm coming home.

I tossed the phone down next to me and ran my hands through my hair. Whatever peace I'd fought for since coming here was now shattered, but with Mara came hope. How the fuck, out of all the people to crash on this particular mountain, did I end up with Thomas O'Malley's daughter? Fate was a fickle bitch, but maybe this time, she wouldn't fuck me over.

Chapter Three

Mara

I'd fallen asleep almost immediately last night, but this morning, as I stretched and breathed in deep, Rocky's musky scent seemed to wrap around me and hold me close. Something about that scent called to me. As I'd studied him in the firelight last night, I'd noticed he was rather sexy for an older man. He had to be close to my dad's age, or how old my dad would have been if he were still alive. The rage I'd seen on his face should have scared me, but for some odd reason, I felt safe with him. Maybe because he pulled me from the wreckage like a hero saving a damsel in distress? Or maybe it was because he'd known my dad. Whatever the case, I didn't think Rocky would hurt me. Not intentionally anyway.

As much as I would have loved to wallow in the bed a while longer, I could hear Rocky moving around downstairs. I kicked off the covers and shivered as the cool air ghosted over me. The fire had died out at some point last night, and the room now held a chill. Frost covered the windows, and the floor was icy under my bare feet. I quickly walked into the adjoining bathroom and started the shower. Pushing the door shut, in hopes of trapping the steamy air, I stripped out of the T-shirt I'd stolen from his dresser last night to sleep in, stepped out of my panties, and entered the standing shower. No tub for my mountain man.

My mountain man? Get a grip, Mara. The man rescued you. It doesn't make him yours.

I sniffed at Rocky's shower gel and shampoo, smiling when I recognized the scents that clung to his sheets. It seemed I was going to smell like him today. I shampooed my hair, wincing as my fingers pulled through tangles. I hoped he had a brush I could borrow, or my hair was going to look like Molly Grue's. As much as I loved *The Last Unicorn* -- and yes, at nineteen I still watched it at least once a month -- I really didn't want my hair sticking up like hers. Especially not with Mr. Sexy Mountain Man trapped in this cabin with me.

I'd never thought I had a type when it came to guys. I hadn't really dated much, had never truly been interested in anyone, but then I'd never met a guy like Rocky before. He was just so… commanding. And it wasn't just his massive size. Yeah, the guy was packed with muscle and was tall as a damn tree, but it was the way he carried himself, the way he spoke. It was possible that some of that just came from being older than me, but I'd been around plenty of people my parents' age before and I'd never felt anything like I did when Rocky was around. When he spoke, I wanted to listen. If he said to do something, part of me wanted to obey without question. It made me wonder if he was like that in the bedroom too.

I lathered my hands and started washing my body. My nipples were hard and sensitive from the cold air in the bedroom. Just the slight touch of my fingers as I washed felt amazing. After the day I had yesterday, what I needed was some stress relief. Even though I'd made myself come yesterday, after last night's revelations, I was wound up tight again. I pulled on my nipples, pinching and tugging. My breasts felt heavy, and I wished Rocky was in the shower with me, his big hands molding to my curves. I trailed a hand down my belly and spread my thighs a little. Leaning against the shower wall, I stroked my clit while my other hand played with my nipple.

Need burned in my veins, my body throbbing and aching. As I pleasured myself, I closed my eyes and pictured Rocky kneeling at my feet. He'd spread me open and use those full lips of his to taste and tease me. His beard would tickle my thighs as he feasted on me, taking me higher and higher, until I shattered under his masterful mouth. My body jerked as I came, a cry slipping out before I could stop it. My heart pounded in my chest as I buried my fingers in my pussy, stroking them in and out, fast and hard. Even though I came, I still wanted more. I wanted to know what it was like to be with a man, to have someone claim me, make my body his in every way. I knew I wasn't going to come again, not by my own hand anyway, so I finished my shower and got out.

As I dried off, I realized I'd left my bag of clothes in the other room. I wrapped the towel around me, but it didn't quite cover my ass, and there was a definite gap in the front. How such a big man could have tiny towels I didn't understand. Opening the bathroom door, I darted into the freezing bedroom and froze halfway across the floor.

My eyes widened as I stared at the man kneeling in front of the fireplace, a blaze going once more. His eyes darkened as he scanned me from head to toe, lingering a while on my mostly exposed pussy. I knew I should cover up, at least pretend to be modest, but the truth was that I liked the way he looked at me. The hunger in his eyes called to me. He rose to his feet, and the bulge in his jeans was unmistakable. His cock was thick and hard, the denim of his pants pressing it to his thigh. He stared at me for so long, not coming any closer, yet never looking away.

My chest rose and fell with labored breaths, and the towel worked its way loose, falling to the floor. The raw need on his face was nearly my undoing. He was a stranger, some random man who had pulled me from my car. I shouldn't want him the way I did. It was crazy to feel this all-consuming need for a man I hadn't known before yesterday. With Sebastian looking for me, I should be worried about getting far from here. Crawling into bed with the man in front of me shouldn't even be a thought in my head, and yet it was there.

"You're playing with fire, little girl," he said, his voice deep and gruff with arousal.

"Maybe I'm hoping to get burned."

His gaze locked on mine. I took a step toward him, but he shook his head, rooting me to the spot. I knew he wanted me, but I didn't know how to make him act on his desire. My nipples were hard and my body trembled, but it wasn't from the cold. That dark gaze of his swept down my body again, lingering on my breasts and pussy, as if he were memorizing me. I wanted him, more than I'd ever wanted anything before.

"Please," I said softly.

"I'm not good for you, little girl. Too damn old for one thing."

"You're not old. And I'm not a little girl. I'm a grown-ass woman."

His gaze caressed my curves again, but he shuttered the heat I saw in his eyes.

"I've done a lot of bad things in my life, Mara. There's blood on my hands. You deserve a guy who won't bring death and destruction home with him." He stared at my breasts again. "And I'm going to tell you right now. If I got my hands on you, had a taste of that honey I see between your thighs, I wouldn't let you go. You'd be mine."

His words sent a shiver down my spine, but if he was trying to scare me away, he was failing miserably. What would it be like to be owned by a man like him? To be claimed so thoroughly, knowing another man would never touch me? Before I could say anything else to try and sway him, he stalked past me and out the door. I heard his booted steps clunk down the stairs. After a moment, the front door opened and shut, and I knew I was alone.

I didn't care what he said. I wasn't a little girl, and even though he thought he was all wrong for me, I was thinking maybe he was just right. I'd sometimes wondered if there was something wrong with me. I'd never once been tempted to have sex with anyone. I wasn't a virgin because I'd held onto it on purpose, I'd just never found someone who made me feel anything. But Rocky... I wanted to feel his arms around me, wanted his cock to fill me.

After pulling on the warmest clothes I'd packed, I dried my hair, then went downstairs. My boots were sitting by the door, and I pulled them on before throwing open the cabin door. A good fifteen to twenty minutes had passed since Rocky left, but the snow had stopped falling and I could clearly see his tracks. I knew it was idiotic to wander off, but I wasn't going to let him run from me. I'd always done what everyone told me to do, but for once, I wanted something badly enough to fight for it. And if that meant trudging through the snow after the stupid man, then that's what I'd do.

The tracks led into the forest. My legs were aching by the time I reached the clearing. A frozen lake dominated the area, but there was a hole in the ice not far from a pile of familiar clothes. What the hell? Barefoot prints trailed from the clothing to the ice-covered lake. The man wasn't really dumb enough to go swimming right now, was he? What happened if he drowned? Or died of hypothermia?

Rocky rose from the lake, water cascading down his body. He braced his hands on the ice and lifted himself out of the hole. He stalked forward, a glare aimed my way. Even soaked with water that had to be freezing, his cock was still hard. I couldn't help but look. It was even bigger than I'd thought, and my thighs clenched at the thought of him sliding it inside me.

"What the fuck are you doing here?" he asked.

"You ran off."

"I left for a reason."

I licked my lips and tried to drag my gaze back up to his face, but I stopped along the way to admire his eight-pack abs and a chest that was so broad and heavily muscled that I longed to run my hands over it. I'd already been wet from the looks he'd given me in the bedroom, but now my panties were soaked.

"I'm not a child, Rocky. I know you're older, but there's nothing wrong with us being together."

He began pulling on his clothes, and I was a little dismayed that he was covering all that perfection. When he was finished dressing, he grabbed my hand and began dragging me back toward the cabin. I stumbled along in his wake, but he either didn't notice, or was too angry with me to care. I didn't know how much time had passed before we reached the cabin. My face was numb from the cold as he pulled me up the porch steps and shoved me into the cabin. The door slammed shut, and I heard the bolt slide into place.

"You really want me?" he asked. There was a hard edge to his voice I hadn't heard before. "You want me to fuck you?"

I swallowed hard and slowly nodded.

He moved closer, his hand gripping my hair and pulling my head back. "Want me to force you to your knees and fuck that sassy mouth with my big cock? Thrust it down your throat until you gag?"

A whimper slipped through my lips.

Rocky leaned in closer. "Want me to bathe that pretty mouth with my cum, then flip you over and fuck that pussy of yours long and hard?"

Oh God. No one had ever talked to me that way before. His roughness should have scared me, but if anything, it just made me want him more. All the filthy things coming out of his mouth made my pussy clench.

"How many cocks have been in that sweet pussy, Mara? One? Three? How many lovers have you had?"

I stared at him.

"Answer me."

"None," I said softly.

He froze and his eyes dilated a little. "None?"

I bit my lip.

His other hand slid between my legs, cupping me. "Are you telling me this is a tight little virgin pussy?"

"Yes."

He growled and abruptly released me. "Fuck," he roared.

I stumbled back a step and stared at him wide-eyed. Rocky stood facing the fireplace, his fists clenched at his sides. I didn't understand why he was so upset that I was a virgin. Just because I'd never been with anyone didn't mean that I didn't know what I wanted. And I wanted him.

"We need off this mountain," he said. "If we stay here one more day, I won't be able to stay away. I will fuck you, hard and deep, and more than once. I will take you every way I can, fill you with my cum over and over. I will claim that pussy of yours thoroughly, and no other cock will ever be inside you again."

His shoulders rose and fell with the force of his labored breathing.

"You don't want that, little girl. I would want to possess every inch of you, and I'd end up breaking you. I'm not a gentle man, I don't have a soft touch."

I didn't recall asking him to be gentle. When he turned to face me, I saw that his mind was made up. No matter how much I begged, he wasn't going to touch me. And if getting away from me -- from temptation -- meant driving down a treacherous mountain in fresh snow, then that's what he was going to do. I only hoped he didn't kill us in the process.

"Get your things," he said gruffly.

I stared at him a moment longer, then hurried up the stairs. I stuffed my clothes from yesterday into my bag, then carried it downstairs. Rocky pointed at the couch, and I sat while he disappeared from the room. I heard him stomping around in his bedroom. He'd already banked the fire down here, but the room was still warm. When he came down a while later, with a canvas duffle slung over his shoulder, and a fierce expression on his face, I noticed he'd buzzed his hair short and trimmed his beard.

"You slept in my shirt?" he asked.

I slowly nodded, wondering if it would make him angry.

He closed his eyes, his nose flaring with every breath. When he opened his eyes again, he looked to be back in control. He stomped through the living room and flung open the door. I hastily followed after him, my breath frosting the air as I stepped onto the porch. Rocky locked up the cabin, gave it a lingering look, then led the way around back. I hated that he felt the need to leave before he was truly ready. He hadn't asked for any of this, for an unwanted guest. But he'd saved me, and seemed intent on keeping me safe. There was a garage set back away from the cabin. He entered a code on the panel by the door, and the door lifted.

I peered around him and saw a huge black truck parked inside, along with a snowmobile. The tires on the truck already had snow chains on them, and it was lifted. I didn't think getting through the snow would be an issue with the monstrous vehicle. Rocky unlocked the truck, then helped me inside. His hands lingered at my waist a moment, almost as if he were reluctant to let me go, then he clicked my seat belt into place. He rounded the truck and opened the door. He tossed our bags into the back seat before sliding into the driver's seat.

The truck engine rumbled when he turned it on. Rocky carefully backed out of the garage onto the snow-covered drive, pushed a button to close the garage door, then began slowly making his way down the mountain. I knew we were creeping along because of how deep the snow was, but the truck didn't slip once. The winding road down the mountain hadn't been cleared yet, and I worried for our safety, but Rocky seemed to have everything under control.

I found myself checking the side-view mirror every few minutes. I knew it wasn't likely that Sebastian would be behind us, but it didn't stop me from looking. It didn't take long for Rocky to catch on. He reached over and placed his hand on my thigh, giving it a squeeze. My head whipped around in his direction, but his gaze was fastened on the road in front of us. That single touch was enough to make me tingle, despite my fear that we were being followed.

"Only someone who lives around here and knows how to handle weather like this will even attempt to drive on these roads," he said. "The Rossi family isn't going to be coming after you just yet."

"But you think they will eventually, don't you?"

He shrugged and removed his hand. "Truthfully, from what I know of Sebastian Rossi, he's a spoiled shit who thinks he can have whatever he wants. If he wants you, he's going to come for you. Or send someone."

"You said you're taking me out of state. Won't it be hard for him to find me once we leave this area?" I asked.

He glanced my way. "You have a cell phone?"

"In my bag."

He held out his hand. I unbuckled my seat belt long enough to scrounge my phone out of the bag in the back seat. I plopped back down on my butt, handed him the phone, then buckled back up. Rocky turned the phone on, then turned it toward me.

"Unlock it."

I placed my thumb on it and the screen opened for him. He grunted as he scrolled through heaven only knew what, then before I realized what he was doing, he'd rolled down his window, popped out the SIM card, and chucked the phone out onto the mountain road. I shrieked and lunged in his direction, but he threw his massive arm across me, pinning me to the back of the seat.

"Why did you do that?" I demanded.

"Your phone has GPS. And if the Rossi family paid for that phone, I'd be willing to bet they have other ways to track it. There are apps where you can track someone, not to mention the phone company would give them information if you're on the Rossi account."

My shoulders slumped. I hadn't even thought of that. I apparently sucked at this running away thing. What would have happened to me if I hadn't crashed and found Rocky? Would Sebastian have caught up to me quickly and made me pay for what I'd done to him? I wouldn't have stood a chance.

"They may find your car wrecked on the mountain, assuming it's not buried, but the snow covered our tracks back to the cabin. They won't know for sure what happened to you. When they track the phone to this road, they'll assume you got a lift down the mountain," he said. "But they won't know where you're going from there."

"So I'm safe once we leave Colorado?"

"Should be. Unless they have some other way to find you."

"Like what?" I asked.

"Trackers can be placed pretty much anywhere. You can have one in your shoes, somewhere in your bag or the hem of your clothes. I'd imagine they had one on your car."

My eyes widened and my jaw dropped. "Who the hell does stuff like that?"

"Besides the government? Pretty much any crime family worldwide."

That didn't make me feel better. What if they'd planted those tracker things in my clothes or shoes? What if... I drew in a sharp breath.

"I'd know if they'd microchipped me like a puppy, wouldn't I?" I asked.

His gaze slid my way before returning to the road. "Not necessarily."

I felt my face pale. That seemed a bit extreme, but what if they really had done that to me? What the hell had my mother gotten me into? I'd known from the beginning that the Rossi family was bad news, but it hadn't really hit home until now just how much trouble I was really in. Would Sebastian go so far as to kill me if he found me? If he was capable of raping his stepsister, I wouldn't put it past him to cross that line too. It was obvious to me that he was a monster.

"Where exactly are we going?" I asked. Not that it really mattered. Anywhere but here sounded good to me.

"I'm part of the Dixie Reapers MC. My home base is in Alabama. If anyone can help me protect you, it's my brothers. Anyone other than your family going to miss you right now?" he asked.

I shook my head. "I've never been very good at making friends."

Rocky was quiet for a few minutes. I wasn't sure if he was just concentrating on the road, or thinking things over. The last thing I wanted to do was distract him while he was driving down this treacherous highway winding around the mountain. We'd been on the road for a while when my stomach began to rumble. I bit my lip and stayed silent, not wanting to be more of a burden than I already was, but Rocky must have heard it and pulled over at the next little town.

We drove down the main strip, and I admired the stores along the way. It seemed like a quaint place, the type you'd see on a greeting card, or on one of those Hallmark Christmas movies. The streets had been cleared, as well as the sidewalks. It amazed me that we'd been on the road for so long, and yet were still at a high enough elevation for there to be snow on the ground. It was still early in the year for snow, but Colorado seemed to be getting more than its fair share already. I wondered what the weather was like in Alabama. I'd never been down south before.

Rocky pulled to a stop in front of a diner. I remembered how far down the ground was and waited for him to come around and help me out of the truck. His hands went around my waist, and I placed my palms on his massive shoulders as he lifted me off the seat and set me down on my feet. He was so close I could feel the heat coming off his body, but all too soon, he moved away. After shutting the door and hitting the locks, he took my hand and led me inside.

A waitress waved at us. "Sit anywhere you'd like."

Rocky led me to a booth in the back corner, then he claimed the seat along the wall, where he could see the entire diner. I eased onto the seat across from him. He scanned the area inside and outside before his gaze rested on mine.

"I'll have to take off the snow chains before we leave. Roads should be pretty clear from this point on. We'll eat, then you can sit and enjoy some coffee or something while I take care of it. No sense in you freezing while you wait for me."

I nodded. I'd never dealt with snow chains and didn't have a clue how they went on or came off. I hadn't even realized he'd have to take them off partway down the mountain. Even though the Rossi family spent most of their time in New York, my mother and I had stayed in their Beverly Hills mansion once she'd married Carl Rossi. There were times, after I'd gotten older, that she'd go with him to New York and other places, but I'd remained in California. It was only during occasional family trips, like this one, that I'd gone anywhere with them.

The waitress came over and dropped off two menus, some rolled silverware, and two glasses of water. "I'll be back in a few minutes, after you've had time to look at the menu. Just holler if you need anything."

Rocky opened his, and I reached for mine. I was starving, so of course everything looked good. I could have ordered one of everything, but my thighs were chunky enough already. A salad wasn't going to cut it, though. I really did need to diet and exercise more, but I honestly just loved food too much. All kinds of food. I had a healthy appetite, always had. Even when I was little, I'd been a little fatter than most of the kids in my class. I'd been teased a lot, and even now received some snide comments when I went out places.

Our waitress came back over, her pad in hand. "Do you know what you want or do you need more time?"

"Mara?" Rocky asked.

"Um, I think I'll have the meatloaf with mashed potatoes and carrots, and can I get some corn bread with that? Oh, and a Coke if you have it."

The waitress smiled, nodded her head, and wrote down my order, then turned to Rocky.

"I'll have two of your deluxe cheeseburgers, fries and onion rings, and a glass of sweet tea."

I had no idea where he was putting all that food. I mean, yeah, the guy was freakin' huge, but he was also solid muscle. How could he eat like that and still look that good? My expression must have said as much because he grinned and winked at me.

"I'm a growing boy," he said.

I snorted. "If you grow much more, they'll have to reconstruct the buildings so you can get in and out of them."

He shrugged. "I already duck for most doorways."

I leaned back in the booth. I'd known he was a lot taller than me, but just how tall was he? Not that it took much to dwarf me. I was barely over five feet. I'd gotten my height from my mom, but little else, thank goodness. I really didn't want to be anything like that woman. And if I found out she'd known what would happen to my dad, or had a hand in it, I just might kill her with my bare hands.

"It's about twenty hours from here to where we're going," Rocky said. "I want to get as far from this area as we can, and then we'll pull over for the night. You only have winter clothes with you?"

I nodded.

"You'll want something a little cooler to go with your jeans once we start out down through the southern states. Once we get to Kansas, I'll stop at a Wal-Mart or something, let you pick up a few shirts and anything else you might need. You can't have much in that bag of yours."

"I have the outfit I wore yesterday, and one more. That's pretty much it. I didn't really have much of a plan other than to get away. I didn't care where I went, as long as it was far from Sebastian. If I'd gone home, he'd have followed me there."

"So you were just going to drive until you found a place that looked good?" he asked.

"I guess."

He leaned his forearms on the table, crossing them in front of him. "Are you wanting to completely disappear? Start over?"

"The thought did cross my mind, but I don't have those kinds of resources."

"With the Rossi connections, even if you changed your name, they would eventually find you. We'll talk to Torch when get to the Dixie Reapers compound. He's ex-military, and I'm pretty sure he's done off the books work for the government over the years. If anyone can figure this shit out, it's him. In the meantime, I have Wire working on unraveling the fucked-up mission that killed your dad."

"Thank you," I said softly. "For taking me in, and for helping me."

"Anything for Thomas O'Malley's kid."

Well, that certainly put me in my place. I knew he found me attractive, but if he insisted on seeing me as Thomas' kid, then he'd never act on those feelings. And I wanted him to, so badly. I'd never been tempted to lose my virginity until now. I wanted Rocky to be my first. There was something about him that pulled me in, made me feel safe, and I just knew that it would be perfect if I were to give myself to him. If it was really going to take twenty hours to reach our destination, then I had some time to work on him. He'd either give in, or tell me to fuck off. At least I'd know for sure where I stood with him.

Chapter Four

Rocky

I'd not stopped driving, except for gas and food, until we reached Wichita, Kansas. We'd been on the road for over eight hours, but I'd wanted to put as much distance between us and the Rossi clan as I could. Mara had napped off and on, and my eyes were starting to feel like sandpaper, but I'd pushed through. Stopping at a Target gave us a chance to stretch our legs, and Mara the opportunity to buy more clothes. I'd sent her off for whatever girly shit she needed, while I grabbed a small rolling suitcase for her new things. It didn't take me long to find her in the lingerie department.

Seeing the pink, lacy bra in her hands made me audibly swallow as I imagined the scrap of cloth cupping the rather spectacular breasts that peeked through the V-neck of her sweater. Whatever she was wearing right now seemed to barely contain them. I willed my cock into submission, not wanting to walk around the store with a tent in my jeans. Maybe it had been too damn long since I'd had a woman, but something told me it wouldn't matter if I'd gotten laid last week. There was just something about Mara. She was curvy as fuck, just the way I liked a woman. And the innocence in her eyes made me want to corrupt her.

I set the suitcase into the shopping cart she was using and tried my damnedest not to think about her wearing any of the things she'd picked up since I'd left her in the shoe department an hour ago. The panties now in her hands were so sheer they wouldn't hide anything. She studied them, holding them up to the light, before tossing them into the cart, then reached for another pair made of black lace.

"Are you doing this on purpose?" I asked.

She turned to me with wide, innocent eyes, the lace panties clutched in her hands. But that look was a little too innocent. Yeah, the minx knew exactly what she was doing. She'd made it no secret she wanted me, but I wasn't the right man for an innocent virgin like her. I turned away from her, surveying the area. I didn't think it was likely that Sebastian Rossi could find us here, but the Rossi family had eyes everywhere. If anyone recognized Mara, we were screwed. Not that Target was really the type of place millionaire criminals liked to shop. They had a tendency to lean more toward silk shirts and custom-made suits. We were surrounded by moms and teens, and the occasional disgruntled dad following his family, each step labored, as if he'd rather be anywhere else.

"I'm almost done," she said.

I looked into the cart that was nearly overflowing with clothes and shoes. I couldn't imagine what else she could possibly need. As she left the lingerie department, tossing in some sleepwear that I knew was designed to kill me, I trailed behind her. It was another half hour of her tossing things into the cart before we were able to check out. I had no idea how long we'd been in the store, but it felt like forever. Now I knew why my friends had always declined to shop with their women. This was insane. How could one woman need so much shit?

The cashier rang up the total, and my eyebrows shot upward when it came out to almost four hundred dollars, but before I could reach for my wallet, Mara was pulling cash from her pocket. That must have been what she'd gotten out of her bag before we'd come into the store, but I hoped she wasn't using everything she had. It wasn't like she could access the funds in her account or use her credit cards. Not unless she wanted to lead Sebastian right to her location.

She pulled five one-hundred dollar bills off the roll, then shoved the rest back into her pocket. It looked like she had maybe another five hundred. It wasn't going to last her long, not unless I found a way to get Sebastian off her trail. If Torch didn't have any ideas, I'd have to hope that whatever Wire had come up with would incriminate the entire Rossi family. Even if she went on the run, they would eventually catch up to her. She just didn't have the resources she would need to stay ahead of the Rossi family, or those in their employ. Their reach was far and wide, spanning continents, and Mara didn't stand a chance. Not on her own anyway.

I loaded her things into the back seat of the truck, then drove to a small town a little farther down the highway before pulling into a motel. I was exhausted, and Mara probably was too. It was past time for dinner and some sleep; then we'd get a fresh start in the morning. The Sleepy-Daze Motel looked like it had seen better days, but it would do for tonight. Mara waited in the truck while I got a room key, then I pulled around to the back and parked in front of room 117.

"We'll take all your things inside, and you can pack your new suitcase, then use your old bag for your dirty clothes until we reach the compound. Then you can do some laundry," I said. Not really having any idea where she'd stay once we got there, but we'd figure that part out later.

I helped her carry everything inside, but I froze in the doorway and silently cursed. One. Fucking. Bed.

When the asshole behind the counter hadn't asked if I wanted one bed or two, I assumed all the rooms came with two. Guess that just went to show what happened when you assumed shit. Mara pushed at me, and I entered the room fully, giving her enough space to step inside. She dropped her stuff on the bed but didn't comment on our accommodations.

"You want to eat in or go out?" I asked. "I saw a burger place a few lights back. I could swing through and pick up something, or there was a Waffle House on the corner."

"Burgers are fine," she said. "I'm going to sort this stuff out, then take a quick shower while you're gone."

I nodded. "Anything special on your burger?"

"Everything with double bacon and extra cheese." She smiled. "And I want fries. Do you think they have shakes?"

I shrugged.

"If they do, get me a chocolate one. If not, any type of soda is fine."

"All right. I'll be back in a bit. I'm taking the room key with me in case you're in the shower when I get back. Don't step out of the room for any reason. This area looks safe enough, but you never can tell."

"I won't," she promised.

I stared at her a moment before heading back out to the truck. She was giving me another of those *I'm so innocent* looks that I didn't buy for a minute. There was no doubt she was naïve, and yes, she was a virgin, but I could see the naughtiness lurking inside her, and it called to me. The look in her eyes, the curves of her body, made me want to bend her to my will, command her to do things a good girl would never dream of. My cock started getting hard just thinking about urging

Mara to her knees, and I groaned, then readjusted myself as I climbed into the truck.

For a small town, the burger place was packed. The drive-thru said it was closed for maintenance so I had no choice but to go inside. There were at least six groups ahead of me, maybe more. Most were high school kids, and I wondered if this was the local hangout. Every small town had one. With everyone clustered together, it was hard to tell which couples were on a date and which ones were out as a group, but I slowly got closer and closer to the counter.

By the time I placed my order, received my food, then had them correct the parts they'd screwed up, it had been over a half hour since I'd left Mara at the motel. I didn't like leaving her for so long, not knowing if there was a way for the Rossi family to track her. Ever since she'd asked if they could have microchipped her, I'd kind of wondered if maybe she did have a tracker on her somewhere. Without the right equipment, there was no way to tell, and the only way to remove one would be to cut her open. That wasn't something I was anxious to do.

I let myself into the motel room and heard the shower running. She'd left the door cracked and light spilled out, as well as a cloud of steam. I set the food on the rickety table near the window and sprawled in one of the chairs. A noise caught my attention, and I focused on the bathroom, thinking Mara had called for me.

"Rocky," she moaned.

I fisted the arms of the chair as I listened to her whimper and moan some more. Before I knew what I was doing, I was up and moving, crossing the small room and stopping outside the bathroom door. I pushed it open farther, my mouth going dry. The shower curtain wasn't closed all the way, and Mara was leaned back against the tiled wall, her legs splayed and her fingers playing with her pussy. She drove them in and out as she called my name again, her eyes closed and a look of bliss on her face. *Fuck. Me.* My cock went from semi-interested to hard as a steel post in a matter of seconds.

I needed to turn around and walk the fuck out, but instead my feet seemed to have a mind of their own as I moved farther into the small space. I pushed the curtain open wider. Reaching for my belt, I unfastened it, then my pants, pulling my cock out. My gaze was fastened on the fingers driving in and out of her as I fisted my dick, giving it a stroke.

A startled gasp had me looking up, and I caught her gaze. She seemed surprised to see me there, but she didn't stop fucking herself. Her nipples hardened further, and I growled softly.

"Pinch those pretty nipples," I said.

Her free hand reached up and cupped her breast, rolling the nipple between her fingers. She whimpered, and her legs spread farther. I was playing with fire and I knew it, but fuck if I cared right then. My heart started to thud heavily in my chest as I got closer to coming. Mara stroked her clit and came, screaming my name. Fuck if that didn't turn me on even more.

Her fingers slid free of her pussy, and she dropped to her knees in the bottom of the tub, panting and looking spent. Seeing her there was almost my undoing. I growled again, stroking harder and faster, but I knew my hand wasn't what I really wanted.

"Come here, sweet girl," I said, my voice more growl than anything.

She leaned closer, and I reached out, gripping her hair and tipping her head back a little.

"Open," I demanded.

Her eyes dilated as her lips parted. I thrust into her mouth, using shallow strokes until she was taking damn near all of me. Jesus but her mouth felt like fucking heaven. I angled her head a little more and slipped in farther. Fucking her mouth with long, deep strokes, I knew I wasn't going to last but another few seconds.

"I'm about to come, sweet girl. Can you swallow for me?"

She hummed, and I took that to mean yes. With a grunt, my release hit, spurt after spurt of hot cum filling her mouth. Some dribbled from the corner of her mouth, but she took it all. When I had nothing left to give, I pulled free of her mouth and helped her stand up. She rinsed her face off, then blinked at me as if she couldn't quite believe that had just happened.

I tucked my cock back into my jeans and zipped up, then fastened the button and my belt. I wasn't quite sure what to say. The way she'd taken my cock was better than anything I'd felt before, but I knew it was wrong to want her the way I did. Not only was she too damn young for me, I had too many demons that I battled every night in my sleep, which she'd find out soon enough if we had to sleep in the same damn bed.

I stared at her a moment before turning and walking out. I sprawled in the chair again, wondering if I'd just damned myself to hell. Now that I'd had a taste of what it would be like to fuck that sweet girl, I knew I wanted her more than my next breath. But she deserved better than a broken-down Marine. What the fuck would Thomas say if he knew I'd just done that with his little girl? He'd probably put his fist through my face and tell me to stay the fuck away from her. But I didn't know if I could. Walking out of that bathroom had been damn hard, when all I'd wanted to do was strip my clothes off and climb into the shower with her.

She appeared in the bathroom doorway, a towel wrapped around her body. The white terry cloth didn't quite meet since she had such a luscious figure, and I fought for control. She slowly came closer, stopping in front of me, close enough to touch.

"Rocky, I know you want me. And I know that you don't *want* to want me. But I'm not some little girl. Just because I'm inexperienced when it comes to sex, it doesn't mean that I don't know what I want. I want *you*."

"You don't know what the fuck you're asking for, Mara. If I take you, if I claim that virgin pussy, I'm not letting you go. You have no idea who I am, what I've done, or what I'm still capable of doing."

Mara stared at me a moment, and then she sank onto the edge of the bed, facing me with her hands clasped in her lap. "You seem to think that being claimed by you would be the worst thing in the world. Let me ask you something. What exactly does it mean to be claimed by you?"

"You'd be mine. Forever."

She nodded. "I know we don't know each other very well, but I also know you're a good man. You can deny it all you want, but a bad man wouldn't be haunted by what happened while he was serving his country. A bad man wouldn't have pulled me from that car and taken care of me. A bad man wouldn't be helping me right now, making sure that Sebastian Rossi doesn't get his hands on me. So say what you want, but you're a good, honorable man, Rocky. So while to you, claiming me forever might be a bad thing, it sounds pretty good to me."

I opened my mouth, but she raised a hand and stopped me.

"When I was only nine years old, I lost the only person who ever loved me. My mother and stepfather have pretty much ignored me except for when they want to show off their perfect family. My stepbrother tried to rape me, and would have succeeded if I hadn't stabbed him. I have no friends, and while you say I have a grandmother out there somewhere, I've never met her. I have no one, and I haven't had anyone for a really long time. So if you're going to threaten me with something, you're going to have to do better than that."

She stood and walked over to her suitcase, which she'd packed while I was gone. Then she pulled out some clothes and disappeared back into the bathroom, the door shutting behind her with a *click*. I'd killed men, women, and children too, and yet she still thought I was a good man? The blood on my hands ensured they would never be clean again. I shouldn't want to touch her with hands that taken life after life, even if it was in the line of duty. But Mara's sweet, innocent nature called to something inside me; it pushed back the darkness.

While she got dressed, I pulled out the food I'd purchased for us and set everything out on the table. Her milkshake was melting, and my soda tasted watered down. The bathroom door opened, and my gaze jerked in her direction. The silky tank and shorts she'd put on showed a lot of skin. Her breasts bounced with every step, and I had to look down at my food to keep from going to her. I didn't care what she said. She deserved better than me. Even if it killed me, I'd stay away. What happened in the bathroom was a mistake, one I wouldn't be repeating.

"Thank you for dinner," she said softly as she sat across from me.

I nodded and picked up one of my burgers, taking a big bite. She didn't complain that the food had cooled, or that her shake had melted. Mara ate every bite, and then gathered our trash and threw it all away. There were shadows under her eyes and without a word, she pulled back the covers and slid into bed. I pulled some clean boxer briefs from my bag, took a quick shower, then cut off the lights in the room. Lying next to her was going to be hell on my control, but I knew if I didn't get some sleep, we wouldn't get very far tomorrow. And the sooner we reached my brothers, the better.

I tried to stay on my side of the bed. Sprawled on my back, one arm under my head, I stared at the ceiling. It didn't take long before Mara was plastered to my side, her leg thrown across mine, and her head on my shoulder. Her arm went across my waist, and I sighed, knowing it was going to be a long-ass night. I curved my arm around her and held her close, her scent teasing me. Slowly, the tension in my body loosened, and my breathing evened out.

Her words about the life she'd led circled my mind. Knowing she'd been alone for so long made my heart hurt for her. The fact her mother didn't seem to care about her made me wonder why she'd kept Mara all these years. She had to have known that if Thomas' mother knew about Mara, she would have taken in the child. Had she kept her out of spite? Or was there more going on? I hated having so many questions and no answers, but once we reached the Dixie Reapers compound, I was hoping Wire could shed some light on a few things.

Sleep eventually claimed me, and fuck if it wasn't the most peaceful night I'd had in ten years. No way in hell I was going to analyze that, though. Some things were better left alone.

Chapter Five

Mara

It took a couple days to reach our destination, and by then I was tired and cranky. Rocky hadn't touched me since that first night at the motel in Kansas, not willingly anyway. He let me sleep in his arms both nights we were on the road, and each of those mornings I woke to his cock poking me in the ass and his hand cupping my breast. I'd thought that maybe understanding my life a little more would have proven to him that he was exactly what I needed, but if anything, he seemed to distance himself further. The moment he realized I was awake, he'd roll out of bed and do his best not to touch me.

Sitting in the truck, so close and yet so far from him, hadn't been easy. I'd worn one of the few dresses I'd purchased, hoping to entice him, but he had barely spared me a glance. I was glad we'd finally reached our destination. I didn't know what I'd expected when he said we were going to a compound, but the large metal fence topped with what looked to be barbed wire gave me pause. Were they trying to keep something in or keep everyone else out? And if they didn't like strangers, how were they going to react to me being here? Rocky pulled through the gates and stopped in front of a large building with a long porch across the front.

A man stood leaning against a porch post, a cigarette in his hand, and his gaze fastened on Rocky's truck. Those dark eyes didn't seem to miss anything, and I wondered who he was. There was a leather vest over his shoulders that said something on the front I couldn't read from so far away. Rocky turned off the truck and got out, but I wasn't about to move until someone said I should. While I knew Rocky was a Marine and something of a badass, the man on the porch gave off the danger vibe. I was starting to question if it had been wise to come here.

They spoke for a few minutes, and Rocky gestured toward the truck. I hoped they weren't talking about me, but something told me I wasn't that lucky. The scary-looking man came down the steps and followed Rocky over to my door. When Rocky opened it and pulled me out, I stumbled and clutched at him. He didn't even look at me, and I released him quickly, taking a step away.

"Venom, this is Mara. She needs our help," Rocky said.

Venom stared at me for a few minutes, and I stared back, my heart hammering in my chest. I wasn't sure I even blinked. After a moment, his lips tipped up on one corner.

"It's nice to meet you, Mara. The simple fact you got Rocky off that damn mountain makes you more than welcome here. My old lady is inside, along with Torch's woman. While you don't you have a drink with them while Rocky gets the rest of us caught up?" Venom asked.

"Old lady?" Was his grandmother inside?

Venom turned an amused glance toward Rocky. "Did you tell her anything about where you were bringing her?"

Rocky shrugged.

No, the man hadn't told me much of anything. Where exactly was I? The stitching on Venom's vest said Dixie Reapers MC with his name and VP. I didn't have any idea what any of it meant, and I was starting to feel a little like Alice down the rabbit hole. Except, I had a feeling this was far more fucked up than

Wonderland. What had Rocky gotten me into by bringing me here?

"Ridley is my woman," Venom said. "My kids are in there too if that makes you feel any better about going inside. You're safe here."

I nodded and followed them inside. If there were kids in there, then it couldn't be too scary, could it? The interior was dim, but I saw two women sitting at two tables in the corner, a baby in a carrier on one of the tabletops. There was a little girl who looked about three sitting near the baby, a coloring book and crayons in front of her. Rocky urged me over toward them with Venom at his side.

"Baby girl, Rocky's home, and he brought a guest," Venom said.

The blonde looked up and smiled. "I'm Ridley, and this is Isabella. Come sit with us while the men go talk. Rocky hasn't been home in forever so I'm sure they have a lot to discuss."

"I'm Mara," I said as I sank onto a chair.

"Want something to drink?" Ridley asked.

"Um, a soda would be fine. Any kind is okay."

"Johnny," Isabella called out to a man behind the bar. "Bring Mara a Coke."

"So, are you Rocky's old lady?" Ridley asked. "He was single when he left here, but it doesn't surprise me he'd bring someone home."

My cheeks flushed. I still didn't know exactly what an old lady was, but it was obvious that Ridley and Venom were together, and she assumed that I was with Rocky in that same way. As much as I would love to be Rocky's, I doubted that would ever happen. The man had made it clear that he thought it was a bad idea.

"He's helping me," I said.

Ridley snickered.

"Why is that funny?" I asked.

"When I came here, I was running from my mom and stepdad. They had very bad things planned for me," Ridley said. "My dad is part of the club, and I thought he could help me. What I didn't count on, was Venom. One look and I was hooked. I knew I wanted that man to be my first, last, and only." She waved at the kids. "You see how that turned out."

"And my father traded me to Torch for services rendered. He had good intentions, though. My dad is in a dangerous line of work, and he wanted someone to protect me." Isabella smiled and showed off her baby bump. "I think it's safe to say I've been well and truly claimed."

My eyes were wide as I stared at them.

"So, has Rocky claimed you?" Ridley asked.

"No. Not for lack of trying on my part."

Isabella smiled widely. "Then you do want him?"

I nodded. "He's doing his best to avoid me, though. We had to share a bed on the way here from Colorado whenever we stopped at motels, and I'd wake up in his arms every morning, but then he'd move away and act like nothing had happened. It only took us three days to get here, but it was enough for me to know I want more with him."

"And he knows you want him?" Ridley asked. "Because, while I don't know Rocky as well as the others, he isn't really the type to keep his hands to himself. If he sees a woman he wants, he takes her."

My cheeks burned. "He said…"

Ridley grinned at my discomfort and leaned in closer. "He said what?"

"He said if he claimed my virgin pussy that I was his, and he wouldn't let me go," I mumbled, embarrassed beyond belief.

Ridley cackled, and Isabella seemed to find my situation humorous.

"Do you want him to claim you?" Isabella asked.

"Yes, but he's being stubborn. He thinks he's all wrong for me. I don't care about our age difference or all the things he thinks he's done that were so horrible. He's a good man, whether he believes it or not."

Ridley and Isabella shared a look, both of them grinning.

"I think it's time we bust up Church," Isabella said.

"Torch is going to spank you," Ridley said. "Remember what he said last time we barged in there?"

Isabella shrugged. "He won't hurt me. He may be all gruff and growly in front of his men, but at home he treats me like I'm made of glass."

"Um, what do you mean by Church?" I asked.

"The Dixie Reapers are an MC," Ridley said. "Do you know what that is?"

"Not really."

"The men in this club are bikers," Isabella said. "The leather vests everyone wears are called cuts. Ridley and I each have one too, but ours are a little different. Mine says Property of Torch and hers says Property of Venom. Like our tattoos," she said, showing off her arm.

I stared and couldn't quite understand what I was seeing. "You let him brand you?"

"It's part of this way of life," Ridley said. "And if you want to be Rocky's, then you'll wear one too. It lets anyone who meets us know that we're taken. If they see our Dixie Reapers cuts when we're out, they'll know they'll get their asses kicked for messing with us. It's a way of protecting us. And the guys are a bit territorial, so I think it's a big turn on for them when we wear their names."

I tried to absorb what they were telling me. If I were to let Rocky claim me, then I'd have to get tattooed like a pet, and wear something that claimed I was his property? I wasn't certain how I felt about that. The women in front of me seemed content, happy even. But their men had marked them like possessions, some trophies to be carried around. Was that what I wanted?

"They own you?" I asked. "Like, they order you around, and you have to do whatever they say?"

"If Torch tells me to do something, it's usually for my own good," Isabella said. "He would never tell me to do something that would hurt me, and he would never try to tear me down. He loves me, and I love him. We may not have what some consider a conventional relationship, but it doesn't make it any less than what people outside these gates have. I mean, we're married, but there's a huge age difference between us and the whole property thing. Your average person on the street might not be as accepting of this life, but Torch treats me well."

"I grew up in this way of life," Ridley said. "My daddy was a biker long before I was ever born. Venom talks a good game in front of his brothers, but when it's just the two of us? He's a completely different man. Oh, he's still bossy, but I don't exactly mind following his orders in the bedroom. I know that he loves me, and he adores our kids. Being his old lady isn't just about him owning me. I have his protection, and the protection of this entire club. There isn't anything any man here wouldn't do for me or my kids."

"You don't feel degraded?" I asked, genuinely curious. "I'm not trying to offend you, either of you, I just want to understand. I guess the concept of being property is a little weird to me."

Ridley looked at Isabella. "How else can we explain this?"

"Torch is the President of this club," Isabella said. "And it used to be the most important thing in his life. It's still really important to him, and he'd gladly die for anyone who's part of the Dixie Reapers. But as his old lady, as his wife, I come first, and so will our children. He may claim me as his property, but I also know that he's completely devoted to me and would die for me. When he claimed me, it was so much more than a marriage. It's forever. Once he inked me as his, that was it. I became his, but he also became mine."

"I think I understand." And I did, a little. The tattoo, the cut, they were just words, just symbols. A sign to others to back off.

"Still want Rocky?" Ridley asked.

"If he claims me, it's forever," I said. "No matter how much trouble I bring with me, he wouldn't turn me away? He wouldn't abandon me?"

Isabella's gaze softened. "No. He wouldn't abandon you, and neither would anyone else in the Dixie Reapers. You'd be family, to all of us. Something tells me that you need that almost as much as you need Rocky."

Isabella saw more than I wanted her to, but it wouldn't be long before everyone here knew my story. Rocky was likely talking to Venom about it now, and possibly others. These women seemed nice, and I wondered if maybe I could have friends if I stayed here. Would it hurt to open up to them? To tell them at least a little bit of what I'd been through? I didn't know if their men would like that, though, and I certainly didn't want some big, badass biker to toss me out on my butt. Something about the way they watched me, the look in their eyes, said that I could trust them.

"Rocky rescued me," I said. "My stepbrother tried to rape me, so I ran. I ended up crashing down the mountain when something ran in front of my car, and Rocky pulled me from the wreckage. He took me to his cabin and took care of me."

Their eyes were wide. I didn't know how much more I should say. Would Rocky, or their men, want them to know who my stepbrother was? Or that Rocky had served with my dad? I didn't know what was and wasn't allowed. If these were just random women I'd met, it would be different, but they were part of a lifestyle I didn't really understand that well. The last thing I wanted to do was get them, or me, into trouble. I had enough of that already.

"Why do you want Rocky?" Ridley asked. "Because he rescued you?"

"I've never really been interested in guys. But with Rocky… he makes me feel things I've never felt before, and he makes me feel safe. I haven't felt safe in so long. It's not just that, though. He's the only guy I've ever desired. I'm nineteen, and I've never wanted to feel a man's hands on me until now. That has to mean something, doesn't it?" I asked. "I want him to be my first, my only. He doesn't want me, though. Or at least he doesn't want to want me. I know I make him hard, but maybe any woman can do that. You said he's never had trouble getting a woman, so maybe I'm seeing a special connection that isn't even there."

I stared at the table, feeling dejected. I had absolutely no experience with boys my age, much less a man like Rocky. Even if there was a way to make him act on his attraction, I didn't know if I should. If he used me, then tossed me away, I think I'd feel even worse than I already did. Maybe it was better to leave things as they were. I had no idea what was going to happen to me, or where I would go when I left this place. I'd watched enough movies to know I shouldn't use my credit cards, and I only had five hundred left in cash. That wasn't going to get me very far.

"You really want Rocky?" Isabella asked.

"Yeah, but I don't want to force him to be with me. He either wants to or he doesn't, and right now, it seems like he doesn't. I don't know why I thought he'd be any different."

"Different from what?" Ridley asked.

"From the other guys I've known. My stepbrother is the only one who's ever wanted me like that."

Fire flashed in Ridley's eyes. "Trying to rape you isn't even nearly the same thing as wanting you. What he did was horrible and wrong. It was the violent act that was getting him off, not because he desires you."

"Then I guess no one has ever wanted me like that," I said. "Why would they? I'm just this big fat disgusting blob. My ass jiggles; my stomach jiggles. I'm so far from sexy it's not even funny."

Tears blurred my vision, but it was hard to miss the huge man kneeling beside me. Rocky lightly gripped my chin and turned my face toward him. I blinked, but the tears just slipped down my cheeks faster. Something was different. He was wearing one of those leather vests. A cut, with his name on the front.

When I focused on his face, the intensity of his gaze made my breath stall in my lungs.

"You think I don't want you? That you're undesirable?" he asked.

"No one's ever wanted me," I said softly. "Why would you be any different?"

"I'm going to say this once, and once only, so listen carefully," he said. "I happen to love the fact that you're fuller figured. Your curves drive me crazy and make me want to do things I shouldn't. You're beautiful, Mara, inside and out. And you deserve someone better than me. You need someone who can give you the white picket fence, kids, and normal life. My life is never going to be normal. Danger is all around me all the fucking time, and I don't want that for you."

"I stabbed Sebastian Rossi," I said. "He's going to come for me. The entire family may come for me. I don't know what you do here that's so dangerous, and I don't need to know. But do you honestly think I'm safer out there, on my own, than here with you? You think some random guy on the street will be better at protecting me than a Marine?"

"I'm not in the Marines anymore."

"Once a Marine, always a Marine," I said, quoting something I'd heard my dad say when I was younger.

He smiled faintly.

"If you want me," I said, "then take me. I'm yours for as long as you want me, but I'm kind of hoping you'll decide you don't ever want to let me go. Because I already know that I want to keep you. I want to wake up every morning with your arms around me, and I want to go to bed every night the same way. I know that I'm younger than you, but I'm not a child,

Rocky. I know what I want, and I want you. The question is do you want me too?"

He stared at me for several heartbeats, not saying a word. Rocky looked at someone over my shoulder, but I didn't dare turn to see who it was. When he focused on me again, there was a determination in his eyes.

"If we do this, then it's all or nothing," he said. "You'll be mine, completely."

"Does that mean I have to get one of those tattoos like Ridley and Isabella have? Because I'm kind of scared of needles."

"Yeah, you'll be inked. Among other things."

The heat in his eyes told me well enough what those other things would entail. I was actually looking forward to that part, but the tattoo I could live without. I'd never once been tempted to get one, and I didn't much want to get one now. But if it was required in order for me to be his, then I would do it. For him. I just hoped they had a soundproof room because I was probably going to scream the building down.

"Okay," I agreed.

"Zipper's out on a run," a voice said behind me. "Won't be back for another day or two."

"Then I guess the ink can wait," Rocky said. "You ready to be mine, baby?"

I nodded, a flutter of excitement in my belly.

"Can't very well claim her in your room here," the voice behind me said.

Rocky frowned. "That's all I have right now."

"What about the yellow house?" Isabella asked. "No one has wanted it because it's so small, but it might be just right for them."

"What yellow house?" Rocky asked.

A man with silver hair stepped forward where I could see him. The stitching on his cut said he was the President of the MC.

"She's talking about that small cottage out past Venom's house. I had the Prospects pull out the old carpeting and put in laminate flooring, they repainted inside and out, and we put in new appliances. Now that more people are settling down, I thought we should get more homes ready," the man said.

"Everyone else already picked a house?" Rocky asked.

The man shrugged. "Those who already had old ladies had homes, and Venom and I already had homes. But I wanted to be prepared. It's just the first house we fixed up. Everyone complained when they heard which project the Prospects were working on, claiming the house should have been torn down."

"What's wrong with it?" I asked.

"It's in good shape," the man said. "But it's a three-bedroom one-bath home. The rooms are a little on the small side since the house is only around fourteen hundred square feet. Isabella and Ridley picked out the colors. The outside is yellow with white trim and black shutters."

"It's really cute," Ridley said. "There's a small front porch with flower boxes on either side of the steps. The backyard is already fenced and has a deck. There's a small sunroom at the back too."

"It sounds really nice," I said. And it really did. I'd never wanted some huge, ostentatious house like the Rossi family owned. I liked the idea of a small cottage. Something cozy.

"It's not furnished," Isabella said. "But we could get it done quickly."

"Bella," the older man said with a tone of warning.

She smiled brightly at him. "I just need about two or three hours, a handful of Prospects, and a few trucks."

The man motioned toward me. "Mara might want to furnish her own home."

Pick out furniture? I'd never gotten to select my own things before. The idea was intriguing. Until Rocky had taken me shopping in Kansas, I'd never even been allowed to choose my own clothes. It had been a freeing experience.

Rocky made me look at him again. "Do you want the house, Mara?"

"Can we go see it?" I asked. I already knew I wanted it, but I still wanted to see what it looked like.

The older man snapped his fingers at Johnny. The younger man retrieved something from a box hanging on the wall behind the bar, then came over and dropped a set of keys into Rocky's hand.

"Come on, sweet girl. I'll take you to see the house, then we'll decide what to do." Rocky stood up and pulled me to my feet.

I followed him out to his truck, and he boosted me onto the passenger's seat. He backed out and pulled down a road that looked like it went on forever. It twisted and turned. He pointed out Ridley's house and kept going. Another two minutes went by, and he pulled down a gravel drive to the most adorable house I'd ever seen. It was just as they had described, except the front door was a deep red with a brass knocker. I fell in love instantly.

Rocky helped me down, and we walked up the steps. The porch was pretty small, but could probably hold a rocking chair or two. There was a black wrought-iron railing around it and down the cement steps. The planters on either side were tiered with three sections on each side. It had to be the cutest home I'd ever seen. When I'd been little, I'd dreamed of having a house like this one day.

He unlocked the door, and we stepped inside. The laminate flooring looked like pine faux wood. It was in every room except the bathroom, which had neutral-colored tile on the floor and inside the tub-shower combo. It was a tiny bathroom compared to what I'd grown accustomed to, only about fifty square feet, but the pedestal sink, toilet, and tub looked new. An oval mirror hung over the sink, but I didn't see anywhere to store towels or other bathroom things. It would probably be a little cramped for a guy Rocky's size, but I thought we could make it work.

Rocky opened the small closet in the hall, which had shelves nearly top to bottom. "Looks like a linen closet," he said.

I peered into the bedrooms. The first two were really small, but would be fine for kids. My cheeks flushed as I thought about having kids with him. The last bedroom was a little bigger and had three windows. It would probably hold a king-size bed, dresser, and possibly one other piece of furniture, but that was about it. It was small for a master bedroom, but not bad overall. There were his-and-hers closets, and though small, they were adequate. Another door drew my attention, and I opened it, stepping down into the sunroom. French doors led into the dining room.

"The kitchen isn't too terrible," Rocky said, looking into the room off the dining area.

It was long and skinny, and the washer and dryer took up space along one wall, but there was a pantry and tons of cabinets. The walls were a soft butter color, and the counters, cabinets, and appliances were all white. The only window was at the opposite end of the room over the sink, so the room was a little dreary, but there were two ceiling lights to brighten the space.

"I know it's not what you're used to," Rocky said. "But I think it has potential."

With the exception of the kitchen, and the sunroom, which was a pale green, the rest of the house had been painted a taupe color. It would make buying furniture easy, since just about anything would match.

"I love it," I told him honestly. "And we don't need a lot to start. Obviously, we need a bed and some sheets, but as long we have a place to sleep, maybe some towels so we can shower, then we can get the rest later."

Rocky leaned against the wall, pulling me toward him. His booted feet were spaced apart, and I stepped between them, pressing my body to his.

"You're sure about this?" he asked. "There's no going back. We do this, and that's it."

"I'm sure," I said softly.

"It's a big decision, Mara. We barely know one another. The life you've led…" He shook his head. "I'm taking advantage of you, and I know it. Doesn't stop me from wanting you, but the last thing I want is for you to wake up one day and regret choosing this path. You could go to school, have a career, lead a regular, normal life like anyone else out there."

"Rocky, what part of my life has ever been normal? For some reason, my dad kept me a secret from his family. My mom is hiding things and married into a family of criminals. My stepbrother tried to rape me and is likely out to kill me now. Why would I want normal when I don't even know what that is?"

"Fair enough."

"I have some money we can put toward the things we'll need," I said.

"Keep your money, Mara. You're mine, and I take care of what's mine. You want furniture, bedding, and whatever the fuck else we need, I'll buy it. You want to go out with the girls, I'll give you money. As of now, you're my woman, my old lady, and that makes it my job to take care of you."

It sounded almost like I was trading one cage for another, but anything was better than being with the Rossi family. Rocky might sound all possessive and caveman-like, but I didn't think he'd ever do something to hurt me. And part of me kind of liked his alpha attitude. With my stepfather and stepbrother, they demanded people follow their orders. But with Rocky… the commanding tone he had made me want to obey. Like in the shower that night. My body responded almost before the words even registered. Maybe that should have scared me, but it didn't.

His hand fisted in my hair, and he dragged me closer. "Mine."

His lips closed over mine, and I clung to him, my knees going weak as his tongue swept into my mouth. His kiss said I was his, that he owned me. It was dark, dangerous, commanding. Seductive. A whimper escaped me, and I squeezed my thighs together as a tingle started down low. I wanted him, more than I'd ever wanted anything. And now he was mine. I'd wear his mark, bow to his demands, and in that submission I'd finally experience freedom.

He set me away, his eyes burning with desire. The bulge in his jeans couldn't be ignored, and I reached for him, but he captured my hands and held them tight.

"You touch me, and I will fuck you here and now. You don't want me taking your virginity up against the wall, sweet girl. I want a bed, and I want the time to claim you properly."

My heart hammered in my chest. Rocky took my hand and led me back out to the truck, stopping long enough to lock the house. He sent a text to someone and then pulled out of the driveway and toward the front of the compound. Two more trucks met us there and followed as we pulled out of the gates. Now that he had a mission, I didn't think anything was going to stop him. Little did I realize that the Marine wanted in my pants so badly that he bought everything he'd need to give me a night to remember, and he managed to do it all in less than two hours. While he and two other men set up the bedroom, I hung the shower curtain and put down the bath mat. I stocked the hall closet with towels, and put our things away. The entire time, my heart raced, and there was a flutter in my belly that seemed to only grow stronger as the minutes ticked by. When Rocky called me to the bedroom, I knew that my life was about to change forever. I just didn't realize how much.

Chapter Six

Rocky

Mara stood in the bedroom doorway, her gaze darting around the room. As badly as I wanted her, I also wanted tonight to be special for her. The Prospects had helped put the king-size bed together, as well as the dresser. I'd bought two fluffy pillows and one of those bed in a bag sets. It wasn't anything fancy, just a navy blanket with aqua swirls, and matching aqua sheets. I'd tried to pick something Mara might find pretty, without having to sleep under flowers and shit. So her feet wouldn't be cold in the morning, I'd picked up the matching rug, and it lay beside the bed on her side.

Three jar candles were scattered across the top of the dresser, and I'd lit them; the eucalyptus and mint scents filled the air. I'd shut off the light, so only the glow of candlelight lit the area. I also had put a candle on each bedside table, but Mara didn't know about the stuff I'd hidden in one of the drawers. We'd picked up the furniture at a warehouse on the edge of town, then stopped at a Target on the way back for everything else. While she'd been picking out towels and shit, I'd made a quick side trip down another aisle. I'd left the Prospects with her, and they'd done a good job keeping her occupied.

The windows had those cheap three-dollar blinds up, but I'd made sure they were closed so we'd have some privacy. I'd buy her better ones, but these were fine for now. The silvery light of the moon tried to break through them, but no one could see in, and that's what mattered. Not that I thought my brothers would pull that shit, knowing that I was going to claim my woman tonight. Everyone would give us some space.

"How did you get all this without me knowing?" she asked.

"I made sure you were distracted."

She smiled softly. "Thank you, Rocky. This is amazing."

"I can be an asshole, but I'm not a complete asshole. You deserve for tonight to be special. I've never been much of a romantic, and I can't promise that you'll get stuff like this all the time. I just... I didn't want you to look back on tonight and be disappointed."

Mara moved closer, her hand coming up to rest on my chest. "I won't be disappointed. Even without the candles and stuff, I still wouldn't have been. All I need is you, Rocky. If you'd taken my virginity in that cheap motel in Kansas, it still would have been a good memory for me."

I cupped her cheek, my thumb caressing her soft skin. "Your daddy was a good man, and I don't know that he would approve of us being together, but I promise that I will always take care of you. I'm sure I'll make mistakes along the way, but I will never knowingly hurt you."

"I don't understand really about all this MC stuff, but I'll try not to embarrass you."

"Sweet girl, you could never embarrass me."

I kissed her, slow and deep. Sliding my hands under her dress and cupped her ass, lifting her against me. I couldn't wait to strip her bare and feel all those curves against me. *Slow and steady*, I reminded myself. It wasn't a race. She wasn't some club slut that I could flip over, fuck fast and hard, and walk away. She was mine, my woman, and I was going to treat her right.

Oh, she would get it hard, but I was going to savor every moment, every inch of her soft body. This wasn't just a first for her. I was far from a virgin, but it was my first time with a woman who mattered.

Her legs came around my waist, and I could feel the heat of her pussy even through my jeans. I eased one of my hands down her round ass until my fingers could slide under the edge of her panties. She was already soaked. I pulled my hand free and stopped kissing her long enough to suck her cream off my fingers. Her eyes dilated, and her lips parted as she watched me.

I let her slide down my body until she was standing. "Take that dress off, sweet girl. Let me see you."

She took a step back and pulled the dress over her head. It dropped to the floor, leaving her in the lacy pink bra and panties she'd purchased a few days ago. I could see her nipples through the material, hard and begging for my attention. I gripped her waist and pulled her closer, lowering my head to brush my lips across the swells of her breasts. My nose traced a path down into her cleavage before I latched onto a nipple, lace and all. I used my tongue to rub the material against her, sucking and licking until she was whimpering in my arms. Her body trembled, and I couldn't wait to hear her screaming my name.

I switched to the other while my hand teased her through her panties. They were drenched, and I couldn't wait to get them off her. Her little clit was so hard it was sticking out, the faint bump outlined by the lace molded to her. I rubbed it slowly while I feasted on her breasts. Mara began panting for breath, her body tight, and I knew she was close to coming.

"Take off the bra," I demanded.

Her hands shook as she unfastened the clasp and tossed the garment aside. Her breasts bounced as she freed them, and I groaned at how damn beautiful they were.

"Offer them up to me, baby. Let me suck on those pretty nipples some more."

She cupped her breasts, lifting them toward me. I latched onto one, drawing the peak into my mouth and sucking on it. She was getting wetter by the minute, and I wondered what would push her over the edge. Switching to the other side, I nipped her lightly before flicking the rosy tip with my tongue. Mara cried out, so damn close, and yet she still didn't come.

"If you don't want me to tear your panties, you should take them off," I said.

It only took her a moment to shimmy out of them, and as I reached for her pussy again, she spread her legs. I loved that she was so eager for my touch, so ready to obey my every command. She was mine, and soon I would own every inch of her body. I'd mark with her with my mouth and with my cum. I wanted to fuck her any and every way that I could. Wanted to take her deep, and hard, and fill her up until she knew she belonged to me.

I teased her slit, then circled her clit. Her fingers curled around the back of my neck as I lavished attention on her breasts, as if begging me not to stop. I sank a finger deep into her pussy, feeling how fucking tight she was. I damn near exploded in my jeans just thinking about being inside her. She was going to squeeze me so damn good. I fucked her with my finger, long, deep strokes while my thumb rubbed against her clit. Her nails bit into the back of my neck as she gasped. Her pussy clamped down on me, and she came with a loud, keening cry. I didn't stop, my finger stroking in and out of her, wanting her to come again.

She shook and trembled, barely able to stay upright as she came a second time. I eased my finger out of her and pulled away. Her breasts were rosy from my lips, and she had whisker burn from my beard. I knew they'd be tender tomorrow, but before I was done with her tonight, she'd be feeling me everywhere tomorrow. Lifting her into my arms, I carried her to the bed and laid her down.

I grabbed the back of my shirt and pulled it over my head, throwing it to the side, then I kicked off my boots. It only took me a moment to strip completely bare. My cock was so fucking hard. The head was ruddy and had a steady stream of pre-cum leaking from the slit. As much as I wanted to bury myself inside her, I wasn't done just yet.

Gripping her thighs, I pulled them apart, as far as they would go, before kneeling next to the bed. She lay limp, breathing hard, her eyes only half-open. Little did she realize that we'd barely even begun. I might be thirty-nine and getting older by the minute, but I could still go all damn night, especially knowing that she was mine and only mine. My cock would be the only one she ever knew.

I lowered my head and lapped at the lips of her pussy. Her skin was so damn soft, and her flavor burst on my tongue. I slid my hands up her thighs and spread her pussy open, admiring the view for a moment. She was so pink, so damn wet, and the prettiest thing I'd ever seen. I couldn't wait to see her wrapped around me while I fucked her.

I took my time, teasing and playing. I drove her wild with my lips, teeth, and tongue, until she was begging me for more.

"Play with your nipples, sweet girl. Pinch those pretty girls and make yourself feel good."

"Rocky, I need you."

"And you're going to have me. When I'm done playing."

My lips closed around her clit while I fucked her with first one finger, then two. I curled the digits inside her, rubbing against that secret spot that made her go wild. She came so fucking hard she soaked me and the bed, and I loved every second of it. When I didn't think she had anything left to give, I stood up. Wiping my beard with my hand, I stared down at her. So damn beautiful. Her body was flushed from coming, her pussy wet and ready.

I reached for her and rolled her over onto her belly. "Hands and knees, sweet girl."

She did as I said, not questioning me for even a minute. I reached into the bedside table drawer and pulled out a bottle of lube. She was wet as fuck, but every little bit would help. From what I'd heard about virgins, there was no getting around hurting her this first time, but I wanted to make things as good for her as I could. A box of condoms sat inside the drawer, and I stared at them a moment. I'd picked them up on the off chance I couldn't keep my hands to myself, but the more I thought about it, the less I liked the thought of using them. Mara was mine, and I wanted to feel all of her. I was clean, and since she was a virgin, I knew she was too. Mara was mine, and I didn't see any point in using the latex that I knew would just diminish our pleasure. My heart pounded as I thought about the other repercussions of going in bare, but she was mine. Forever. Whatever happened, I would be okay with it.

I lubed my fingers and plunged them into her pussy, stroking a few times, before slicking my cock. I tossed the bottle onto the bed before reaching for Mara.

I gripped her hips and lined my cock up with her pussy. Her lips parted as the head of my cock slowly pressed against her. I was only about an inch inside her before she started whimpering and squirming under me.

"If you don't hold still, this might hurt more," I told her.

I'd broken out in a sweat by the time I finally sank all the way inside her. She didn't so much as flinch as I bottomed out, my balls slapping her clit. I'd expected tears, but all she did was push back against me.

"You okay, baby?" I asked.

"So full," she said softly. "Don't stop."

I pulled back, my cock shiny from the lube and her juices, a hint of blood along the shaft, then I surged back inside her. Watching her pussy swallow my cock was fucking hot. I used long, slow strokes, nearly pulling all the way out before filling her all the way again. Her pussy rippled, and she squirmed, as if trying to take me deeper.

"More," she begged.

I cupped her ass cheeks and spread them, watching as I took her harder, faster.

"I know you've played with yourself like a naughty girl," I told her. "What did you do besides putting those fingers in your pussy?"

She whimpered but didn't answer.

My hand cracked against her ass, turning it pink and making her gasp.

"Tell me," I demanded as I fucked her.

"I-I-I played with my nipples," she said.

"What else, baby?"

"And my c-clit."

I squeezed her ass cheeks, then reached for the lube. I let some slide down the crack of her ass before tossing the bottle again. She flinched at the cold liquid but didn't complain.

I trailed a finger between her ass cheeks. "And did you play back here?"

"N-no."

I circled her anus, teasing the tight little hole while I drove my cock into her pussy again and again.

"I'm going to fuck you here one day soon," I told her, pressing against the tight muscle, massaging it until my finger slid in up to the first knuckle. *Fuck*! It's like her body was made for this, for me. "It's going to feel so good, baby. You want that, don't you? Want my cock in your ass?"

"Yes," she said, her voice needy as she pushed back against me again.

"What do you want, baby? I'll give you anything you desire."

She whimpered again.

"You want my finger in your ass while I fuck this sweet pussy?" I asked.

She nodded, and her hands gripped the bedding tight.

My cock worked her pussy, going harder with every stroke, while I played with her ass. It didn't take long before she was taking my entire finger. I could feel her pussy getting hotter and wetter. As I pounded into her, I started working on adding another finger to her ass. I'd never been so fucking hard in my life, watching her pussy swallow me whole while my fingers drove into her at the same time. Almost made me wish I had two dicks.

"Feel good, baby?" I asked.

"So good. Make me come, Rocky. I need it so bad."

I fucked her harder, slamming into her, claiming what was mine. I felt her pussy clench down on my cock the same time her ass gripped my fingers, and then she was screaming my name. As her release tore through her, I let go. I roared as cum shot out of me and into her tight pussy. I pounded it into her, wanting her to take every fucking drop. Even when I had nothing left to give, I kept thrusting.

"Rub that clit, baby. Make yourself come again. Let me feel how much you want me."

She did as I said, and I kept fucking her with my cock and my fingers until she came again. Her body slumped to the bed, and I eased out of her. She looked well-used with her ass red and her pussy dripping my cum. It was an image I wanted to remember for years to come.

I trailed kisses down her spine. "You did so good, baby."

I nipped her ass cheek before pulling her up and into my arms. I carried her down the hall to the bathroom and set her down on the closed toilet while I started the shower. She looked a little dazed, and I wondered if it had been too much for her. When the water was the right temperature, I helped her over the edge of the tub and joined her, then pulled the curtain closed.

I washed her gently, wanting to take care of her. As she leaned against the shower wall, I quickly washed myself and rinsed. After I shut off the water, I dried us off and carried her back to the bedroom. Jerking the covers down to the foot of the bed, I laid her down, then covered her up.

"You okay, sweet girl?" I asked.

"Mm-hm." There was a smile on her face, and she looked completely satisfied.

I blew out the candles before climbing into bed with her. She lay on her side, facing the wall, and I curled my arm around her waist, bringing her back against my chest, her ass snug against my cock.

"Did I hurt you, Mara?" I asked, hoping I hadn't taken things too far. She'd seemed to like everything I did, even wanting more, but this had been her first time. I probably should have taken things slower, been easier on her. I'd never been with a virgin before, and I didn't know how far was too far.

"It was perfect," she said, her voice drowsy.

"Get some sleep, baby. I have every intention of waking you before morning to do that again." I kissed her shoulder. "One of these days, I'm going to have you suck me off, then I'm going to fuck that gorgeous pussy of yours before taking your ass."

She moaned and rubbed her ass against me.

"I take it you like that idea."

She nodded.

I smiled in the darkness and wondered if maybe Fate had known exactly what she was doing when she sent Mara crashing down my mountain. I could almost believe that she'd been made especially for me.

Chapter Seven

Mara

I slowly came awake the next morning, my body aching in the most delicious way. Rocky had woken me three times last night and into this morning. I'd thought him claiming my virginity would hurt more, but I'd only felt a twinge of pain that first time. My pussy had burned as he stretched me wide, but it had felt so damn good to have him inside me. Little did he realize that he'd made a lot of my fantasies come true. We hadn't done anything too crazy, but there was a list of things I wanted to experience. I'd been reading romances since I was thirteen, the hotter the better, but none of them had prepared me for how amazing it was to actually have sex. I'd thought they were all just made-up stories and complete bullshit. Rocky had proven me wrong. Or maybe it was because of the incredible man who had claimed me.

I shifted and the way my thighs stuck together sent a flash of panic through me. Not once had we discussed birth control. Obviously, I was clean, not having ever been with anyone, but I didn't know about Rocky. I didn't think he would have taken me bare if he'd been carrying an STD, though. As much as he tried to take care of me, that didn't seem like something he would do. I felt stupid for not asking him last night. Still, that wasn't the only issue. I didn't know if he wanted kids. Hell, I didn't know if I wanted kids. I hadn't exactly had a stellar upbringing. What if I sucked at parenthood as badly as my mom had? Not that it would matter if he kept taking me without a condom, because sooner or later I would end up pregnant.

It was something we should have discussed before anything happened last night, or before that little episode at the motel in Kansas, but I'd been too caught up in the moment both times. Either he had been too, or he wasn't worried about it. I'd always thought guys were paranoid about knocking someone up. Did Rocky think I was on birth control, even though I'd been a virgin? I'd heard of girls taking it for years before they had sex, but if he was expecting me to take care of something like that, he should have at least mentioned it. Would he be mad when he found out that I could possibly be pregnant right now?

I'd rolled onto my stomach at some point during the night, and I turned my head to look toward the other side of the bed. Rocky was sprawled on his back, one arm thrown over the top of his pillow and the other resting on the back of my thigh, as if he had to touch me in some way even in his sleep. After last night, I should just be glad he hadn't decided to sleep with his hand on my pussy, or with his cock inside me. He'd been insatiable, but then so had I. While I'd read about being consumed with a need for someone, I'd never actually experienced it until now. Unfortunately, I was feeling the effects of our all-night lovemaking.

Even with the blinds closed, enough daylight was coming through that I could study Rocky. His lips were slightly parted, and his beard was scruffy. He'd shaved the sides and back of his hair, but it was still longer on top and was sticking out every which way. I couldn't ever remember seeing a man rumpled from sleep. It was kind of sexy. He was too rugged to call him beautiful, but to me, Rocky was the most handsome man I'd ever seen. My heart fluttered every time I looked at him, and butterflies flitted around my stomach every time we touched.

And now, he was mine. I might be the one who would be inked and branded as property, but by claiming me, he'd given me a gift. Him.

A soft rumble escaped Rocky, and he rolled toward me, wrapping both arms around my waist and dragging me closer. As he pulled me across the bed, my body turned until we were lying chest to chest. He was cuddlier than I'd expected. Not in the soft teddy bear kind of way, but more in the "I want you as close as possible" kind of way. Who would have thought such a big, growly man would want to snuggle in bed? I ran my hand up his arm, admiring the muscles that bulged even in his sleep. I had yet to see him exercise, so I had no idea how he'd stayed so fit. Then again, pulling a woman from a wrecked car, then finding out she's on the run probably had put a cramp in his usual schedule.

Despite how sore I was between my legs, feeling his hard cock press against me was enough to make me wet. As much as I wanted him, I didn't think I could go another round right now. My body needed a break, even if it didn't think so. If we kept at it, I wouldn't be able to walk for a week. I guess there were worse things in life, like running from Sebastian, but being bedridden didn't sound like much fun. Not even if the hunk lying next to me was in the bed with me.

His arms tightened around me, and I felt his lips brush the top of my head.

"Morning, sweet girl," he said, his voice a deep rumble.

"Morning, Rocky."

"You sleep okay?"

I smiled a little. "Yeah. Once you let me sleep, that is."

He chuckled. "I won't apologize because I'm not sorry."

I wasn't either. I'd enjoyed every minute of last night and this morning, and I hoped we had many more nights and days like that. Now that I'd had a taste of him, I wanted more. There were so many things I wanted to try, and I hoped he'd be up for it. He'd taken me hard and deep, nearly consuming me. I'd loved every minute of it. The commands he'd given me, demanding my obedience, had sent a shiver of pleasure through me. He was definitely all alpha male. I couldn't see him ever being submissive. If anyone in this relationship would get tied up, no doubt it would be me. And I didn't have a problem with that at all.

"Sore?" he asked.

"Yeah," I said softly. My cheeks flushed as I remembered exactly why I was so sore. I'd been well and thoroughly used. Maybe used wasn't the best word. Pleasured? I was fairly certain I'd been as close to heaven last night as I was ever going to get. I'd seen stars, felt the earth move, and every other thing that happens in romance novels that you swear just doesn't take place in real life. Apparently, it did when you had a man like Rocky between your thighs.

"I'll fill the tub with some hot water. You should soak for a bit. I should have been easier with you last night." He smoothed my hair back. "I'd have stopped anytime you wanted me to. Don't ever feel like you have to give into me if it's not something you really want. At least, as far as the bedroom is concerned."

"Last night was perfect," I said. My cheeks flushed. "But I think I need a break this morning."

Rocky tipped my chin up so that I had no choice but to look at him. "I may be a demanding bastard, but I never want to hurt you. If you tell me you're sore, then I'll wait until you aren't. It's not just about me getting off. I want you to enjoy it too. My favorite part is making you come."

I'd more than enjoyed it, but I wasn't going to shower him with praise. I had a feeling his ego was big enough already. Any man who could navigate a woman's body as well as Rocky did, and have her scream his name until she was hoarse, already knew that he was damn good between the sheets. I had no doubt countless women had already told him as much, and I refused to be part of the crowd. While those faceless women might have been notches on his bedpost, I was something more. I was his, and only his.

"Maybe you should shower first, in case there's not a lot of hot water."

He kissed me softly. "No, sweet girl. I'm going to take care of you. If I have to take a cold shower, then that's what I'll do. A little cold water isn't going to hurt me. You wait here while I draw the water for your bath. You can soak as long as you want."

His lips brushed against mine again, then he rolled out of bed and walked out of the room. I had to admit, the view was nice. It should be a crime for a man to have an ass that good. Where mine jiggled, his was nice and firm. I'd be willing to bet I could bounce a quarter off it. I wondered if he'd let me try that sometime? Probably not.

"Mara, it's ready," Rocky called out from down the hall.

I shoved the covers off me and got out of bed, wincing as I took my first step. The dull throb I'd felt before was minor compared to what I was feeling now. Maybe a sex marathon hadn't been the best of ideas, even if it had felt incredible at the time. I gingerly walked down the hall to the bathroom, feeling raw and achy. Rocky met me at the door, lifted me into his arms, then set me down into the tub. I gasped as the hot water closed over my feet, the skin instantly turning pink, but it quickly changed to a groan of appreciation as I sank all the way down. The tub was small, but I was short enough the water reached the middle of my stomach. As long as my lower half was submerged, that was good enough.

"Thank you," I said, smiling up at Rocky.

"Call me if you need anything. I'll be in the bedroom."

His gaze caressed me for a moment before he turned and walked away. Tipping my head back against the tub, I closed my eyes and enjoyed the hot water. When my fingers and toes began to prune, I decided to wash and get out. I pulled the plug and stood, then reached for the towel Rocky had hung over the rack. As I stepped over the edge of the tub, I nearly slipped and fell, but managed to catch myself just in time. Maybe we needed one of those rubber mats for the bottom of the tub.

I dried myself gently, still a bit sore, especially between my legs. I hung the towel back up to dry and slowly walked back to the bedroom. Rocky was sprawled across the bed, his hands folded behind his head. His gaze jerked my way as I stepped into the room, and he sprang up out of the bed.

"Feel better?" he asked.

"A bit."

He pointed to the bed. "Lie down and spread your legs."

"Rocky, I don't think I can…"

"Not for sex. I had a feeling you would be sore after your first time, so I picked up something for you."

Curious, I did as he'd commanded, lying back against the mattress and parting my thighs. He pulled something out of the bedside table drawer, then pushed my legs farther apart. I heard a top unscrew, and the scent of coconut filled the air. I had no idea what he was doing, but I trusted him. Cool ointment smoothed across my skin as his fingers brushed over my pussy. He smoothed some more on my inner thighs where I had beard-burn from all the times he'd gone down on me last night and this morning.

"What is that?" I asked.

"Coconut oil."

"And you just happen to know that you can use that on me to make the aches go away?" I asked.

"After the motel in Kansas, I did some research on my phone, in the event I couldn't keep my hands to myself. This was recommended if you had a sore pussy after I took your virginity, but they didn't say whether or not I could put any inside you. I'm going to assume the answer is no."

I started to close my legs and sit up, but he splayed his hand across my belly, holding me down. I relaxed against the bed, feeling a little odd that he was just staring at me while I was wide-open like this. His gaze was hungry as he softly stroked my pussy, rubbing more of the cream into my skin. He couldn't hide his monstrous, hard cock, and I knew he was turned on seeing me spread open like a buffet, touching me yet unable to do more. I was too sore for what I knew he really wanted, but that didn't mean I couldn't still take care of him. I'd managed well enough at the motel, even though I'd never sucked a cock before that. I could do it again.

My heart nearly beat out of my chest as I thought about what I was going to say. There was a scene in a book that I remembered well, and it was something I wanted to try. I'd thought it sounded hot, and completely naughty, when I'd read it. I licked my lips and gathered the courage to ask for what I wanted. His fingers were still lightly stroking me, and while his touch didn't hurt, it was starting to turn me on. I could feel myself growing slick with desire, and if he kept it up, I was going to beg for things I shouldn't right now.

"Rocky."

He looked up at me and his fingers stilled. "Am I hurting you?"

"No, but there's something I want."

"Your pussy can't handle my cock right now," he said.

"Maybe not. But my mouth can."

His gaze darkened, and his fingers trailed up my body to settle at my waist. "Are you sure you want that? I didn't try it last night because I didn't know if you'd enjoyed it at the motel."

"I like the way you taste," I said boldly.

He growled softly and crawled onto the bed, straddling my waist. His cock pointed upward, and his balls brushed against me.

"Tell me what you want," he said, his hand wrapping around his shaft, stroking it up and down.

My breath caught as a bead of pre-cum formed on the tip, and he smoothed it down his cock. "I want you to fuck my mouth."

His strokes quickened. "How do you want me to fuck your mouth?"

"I want you to take what you want, what you need. I want you to fuck me fast or slow, gently or hard… I want you to come on my tongue and down my throat. I want you to do what you did at the motel and keep fucking my mouth even after you've come." I swallowed hard. "I want you to take control."

Rocky moved farther up my body until his thighs slid up against my shoulders. "Open that mouth, sweet girl. Open wide and I'll give you everything you've asked for."

I lowered my jaw. Rocky leaned forward, bracing his weight on one hand, while his other hand fed me his cock. He circled my lips with the head, painting them with his pre-cum, before sliding in a little ways. He teased me, giving me just a bit of his cock before pulling back, then pushing forward again. I reached up and cupped his ass with my hands, trying to urge him on.

"You want it all, baby?" he asked.

I hummed my approval. Rocky braced both hands on the bed and stared down at me. I waited, the head of his cock between my lips. His body was tense, his gaze never leaving mine.

"You wanted it, so I'm going to give it to you," he said. "Every. Fucking. Inch. And you're going to take it all, aren't you?"

He didn't wait for my response before thrusting forward, his cock sliding over my tongue and down the back of my throat. Tears blurred my eyes as he fucked my mouth slow but deep. After a few strokes, I was able to relax my throat and take more of him, breathing deep through my nose every time he pulled back. He curled a hand around the back of my head, holding me as he took what he wanted, used me the way I'd asked. I felt the muscles in his ass bunch and flex with every thrust, and I dug my nails into his skin.

He grunted at the bite of pain, and his strokes became erratic. The first splash of cum hit my tongue before he pushed his cock down my throat. In. Out. My mouth filled up with every stroke, and I swallowed what I could. I could feel it coating my lips and sliding out the corners of my mouth. Rocky didn't stop. Even after the last drop of cum had shot out of him, his dick was still hard, and he still fucked me, just the way I'd asked him to. When he finally pulled away, sliding down my body to straddle my hips, I wiped off my mouth and stared at his hard cock. How the fuck could he still be hard after all that? It didn't look like he'd come at all. I'd always heard that older men had trouble getting it up. Rocky not only didn't have any trouble with that, but the man seemed to stay hard for a really long damn time.

"How are you still hard?" I asked, genuinely curious.

He grinned. "Because you inspire me with that naughty mouth, these sexy curves, your pretty pink pussy, and that tight ass. I could fuck you all day, every day, in every way imaginable. Except I don't think you'd be able to walk if I did that."

I waved a hand at the cock pointing toward the ceiling. "What are you going to do with that?"

"Go take a cold shower and hope it goes down."

"Good luck," I muttered as he got off the bed and headed down the hall.

While he showered, I washed off my face and brushed my teeth. My hair was too knotted to do much of anything with it, so I twisted the mass into a messy bun and put a ponytail holder around it. I went back into the bedroom and finished getting ready. I didn't know what we had planned for today, but I hoped at some point, it would include getting more furniture. Or at least picking stuff out to be delivered later. It would be really nice to have a couch and TV, and maybe some cookware so we didn't have to eat out for every meal.

I was slipping on my shoes when Rocky came back into the bedroom. My gaze traced over him, thinking it was a shame he had to cover up that fine body. I could look at him all day. Of course, then I'd want to touch, which would lead to other things, and I wasn't ready for those other things right now. My body needed to rest, so it was probably best if he put on clothes. He noticed me watching him and smirked as he reached for his bag.

"Like what you see?" he asked.

"A little too much. My belly clenches, and I feel all fluttery, but I'm still aching too much to act on those feelings."

Rocky laughed and came closer, pulling me off the edge of the bed and into his arms. He kissed me hard and deep, before releasing me. I sank into a boneless heap onto the mattress again.

"Good to know you feel that way just looking at me." He smiled.

"What are we doing today?"

"We're going to grab some breakfast, and then we're meeting Wire to discuss what he's found. I probably should have stopped by his room yesterday, but we needed to get this place ready, and then I was distracted."

"If I find out my mother had anything to do with what happened to my dad and you, I'm going to kill her."

He gave me an intense stare. "I'm afraid that honor goes to me."

I wasn't certain if he meant he would actually kill her, or if it was just a turn of phrase, and I decided I didn't really want to know. Part of me wanted to end her life myself, but I knew I didn't have it in me. But if Rocky killed her, it wouldn't be any great loss to me, or the rest of the world. But I didn't want Rocky to go to prison either.

Whatever happened, he had my support. If he wanted to take out Mom and the entire Rossi clan, I wouldn't stand in his way. Hell, I might even hand the weapons to him.

Chapter Eight

Rocky

I'd had every intention of feeding Mara before we did anything else, but a call from Torch had me driving straight to his house. Since our home was still pretty bare, I took Mara with me. If Torch didn't want her to hear what he had to say, then she could visit with Isabella. I hoped the two would become friends. There was still a lot I didn't know about Mara, but I knew she hadn't made friends easily in the past. The way she talked, she'd been lonely for a long time. I didn't understand parents who had kids and then wanted nothing to do with them. Not that my childhood had been perfect, but it was a lot fucking better than Mara's had been.

We pulled to a stop in front of Torch's house, and Mara jumped out of the truck. Isabella threw the front door open and waved for us to come in. I'd barely cleared the doorway before I saw my woman being dragged into the living room. It looked like the women would be occupied for a bit.

"In the kitchen," Torch yelled out.

I locked the front door and followed Torch's bellow. He and Wire were sitting at the table, a cup of coffee in front of each of them, along with a stack of papers and pictures. Torch nodded to the coffeepot on the counter.

"You're going to need some of that," Torch said. "Mugs are to the right of the sink."

I opened the cabinet and had to bite my lip to keep from laughing. It seemed Isabella had made herself right at home, if the collection of mugs was any indication. I saw a white mug with red lips that said *I'm too sexy for my mug*. There was a sparkly pink one that said *I'm the motherfuckin' Princess, that's why*. After pawing through the collection, I found a black mug at the back with a Harley on it. No way I was going to sit with my brothers and drink from a mug that looked like it had been doused in glitter.

I poured a cup of coffee, then claimed the chair between Torch and Wire. They let me take a few swallows before Torch nodded to Wire, evidently letting him take point. Wire reached for the papers. He handed me a set of pictures, and I spread them out in front of me. A woman and two men. I had a feeling I knew exactly who these people were, but I wanted confirmation.

"What am I looking at?" I asked.

Wire tapped the first picture. "That's Sebastian Rossi. You mentioned that he's after Mara, so I thought you'd want to know what he looks like. I checked over his records. There were some recent fund transfers that drew my attention. So, I did some digging to see what I could find. Looks like he's paid some men to hunt down your woman. It's a capture order, but I don't know what he plans once he gets his hands on her."

My gut tightened as I studied the asshole responsible for making Mara's life hell. Part of me hoped if he came for her, he'd do it himself. I wanted to end his sorry life. Any man who forced themselves on a woman didn't deserve to draw breath. Not unless they were in prison on the receiving end of attention from a big man named Bart who had a thing for pretty boys like Sebastian Rossi. If this ended with Sebastian in jail, I knew Torch could make sure he received special attention every day for however long he was behind bars.

"He's part of the Rossi crime family, but you already knew that," Wire said. "He's recently gotten pretty involved in the family business. Set up some arms deals in recent years, among other things. While there are some shady dealings with the military, he wasn't in action back when Mara's dad died. Not that he's innocent by any means, but he didn't try to have your team killed."

"And this one?" I asked, tapping the second picture, thinking the man looked familiar.

"Mara's stepdaddy, Carl Rossi. You've probably seen him on TV a time or two. There isn't much that asshole isn't into. If it's illegal, he's either tried or is currently running it. He's a real piece of work. Deals in women, guns, drugs… and he's not afraid to get his hands bloody. I went back as far as I could with his financials. Your team was killed ten years ago, correct?" Wire asked.

"Yeah."

Wire pulled out some papers and handed them to me. Certain amounts were highlighted. "Those checks were made out to Sara Rossi, starting about five months before your team was taken out. So, three months before she vanished with Mara."

My brows lowered as I stared at the paper. "Rossi? But Mara said they were only recently married. Wouldn't she have gone by a different name back then?"

Wire pulled out another sheet. A marriage certificate for Carl Rossi and Sara Jane Wilkerson. "Motherfucker!"

"Yeah," Wire said. "I don't know what those two were playing at, acting like they were getting married a few years ago. According to that, they've been married since before Mara was born. It gets even better."

Wire pulled another document. Sara's birth certificate. My eyes widened as I looked from the date to the one on the wedding certificate. "This says she was fourteen when she married Carl Rossi. How is that even fucking legal?"

"He was thirty-five at the time, and likely paid her family a handsome sum for them to sign off on the wedding" Wire said. "The research I did on the two showed that Sara Rossi was admitted to the hospital within six months of their marriage. For a D&C."

My gaze jerked up to his. "She was pregnant? At fourteen?"

Wire nodded. "Seems Rossi didn't keep his hands off his child bride. Sick fucker. Around the time Sara turned seventeen, she dropped off the radar. From what I've been able to find, she forged documents, giving herself a new name and a new life. As the girlfriend of Thomas O'Malley."

Thomas had to have known who Sara really was, and what she was running from. Had he helped her in some way? I looked at the birth certificate again, and Wire slid another one across the table. This one for Thomas O'Malley. If he'd been with seventeen-year-old Sara, he would have been twenty at the time. Not exactly legal in most states, assuming they were sleeping together at that point, but at least they were only a few years apart in age. If he'd waited another year to date her, no one would have thought anything of it. Wire slowly eased another form in front of me.

Amelia Renee O'Malley.

I looked at him in confusion. "What's this?"

"Mara's real name. This is where the story gets a little more fucked up. I don't know why, but within a few months of Mara being born, Amelia disappeared -- in a way -- and Mara suddenly came on the scene. After age four months, Amelia ceases to exist. No death certificate or anything. But there are no records of Amelia from that point on. No doctor visits, no school records. Nothing." Wire handed me another form. "That's the birth certificate Mara thinks is really hers. While it gives her the same last name as Thomas, he's not listed as the father. Robert O'Malley is. Thomas' brother who died at age ten."

I dropped the papers and rubbed my hands over my face. "What the ever-lovin' fuck is going on? None of this shit makes sense."

"My thoughts? Carl Rossi found them, or was closing in. It's not just Mara's birth certificate that changed, Sara changed her name again at that same time, and they moved. In fact, they moved every six months, up until the night Sara grabbed Mara and they disappeared. Now here's where things get more intriguing. Look at that bank statement again for Carl Rossi."

I picked it up and scanned over it.

"You said Mara moved in June, right?" Wire asked.

I nodded.

"The payments to Sara Rossi began three months before that, and continued up until her supposed marriage to Carl Rossi three years ago." Wire leaned back in his chair. "What I think happened is that he found them and made her an offer she couldn't refuse. But I don't think Thomas would have left his daughter. Not willingly. Do you?"

"No," I said. "Thomas never would have walked away from Mara."

Torch slid a paper toward me, and I scanned over it. First I went ice-cold, then I was burning hot as fury gripped me. It was a letter to my superior a week before the incident, guaranteeing that my team would be placed in a certain position, with no backup, at a specified date and time. It didn't take a genius to figure out that Carl Rossi was responsible for what had happened to my team, for killing Mara's dad.

"He was gay," Torch said. "And Rossi threatened to ruin him. The man was living as a straight guy with a stable family, career military. He was a staunch supporter of conservative officials, and vocally he was all things anti-LGBT. So, Rossi threatened to out him, or he could do the man a favor, get rewarded, and keep his secret. He cashed the check, in case you're wondering. The lives of your team were worth half a million."

I growled and fought the urge to get in my truck and hunt down Carl Rossi. The man needed a bullet in his brain.

"Mara said they lived in poverty," I said. If Sara Rossi was getting paid by Carl Rossi all that time, why had Mara grown up in the worst part of town?

"Sara could have paid for a really nice place with the money Carl was giving her. Ten thousand every month. Unfortunately, Sara has a little problem and living in the seedier part of town not only let her blend in, but gave her easy access. Heroin. I think Carl was also prostituting her to his friends."

Well, wasn't that just fucking perfect? This situation was so fucked-up I didn't even know where to start. I eyed the rest of the papers in front of Wire and wondered what the hell else was in there, and did I really want to know? I didn't have a clue what to do with this shit. I didn't want to keep secrets from Mara, but I also didn't think she needed to know absolutely everything either. She was happy for the moment, and I didn't want to ruin that with this giant pile of crap.

"So, what's the plan?" I asked Torch. I knew he had to have already gone over everything with Wire, which meant he probably had an idea of how he wanted to handle this mess. And honestly, I'd take any help I could get. I wanted Mara safe, but I wasn't stupid enough to go up against the Rossi crime family on my own.

"I'm working on getting pictures of the men Sebastian Rossi hired to track Mara," Wire said. "Once I have those, Torch is going to have the Prospects scout around town and keep an eye out for them. Has Mara done anything that could lead them here to the compound?"

I shook my head. "I tossed her phone out of the truck while we were still on the mountain, and she hasn't used her credit cards."

Torch's eyes narrowed. "You're certain?"

"She's been with me the entire time," I said. "Why?"

"Because when he hired those men, he made a flight itinerary for each. And they were flying into Birmingham. If they don't know where she is, why are they coming to Alabama?" Wire asked.

Fuck!

"Gather anything she had with her when you found her," Torch said. "I'll have a Prospect leave town with it and dump it somewhere. But the damage is probably already done. They likely know the address of the compound by now, and who we are. I have a feeling we'll be hearing from the Rossi family before too long. They tend to buy what they want, and they'll think they can buy us too."

"When is Zipper getting back? She needs to be inked now," I said.

Torch sighed. "Do you honestly think something like a little ink or a cut is going to make Sebastian Rossi back off? He's not going to care that you think she's yours. He wants her, and he'll take her regardless."

I growled, not liking any of this.

"I know my opinion isn't going to be very welcome right now, but I say we let them come for her. Keep her inside the compound where they can't get to her, or if you take her out, take a handful of brothers or Prospects with you. Make sure they can't get to her, even if they know she's here. And then take them out, one at a time," Wire said. "Half our brothers, the two of you included, have military experience. Taking on some hired goons shouldn't be that hard of a task."

"They'll just send more," Torch said. "The only way to make sure Mara stays safe is to take out Sebastian Rossi and his father. Because if we take down the son, the dad will come after us next."

"I shouldn't have brought this shit here," I said. "I wanted help protecting Mara, but this is way bigger than I anticipated. I knew Sebastian Rossi was after Mara, and my gut said that Mara's mom had something to do with my unit being set up, but I wasn't expecting" --I waved a hand over the papers on the table --"all this. It's insane, and I can't ask any of you to take this on."

Torch drummed his fingers on the table. "I know you didn't mean to bring all this to our doorstep, but you did, so now we're going to handle it. I'm going to call Church. We'll let everyone know what's going on and come up with a more concise plan than 'take down the bad guys.'"

"What about Mara?" I asked.

"She can stay here with Isabella. The two seem to be getting along. I'll ask Johnny and another Prospect to come watch over them. One in the house and one outside. It's not likely anyone is getting into the compound, but in case they find a weakness and take us by surprise, the women will be guarded," Torch said. "If Johnny calls, I'll answer even in the middle of Church."

I nodded.

Wire began gathering his things. "I'll meet both of you at the clubhouse. If you're putting Mara on lockdown, you might want to let her know. And then she's going to ask questions."

Why couldn't anything ever be easy? Oh, right. Because easy was boring.

I finished my coffee and then rinsed my cup. Torch did the same, and then we went to find the women. The TV was on in the living room, but they weren't in there. I hadn't heard the front door open. Had they somehow slipped past us? I hoped like hell Mara wasn't off wandering around without protection. I didn't think she'd do something so stupid, knowing Rossi was after her, but there was a first time for everything. A giggle sounded from somewhere upstairs, and I followed Torch up the steps.

A door in the middle of the hall was open with light spilling out. Torch smiled and motioned me forward. I'd seen the man smile before, usually when blood was about to be spilled or he was going to get laid, but this was a look I hadn't seen him wear before, a softer look that took me by surprise. I wondered what was in the room.

He stepped inside, and I stopped in the doorway. I'd noticed Isabella's baby bump, though it was still slight, but I guess I hadn't realized Torch would have a nursery set up already. The walls were a soft yellow with teddy bear decals. A white crib, changing table, and dresser took up wall space. The bear motif seemed to carry over into the bedding, and a white blanket covered with teddy bears hung over the railing.

Mara and Isabella were standing near the dresser, and Isabella was pulling out the tiniest damn clothes. They were all those things with feet that people always put on babies. They were currently cooing over a white one with yellow ducks. When Isabella tried to hand it to Mara, my woman looked like someone was giving her a snake. It made me wonder how she felt about kids. We hadn't discussed it, but after last night, there was a good chance she could be pregnant.

Yeah, I was an asshole and hadn't even asked. I'd just taken her bare, wanting to feel her wrapped around me. The caveman in me had wanted to brand her with my cum, especially since she didn't carry my ink on her body yet. And one day soon I was going to come down her throat, in her pussy, and then I was going to take that delectable ass of hers. My cock started getting hard just thinking about it.

"Bella, I don't think Mara is in baby heaven like you," Torch said.

"Oh." Isabella looked at Mara. "We don't have to look at all this stuff if you don't want to. I just get so excited sometimes I can't help myself. Don't get me wrong, I was scared to death with I found out I was pregnant, but it didn't take long for me to be really happy about it."

"I guess I've just not thought that much about babies," Mara said, casting a glance my way. That look told me enough. Babies made her nervous, and she didn't know how I felt about that. Truthfully, I'd never thought much about kids, but now that I had Mara, the idea of having a baby or two wasn't repulsive. I kind of liked the idea of a mini-Mara running around the house.

"Bella, I'm calling Church," Torch said. "I want you to stay here with Mara. I'm sending over Johnny and probably Ivan. Keep Johnny in the house with you. There's someone after Mara, and we need to make sure the two of you stay safe."

Isabella cupped her belly.

Torch got that soft look again and crossed the room, pulling her into his arms. "You're going to be fine, baby. Just keep Johnny close, okay? Watch movies with Mara or something. I'll be home as soon as I can."

Isabella curled against him. "Love you, Connor," she said softly.

His gaze narrowed a moment, but then he sighed. I figured it had to do with her using his actual name, something no one was allowed to do.

"Love you too, Bella," Torch said.

Mara's eyes held a sheen, and I wondered if the touching scene was about to make her cry. She came toward me, and I wrapped my arms around her. I hadn't given her any soft words, and I honestly didn't have a clue what love felt like. But she mattered to me, and I wanted her to be safe.

"Stay safe," I said softly before kissing her. "Have fun with Isabella, and I'll come get you soon. We'll take some of the guys with us and pick out more things for the house. I want you to be comfortable in our home."

"This is about me, isn't it?" she asked.

"We're going to discuss the situation with Sebastian, among other things. I'm going to protect you, Mara. The only way someone is getting to you is if they go through me first."

"That's not very comforting," she said. "If the choice is for me to go with Sebastian or for you to die, I'm going with him."

"It's not a debate." I swatted her ass. "Be good, and I'll see you soon."

Torch pulled himself away from Isabella, and we left the women in the nursery. Torch seemed to have found that once-in-a-lifetime type of relationship, and I wondered if Mara and I would have that one day. Things were still so new between us, but I did feel something for her. She meant more to me than the random women I'd fucked over the years. She was mine, and I'd kill anyone who tried to take her. That wasn't love, but it was still something substantial, at least to me. I'd never cared about a woman before, never given a shit if she was with a hundred men, and I always kicked them out after I fucked them. With Mara, I wanted her in my bed every damn night, and I wanted to wake up next to her every morning.

Maybe that was love and maybe it wasn't.

Torch rode in the truck with me over to the clubhouse, texting on his phone the entire way. I knew it wouldn't take long for all my brothers to meet us in Church. I only hoped that we could find a solution to this insane problem, preferably before someone got hurt.

Chapter Nine

Mara

Rocky didn't say a word after the meeting he'd had, and I'd spent the last ten days worrying about what was going on. Not a word was said about Sebastian or Rocky's suspicions about what happened to my dad. I wanted him to talk to me, to tell me what was going on, but I didn't know if I should ask. If he'd wanted me to know, he'd have said something, wouldn't he?

The day he'd taken me to Isabella's, he'd come back after his meeting and taken me shopping. We now had a couch, entertainment center, and a sixty-five-inch TV that I still thought was overkill for such a small house. Men and their toys! I'd half expected him to buy some sort of game system and every gadget he could get his hands on, but he hadn't. Once the Internet and cable were up and running, he'd picked up a Fire Stick at the store, and now we had access to movies online.

He'd let me get whatever I wanted for the kitchen, but I was a little clueless as to what we would need. I'd never really cooked before and didn't have any idea what items were used for what. A spatula and spoon were self-explanatory, but why on earth did you need so many different-sized pots and skillets? Wouldn't one of each be fine? We'd ended up purchasing one of those large sets that come in a box, same for our dishes and glassware. Since I didn't want us to starve or live off boxed dinners, I grabbed a few cookbooks as well.

While we were busy getting the house taken care of, Zipper had returned. My tattoo was healing nicely and hadn't hurt as bad as I feared. I'd noticed that

Ridley and Isabella wore theirs on their arms, so I'd opted to do the same. Rocky had asked if I wanted it on my back. Just above my right wrist, I now sported black script that said *Property of Rocky* with small white and yellow roses around it, some were buds and some were fully bloomed. I'd asked Rocky why he chose those. He said he'd looked up flower meanings before we met with Zipper. White was for purity and innocence, and yellow meant happiness. He said that I'd been pure and innocent, and he promised me many happy moments in the future. I wondered if he even realized that he could be a bit romantic at times.

We'd gone out a few times since then, but always with other people. I had enjoyed getting to do things with just the two of us, even though we'd only had a few days together before reaching the compound. No matter how much I begged and pleaded, though, he held firm that we needed extra men with us when we went out. So, here I sat in a darkened theater with Rocky, while a group of Dixie Reapers were within arm's reach. The only thing that made it bearable was knowing they were all miserable since I'd chosen a romantic comedy. The looks on their faces when I'd picked the movie was comical. You'd think I'd asked them to strip naked and run down the street. Although, from what I've learned of these men, they would do that in a heartbeat. Especially if alcohol was involved.

I handed my bucket of popcorn to Rocky and stood up. He wrapped his hand around my wrist.

"Where are you going?" he whispered.

"Bathroom. And no, you can't go in there with me."

He narrowed his eyes and motioned for one of the Prospects to follow me. Ivan had become my shadow lately. I wondered if he was as tired of following me as I was of having him around. He wasn't a bad guy, but it would be awesome if I could go pee without having to announce it to everyone, and then have an escort.

I stepped over Rocky's legs, with Ivan right behind me, and made my way down the stairs, around the wall, and out into the main part of the cinema. People were everywhere, and I threaded my way through the crowd to find the bathroom. I bypassed the main one, seeing a line all the way out the door, and found another one at the other end of the cinema. Ivan stopped just outside the door, and I went inside. I'd expected to stand in line here too, but the place was deserted. After I peed and washed my hands, I leaned on the counter and closed my eyes a moment. It was nice, just standing here alone. I hadn't been alone in a week, and it was starting to drive me crazy.

I heard voices in the hall outside and then a loud thump. I frowned and stared toward the doorway, expecting Ivan to walk in and see why I was taking so long. It wasn't Ivan who came in, though. The man who stepped into the bathroom was scary. His dark hair was slicked back, and his eyes were nearly black. There was a jagged scar down his face, bisecting his eyebrow and going down his cheek and under his chin.

"You can come with me willingly," he said, "or not. Personally, I'm hoping you fight. Orders are not to kill you. Boss didn't say anything about having some fun, though."

Bile rose in my throat. I had no idea what he thought would be fun, and I didn't think I wanted to know. I glanced behind him, willing Ivan to come to my rescue. The man noticed the direction of my gaze and smirked.

"That kid won't interrupt us."

Kid? Ivan was older than me for certain. If he thought a man in his twenties was a kid, what did that make me? Or maybe he was the kind of man who got off on hurting girls. I knew there were sick perverts out there.

The man moved closer. "We need to leave before anyone comes looking for you. So are you going to walk out willingly?"

My heart hammered in my chest, and I did the only thing I could think of. I bolted toward the other end of the bathroom, hoping there might be another way out. I heard him chasing after me, then he gripped a handful of my hair and jerked me backward, nearly pulling me off my feet.

He chuckled darkly. "You were warned."

My eyes widened as I saw a fist coming toward me, then pain exploded in my temple, and darkness closed in. My last thought was that Rocky was right, and I should have listened.

* * *

The smell hit me first. Damp. Mildew. Urine. It was enough to drag me back to consciousness. I tried to lift my hand and discovered my hands were tied down, and so were my ankles. My eyes slowly opened, peering into what looked like a corrugated-steel building. There were windows really high up, and the waning light of day streamed through the grimy panes. I shivered and realized my clothes had been removed, and I was completely naked, bound to a chair.

"There's my darling stepsister," a voice said.

I jerked my head in that direction and saw Sebastian, dressed in pristine slacks, shiny shoes, and a button-down shirt. He'd rolled the cuffs of his shirt, but otherwise looked impeccable as always. I licked my lips, my mouth feeling as dry as the desert.

"Where am I?" I asked.

"In a building I rented from some friends. You're quite a lot of trouble, Mara," Sebastian said.

"Why couldn't you just let me go?"

He smiled and the sight chilled me. "You should be thanking me."

"Why?"

"I could have been like my father and taken what I wanted a long time ago." His smile widened. "Or did you not know about that?"

"Know about what?" I asked. Maybe if I kept him talking, it would give Rocky time to find me.

"My father has a thing for young girls. He bought your mother when she was fourteen. He found her intriguing enough that he married her."

"What are you talking about?" I asked. "My mom and your dad didn't get married until three years ago."

"That's what my father wanted everyone to believe. Your mother is his wife for show. Oh, he wanted her back then, but now that she's older she doesn't hold any interest for him, except to have someone acceptable on his arm. He has to portray a family man to the public. But I know the truth… I followed him, to his private club." Sebastian looked downright evil. "Do you know what he does there?"

I honestly didn't think I wanted to know.

"He fucks young girls. Thirteen- and fourteen-year-old girls that he's purchased from their families or found on the streets. So you see, it could be worse. Oh, I want to fuck you. But I waited until you were older before I made my move. Kids don't hold any interest for me."

Bile rose in my throat as I thought about what Carl Rossi was doing behind closed doors, what he'd done to my own mother. How could I have lived with that monster for three years and never have known? He'd never done anything that would make me think he was capable of such a thing.

"What are you going to do with me?" I asked.

I didn't like the glint in Sebastian's eyes as he stood. There was a rolling cart off to the side, but I couldn't see what was on top. He walked over to it and picked up a sharp-looking knife. Waving it in the air, he came toward me.

"The first thing I'm going to do is make sure that biker you've been hanging out with doesn't want anything to do with you anymore. Once you don't look quite so pretty, I'm sure he'll lose interest."

A whimper escaped me as I eyed the knife.

"Then I'm going to take what I want. I'm going to fuck you until I'm tired of you, then I'm going to let my friends fuck you while I watch. And if you want to fight, even better. We'll enjoy holding you down and making you take it. Maybe I'll even record all those sessions and sell them." He chuckled as if that was the funniest thing he'd ever heard. "When you're useless, I'll send you to one of my family's whorehouses. Even with a scarred face and body, I'm sure we can find some customers to pay for your services."

My stomach churned, and I turned my head, puking all over the floor. Somehow I managed to not get any on me. Sebastian came closer, laughing as if he enjoyed my terror, and he probably did. The cool flat part of the knife slid across my cheek, and I shivered.

He leaned closer, and I felt his breath across my ear as he spoke. "This is your fault, you know? If you'd given me what I wanted that night, I'd have kept you.

My virgin stepsister. My dirty little secret. My own personal fuck toy. If you'd just spread your legs for me, you could have avoided all this. But now I'm going to humiliate you, hurt you, make you wish you were dead. Maybe when you're all used up, I'll finish you off and send your body back to your biker. You let him put his filthy hands on you. And now you're going to pay."

Please hurry, Rocky. Not that I had any idea how he'd even find me. Would he eventually stop looking? It wasn't like he was in love with me. Yes, I was his, but sooner or later he'd find someone else. I wasn't special. I'd never been special. Maybe my daddy had thought so, but no one since then.

The bite of the knife slid across my cheek, and I felt blood run from the wound and drip from my jaw. Tears welled in my eyes, and I ground my teeth together to keep from making a sound. I had a feeling Sebastian would love it if I begged, if I cried out in pain. I didn't want to give him that satisfaction.

"You aren't even going to ask how I know that you've given it up to him?" Sebastian asked, his smile cruel and downright evil. "I did a very thorough exam while you were knocked out. But don't worry. I haven't fucked you yet. I wanted to make sure you were awake for that."

The thought of his hands on me made me throw up again. Sebastian just laughed again, and I felt the bite of the knife on my other cheek. Tears streamed down my face, and soon was I was screaming, just like he wanted. Blood poured from the open wounds on my face, arms, and across the tops of my breasts. Sebastian tossed the knife aside and cupped my cheek with his hand.

"My sweet, beautiful stepsister. Our fun is only just beginning." He stared at my right wrist. "You let him brand you. Before I fuck you, I'm going to burn that mark from your skin. You were supposed to be mine."

"Just kill me," I said. Death would be preferable to what he had planned for me.

"Now what fun would that be? No, I want you screaming while I take what I want from you. Even I have standards, though. I'm not going to fuck you in this filthy place. I have a nice little love nest set up for us."

There was an explosion outside, and the ground shook from the force. Sebastian cursed and turned toward the man who had captured me. He'd been standing in the shadows, watching. Judging from the tent in his pants, he'd been enjoying my pain. Or maybe he got off on hearing all the vile things Sebastian was going to do to me. Another blast made the building shake. I didn't know what was going on out there, but I hoped it was someone coming to rescue me.

The door blew inward, and relief poured through me as I saw Rocky, Torch, and a handful of other men wearing the Dixie Reapers cut. I wanted to close my legs, cover myself, but I was still bound to the chair and unable to move. Sebastian pulled a gun from the back of his pants at the same time his thug drew on the men intent on saving me. Shots were fired, the sound of half a dozen weapons going off at once making my ears ring.

Through my tears, I watched as Rocky approached. His eyes were haunted as he looked at me, then he quickly removed his cut and pulled off his shirt. He slipped the leather back over his shoulders, then started working on the ropes holding me down. Once my arms were free, he slipped the shirt over my head, then freed my feet. I sobbed hard, my entire body shaking, as I fell into his arms.

"I'm so sorry, sweet girl," he said softly. "So damn sorry. I didn't protect you like I promised."

"I should have l-listened."

He pulled back and looked down at me. "This isn't on you. None of this is your fault, do you hear me?"

Torch came over, standing just behind Rocky. "Did he violate you, Mara?"

I whimpered and slammed my eyes shut. "He said he examined me while I was knocked out. He knew I wasn't a virgin anymore."

A growl came from deep inside Rocky as Torch turned on his heel and walked off. A minute later, I heard an inhuman scream. Rocky pressed my face to his chest, not letting me look. Whatever was being done to Sebastian, I didn't care. I wanted him dead. I needed the peace of mind that he would never come after me again.

"I'm going to carry you out to the truck, and then we're going to the hospital. I think this is beyond what Doc can handle. I'm sure they'll have questions, but I'll figure something out. They'll need to clean your wounds, maybe do some X-rays, and see if you need stitches," Rocky said. I heard him audibly swallow. "Are you sure they don't need to do a rape exam?"

"He said he hadn't done that to me," I said softly. "He wanted me to be awake, so he could hear me scream."

A shudder went through Rocky, then he lifted me into his arms and carried me from the building. I closed my eyes, not wanting to see what was happening to Sebastian and his thug. I hoped they died bloody and in pain.

Ivan followed us to the truck and climbed into the back seat. Rocky buckled me into the front passenger seat before getting in on the driver's side. He didn't say anything on the way to the hospital, but he kept glancing my way. At the hospital, he parked outside the ER doors and carried me inside while Ivan parked the truck.

When the ER staff saw my condition, they rushed me into the back. Rocky laid me on a bed behind a curtain and helped me into a gown a nurse provided. My blood seeped through the gown as I lay back and waited for a doctor. Rocky took the seat next to the bed and held my hand, almost as if he were afraid to let go. I'd heard horror stories of people waiting hours to be seen in the ER, but a doctor entered the curtained area within fifteen minutes.

"I'm Dr. Williams. Let's see what the damage is."

He checked out the wounds he could easily see, then peeled my gown down to check the knife marks across the tops of my breasts. I winced at the material stuck to the bloody slashes.

"We have to report wounds like these. What happened?" Dr. Williams asked.

"She was abducted," Rocky said. "The guy cut her up pretty bad before I could get to her. She said that he didn't rape her. Or rather he told her that he hadn't. She was unconscious part of the time."

The doctor looked toward Rocky, taking in the leather cut. "Is this a club issue? One that's been taken care of?"

Rocky nodded.

"I'll see what I can do to keep the police off your doorstep, but no promises," the doctor said.

My wounds were cleaned, and the doctor assessed the damage. If any other man had his hands on my breasts, I had a feeling Rocky wouldn't be happy, but he didn't utter a word of complaint. Probably because the doctor remained completely professional. He touched me, but only out of necessity.

"Do I need stitches?" I asked.

"The wounds look deep enough to scar, but I don't think stitches are necessary. I'm going to treat them, bandage them, and give you some instructions to follow. If it looks like infection is setting in, if they start bleeding and won't stop, then you need to either come back here or see your regular doctor," Dr. Williams said.

"She doesn't have anything to wear out of here," Rocky said. "I brought her in my shirt, but it's covered in blood now."

"I'll get her some scrubs," Dr. Williams said. He studied me a moment. "Are you sure I don't need to order a rape kit?"

"He said he didn't do that to me, and I believe him. He was sadistic enough to want me awake for that part," I answered.

The doctor nodded. When he was finished with my wounds, and had given me a sheet on how to care for them, he went to find some scrubs. They were a little big, but anything was welcome at this point.

Dr. Williams came back after I was dressed. "I was going to write a prescription for you, for pain, but I needed to ask first if you're pregnant."

My heart nearly stalled in my chest. I wanted to say no, but to be honest, I'd had a lot of unprotected sex with Rocky.

"It's possible," I said.

"When was your last period?" Dr. Williams asked.

My cheeks flushed. "About a month ago. It's never been all that regular, but I think I should have had one by now. But I wasn't sexually active until recently."

"How recent?" he asked.

"About a week."

"Week and a half," Rocky said.

Was he keeping track? I glanced at him, but he was staring at the doctor, waiting to see what would happen next. Dr. Williams ordered a blood test, and then I had to wait on results. Thankfully, they were able to run the labs at the hospital, and I didn't have to wait several days like I would have done at most doctor's offices.

Dr. Williams came back a while later, his arms folded. "I don't know if a baby is something you were trying for right now, but the test came back positive. You're pregnant. I've actually never seen such a strong positive result for someone who is barely pregnant. Your hCG level is rather high so there's no margin for error."

The room spun, and I must have started to slip sideways. Rocky's arms came around me, and pulled me onto his lap. I leaned against his chest as I processed what the doctor said. Dr. Williams said something else, but all I could hear was a buzzing in my ears. A small piece of paper was handed to Rocky, and then the doctor left.

Rocky helped me to my feet. He was going to pick me up again, but I held up a hand. "I can walk."

We followed the maze back to the main ER doors. I froze when we stepped into the ER waiting room. I saw Ivan, Torch, and six other Dixie Reapers, their large bodies dwarfing the small plastic chairs. Torch came forward while the others hung back.

"Are you okay, Mara?" he asked.

I nodded. "The doctor thinks I'll be okay, but said the wounds will likely scar."

"Sebastian Rossi has been taken care of. He won't bother you, or anyone else, ever again. I personally made sure of that."

"Thank you," I said softly.

Torch nodded, then turned to Rocky. "Take her home. I know you want to help handle the other problem, but you need to focus on Mara right now. Help her heal."

Rocky held up the paper. "I have to get this filled for her."

Torch took it. "We'll take care of it. I'll have Ivan bring it by later."

"Won't the pharmacy need my insurance information?" I asked.

"We'll pay cash," Torch said. "I'll take it from the Dixie Reapers general funds. You were taken on our watch, so I don't want you to feel responsible. We're taking care of the hospital bill too."

"Thank you," Rocky said.

Torch clapped him on the back. "It's what brothers do."

Rocky and Ivan walked with me to the truck, and once everyone was buckled, we headed back to the compound. I was tired, but I was scared to close my eyes. I was never going to forget the look on Sebastian's face, or his voice as he gleefully described what he would do to me. I wasn't sure that I would ever sleep again, at least not without nightmares. Rocky hadn't said much, but I knew he wanted to know everything. I only hoped that he was patient and would give me some time. I felt like I would break at any moment right now. All I wanted was to curl up with him, feel his arms around me.

At the compound, he dropped Ivan off at the clubhouse before going to our little house. I walked inside and went straight to the bathroom. Part of me didn't want to look, but I needed to know, needed to see. I stepped into the small room and shut the door. Pulling off the scrub top, I stared at my reflection, what parts of me I could see. Blood was already seeping through the bandages so I pulled them off.

The cuts on my face were longer than I'd thought. The tops of my breasts hadn't fared much better. I cried, the salt of my tears burning the wounds. Why would anyone want me while I looked like this? Could Rocky ever look at me again without remembering what happened? Would he see me bloody and tied naked to a chair every time he saw me now? Sobs wracked my body, and I sat on the toilet, wrapping my arms around myself, as if I could squeeze the broken pieces back together.

The door opened, and Rocky came in, kneeling in front of me. His touch was gentle as he nudged my chin up so I would look at him.

"It's over," he said.

"I'm so ugly. You're never going to look at me the same way."

He closed his eyes and breathed out harshly. When he opened them again, there was tenderness there that I had never seen before. He leaned forward and softly brushed his lips against mine.

"I'm going to tell you something, and I want you to listen carefully. I thought you were beautiful the first moment I saw you, even with your wounds from the wreck. They may have healed without scarring, but do you think a few lines on your body are really going to change how I feel when I look at you?" he asked.

"But…"

He placed a finger over my lips. "When I realized you were gone, that the bastard had taken you, I was more terrified than I've ever been before. Thankfully, one of our Prospects was in the parking lot having a cigarette. He saw the man carry you out a side door and put you in a waiting car. If Tyson hadn't seen you, hadn't followed, then I never would have found you. He didn't have reception where you were being held, or I would have come for you sooner."

"What are you saying, Rocky?"

"I'm saying… I think I love you, Mara. I've never been in love before, but when I thought you were gone, that I might never get you back, my heart hurt. If you had died, I would have wanted to die with you. Just as soon as I put an end to whoever was responsible for taking you from me."

"You love me?" I asked in a near whisper.

"Yeah, sweet girl. I love you." He lightly touched my cheek under one of the cuts. "If these scar, the only thing it proves is that you were strong enough to survive. We never have to talk about what happened today, unless you want to. If you need to talk, I'll listen. But I will never push you to share anything as painful as what you went through today."

"He was going to rape me," I said. "He said he'd take me until he tired of me, then give me to his friends. When I wasn't useful anymore, he was going to turn me into a whore."

Rocky's eyes darkened, and his jaw tightened. "Then I'm glad Torch killed that fucker."

"If Sebastian is dead, his father is going to want revenge. All we did was start a war that we likely won't win. Carl Rossi is going to want everyone punished who had a hand in his son's death."

"Torch is going to take care of Rossi. All I want you to do is focus on getting better." He placed a hand over my belly. "You're carrying precious cargo."

"Are you upset? About the baby, I mean?" I asked. "We never talked about kids…"

"I want kids with you, Mara. If you only want one, then we'll take precautions after this one. If you think you'd be happy having another one, then we'll have two. I'm just happy having you in my life, and the fact we created a life together is amazing. Maybe we'll have a little girl as beautiful as her mother."

Rocky kissed me again, slow and tender. When I stood up, he helped me out of the scrub bottoms. After redressing my wounds, he led me into the bedroom and helped me into my pajamas. We cuddled on the couch and watched TV, and when my stomach rumbled, he ordered Chinese for us. I spent the rest of the night in his arms, feeling loved and safe.

Chapter Ten

Rocky

I spent the next week taking care of Mara. We grew closer during that time, but I knew she was still worried about Carl Rossi. When Torch said he had information for me, I didn't hesitate to take Mara with me. There was a chance Torch would ask her to leave the room, but I hoped he'd let her stay. She needed peace of mind, and I didn't know how else to give it to her.

Torch pushed open the door to his house and motioned for us to come in. He gave Mara a slight smile as she entered the house behind me. His place was quiet, and I wondered where Isabella was today. Torch led the way to the back of the house and stepped into an office I hadn't even realized he had. He left the door open as we took our seats.

"I wanted to let you know that the issue with Carl Rossi is being taken care of. I was going to turn him over to the government for that stunt ten years ago, but he's managed to evade the law for so long, I didn't want to chance him walking away."

"So what's going to happen to him?" Mara asked.

"My father-in-law is an interesting man," Torch said.

I snorted. It was a little weird hearing him call a man around his own age his father-in-law, even if that's what Casper VanHorne was. I hadn't met the man, even though I'd been here the day Isabella was first brought to Torch. I remembered thinking she was just a kid, and I didn't understand how Torch could claim her, but she'd only been two years younger than Mara was now. It made me feel a little like a hypocrite.

It was obvious Torch loved Isabella. There might be a huge age difference between them, but it seemed to work.

"So, you've sent Casper after Carl Rossi?" I asked.

Torch nodded. "He's been doing some research the last few days and said he's ready to make his move. If all goes according to plan, by dinner tonight, Sara Rossi will be a widow."

"What's going to happen to my mom?" Mara asked.

"I can't find any direct connection with your mom and what happened to your dad. Yes, she received money from Carl Rossi a few months before she took off with you, and I think she may have known what would happen, but she didn't instigate it."

"She didn't stop it either," Mara said.

"No, she didn't." Torch leaned back in his chair. "Your mother stands to inherit millions when Rossi is taken down. We can leave her alone, keep an eye on her, and see what happens. She may live the rest of her life in peace, or…"

"A heroin addict isn't going to live for much longer," I said.

"He's not wrong," Torch said. "From what we've learned, your mother is in pretty rough shape. She's so far gone, I don't think even rehab would do much good. Likely, she's going to pass before long. If you want her punished for what she did, then I can arrange it. I'm going to leave her fate up to you."

"I don't want her to know where I am, or know that I'm pregnant," Mara said.

Torch looked from Mara to me, his eyebrows raised, and I realized that I'd never told anyone Mara was pregnant. I had a feeling he would say something to me later. I hadn't meant to keep it a secret, but with everything that had happened, it just hadn't occurred to me that I should say anything.

"We'll make sure she stays away from you," Torch said. "You should know that Sara has a will. Wire was able to get a copy. You're listed as her sole heir. Now, with Rossi still alive right now, she's not really worth anything. But once he's taken care of, you'll be a very rich woman after your mom passes."

Mara looked like she'd sucked on a lemon.

"Or not," Torch said, looking amused at her reaction.

"I don't want to touch that money," Mara said. "People have died for it, women have been exploited, and kids were raped."

"When the time comes, we can figure something out," Torch said. "You might want to tuck it away in case of an emergency."

"Is it safe for Mara to leave the compound?" I asked. "I'm sure she's feeling trapped by now. Even though Sebastian is gone, I've kept her on lockdown until Carl Rossi was taken care of. I didn't want him to come after her."

"Rossi knows his son was killed here, but Sebastian must not have been very forthcoming with his father because my sources say Carl can't figure out why Sebastian was in Alabama. If he's noticed Mara is gone, he doesn't seem to care. There's nothing out there about her being a missing person. I honestly don't think Carl is after Mara, but if you want to err on the side of caution, I'll send you a text once Carl is out of the picture," Torch said.

"Will anyone retaliate against the club or the man who's going after Carl?" Mara asked.

"We've made sure nothing can be traced to us," Torch said. "The club is safe, and you will be too."

"Thank you," Mara said.

"You're family, Mara. As Rocky's woman, you're part of us," Torch said. "And seeing as you're pregnant, that baby you're carrying will be part of this family too. Since I doubt you've seen a doctor other than the one at the ER, I'll arrange for you to see Isabella's OB-GYN. She had an appointment scheduled for today, and I'm sure she won't mind you taking her slot."

Mara looked at me and then Torch. "Today?"

He nodded. "You need to leave pretty much right now."

Torch slid a business card across the desk. I picked it up and saw it was for the OB-GYN, with an address and phone number. I knew where it was located. Mara stood up, as did I. Torch remained seated and opened a file on his desk. I knew we were dismissed. Escorting Mara out to the truck, I got us to the doctor's office as quickly as I could, since Torch hadn't given an exact appointment time.

There were a lot of papers to fill out, and Mara kept shaking out her hand. Partway through, I took the clipboard from her and started answering the questions as she gave me verbal response to each prompt on the form. When it was done, I turned it in along with her insurance card and paid her co-pay. If Rossi wasn't going to be around much longer, I had a feeling Mara was going to need new insurance. I'd have to look into it later.

We waited for a half hour before Mara's name was called. They checked her blood pressure and her weight before escorting us to a room.

"The doctor will be in shortly," the nurse said, smiling as she shut the door.

"Nervous?" I asked.

Mara nodded.

"I don't think they'll do much today. Maybe confirm the pregnancy. I may not know much about babies or being pregnant, but I don't think you're far enough along for them to do much else," I told her.

There was a knock on the door then a man in a white lab coat stepped inside. He smiled warmly and offered his hand to both of us. He looked a little young to be a doctor, but if Torch thought he was good enough for Isabella, then the man must be a good doctor.

"I'm Dr. Myron," the doctor said. "It's a pleasure to meet you both. I'm getting more and more Dixie Reapers' ladies these days. You guys must have some powerful swimmers."

Mara bit her lip, and her shoulders shook with silent laughter.

"So, what makes you think you're pregnant?" Dr. Myron asked.

"I had a blood test at the ER. They said it was positive," Mara said. "I don't really know that I needed to come in this early. I had sex for the first time about a week and a half before the pregnancy test was done."

"And when was that?" Dr. Myron asked.

"Three weeks in a few days," I said.

"We won't be able to see or hear the baby at this early stage. Did you complete the form allowing us to receive medical files on you?" Dr. Myron asked.

"Yes," Mara answered.

"I'll want your file from your primary doctor and any OB-GYNs you may have seen in the past. I want to make sure all our bases are covered, and you get the best care. For now, I know that you already had a blood test. I'll need those documents from the ER. They can fax them but may need written permission from you first. Are you on prenatal vitamins?" Dr. Myron asked.

"The ER doctor gave her a thirty-day supply when he wrote the prescription for her painkillers," I said.

"When you received the wounds on your face and arms, did the person responsible hit your stomach or cut you there?" Dr. Myron asked.

Mara shook her head. "I don't think so. I was knocked out part of the time, but my stomach didn't hurt at any point."

"Once I receive the files from the ER confirming your pregnancy, I'll call in a prescription for prenatal vitamins. We'll go ahead and use the ones the ER doctor requested, and if I think those aren't sufficient after future tests we can go from there. Some are stronger than others. For now, you don't really need to change your activities, but I wouldn't do anything dangerous," Dr. Myron said.

"So, no riding on the back of my bike?" I asked.

"I wouldn't advise it," Dr. Myron said.

Mara's head whipped around to face me. "You have a motorcycle?"

Dr. Myron chuckled, and I pointed to my cut. "Did you miss this part of my life?"

"But I haven't seen it," Mara said.

"Torch was storing it for me. Since I've had you with me pretty much everywhere I've gone, I've just been using the truck. Now that the doctor has just vetoed you on riding on the back of the bike, you can ride with Isabella, Ridley, and the kids." I smiled at her. "I promise to take you on ride as soon as you're able to go."

Mara sighed and looked at the doctor again. "When do I have to come back?"

"Why don't we schedule something for six weeks from now? We can listen to the baby's heartbeat then," Dr. Myron said. He looked at me, and there was indecision on his face.

"Spit it out, Doc," I said.

"Were you told why your President and VP chose me to look after their wives?" he asked.

"Figured you were the best," I answered.

"Well, I am pretty good at my job," he said with a smile. "But I think it has more to do with the fact they felt they could trust me to look at their women and not do anything inappropriate."

My brow furrowed.

Dr. Myron smiled a little. "I'm gay. So looking at Mara's more intimate parts isn't going to do a damn thing for me. Not that a doctor should be affected by that anyway, but I thought I'd share that with you, in case it makes a difference."

I scratched my beard. "Well, I appreciate you sharing that, but I didn't think it was an issue with you being a professional and all."

"Good to know," Dr. Myron said. "I'll see the two of you in six weeks. If you have any questions before then, call the office and either a nurse will help you or we can schedule an appointment."

He shook our hands again and stepped out of the room. I helped Mara off the table and went toward the front, stopping at a window near the exit sign to schedule her next appointment. When we were finished, I took her by the ER so she could have her file faxed over. I contemplated taking her home, but she'd been cooped up so much since we came here, except for outings with four or more others with us, I felt bad. Yes, it was for her protection, but I knew it had to be tiresome.

My phone vibrated, and I pulled it out, swiping the screen. There was an encrypted message from Torch's number. We used them often when doing jobs so I entered my code and waited for the message to load.

Torch: Rossi isn't a problem anymore. Kill confirmed.

There was a picture attached of Carl Rossi with a bullet wound through the center of his forehead. I'd thought Casper was going to do it later tonight, but I guess the opportunity presented itself, and he took it. Within thirty seconds of viewing the image, the picture began to pixelate and slowly became unrecognizable, before vanishing completely.

"Everything okay?" Mara asked.

I turned my phone and showed her Torch's text. She smiled, and it looked like the stress just melted off of her. Her shoulders relaxed, her face wasn't as tense. I knew the message would disappear the same as the picture had, so I shoved my phone back into my pocket. I'd known Mara was worried, but I don't think I realized how much until right now. I stopped her next to the truck and put my arms around her. Mara leaned her body into mine and tipped her head back to look up at me.

"You're safe. Sebastian and Carl Rossi are both dead, and no one else wants to harm you. No more hiding at the compound or going out in large groups. You can go places with Isabella and Ridley, or even venture out on your own. I would prefer that you keep a Prospect with you, just in case trouble should come up, but I won't force you to. I know the last few weeks have been a little like being in jail."

"I love you, Rocky, and I know you wouldn't ask me to do something unless you thought it was for my own good. If you want me to take a Prospect with me whenever I leave the compound, I'm okay with that."

"We can do anything you want, just the two of us," I said.

She smiled a little, then pulled me down to whisper in my ear. "You could take me home and fuck me."

I stood up and my gaze skimmed over her wounds. They were mostly healed. "I'll be gentle with you."

She snorted. "I don't want gentle. I want you to fuck me the way you always do. Hard. Deep. Fast. Remind me that I'm yours."

I kissed her, my tongue sliding into her mouth. She melted against me as my hands cupped her ass, and I ground my erection against her belly. If that's what Mara wanted, that's what she would get. And since my cock hadn't been inside her in a fucking week, I was going to make up for lost time.

"I hope you don't plan on walking tomorrow," I said against her lips. "Because I'm fucking you all night long."

She smiled, her eyes lighting up with pleasure. I swatted her ass and helped her into the truck, then drove back the compound like hellhounds were chasing after us. It was time to remind my woman that she was mine, every fucking inch of her, and I was going to taste every part of her. By morning she'd be hoarse from screaming my name.

"I love you, Rocky," she said, smiling over at me as I pulled to a stop in front of our home.

"Love you too, sweet girl."

She followed me into the house, and I'd barely locked the door before Mara had launched herself into my arms. My back slammed into the door as the full force of her body rocked me on my heels. I couldn't help but smile at her enthusiasm and wrapped an arm around her waist as she pressed her lips to mine. I hadn't seen this aggressive side of her before and was both a little amused and a lot turned on. My dick hardened and pressed against my zipper as her legs went around my waist. Even through her jeans, I could feel the heat of her pussy, practically begging to be filled with my cock.

"Bedroom," she said, drawing back.

With a growl, I turned us so that she was pushed up against the door, and I ground my cock against her. "No. Here. Now."

Her eyes dilated, and her lips parted slightly. I kissed her like a man possessed, my mouth devouring hers as my tongue thrust between her lips. I felt her surrender in the way her body melted against me, heard it in the soft sounds she made. Mara's nails bit into my shoulders as she clung to me, and I could feel the hard points of her nipples brushing against my chest. I let my lips trail along her jaw and then lightly bit her neck. She moaned and arched against me, tilting her head to give me better access. I sucked on the soft skin along her throat just hard enough to leave a mark.

I eased away from her, setting her down. My hands braced her until I knew she could stand on her own, then I took a step back. "Strip."

Her breath caught, but she didn't hesitate to obey me. She ripped her shirt over her head and threw it off to the side before kicking off her shoes and shimmying out of her jeans. The bra and panties she had on were my favorites, the lace so sheer it left little to the imagination. When she reached for the clasp on her bra, I reached out to stop her.

"You look sexy as hell in those," I said.

"You want them to stay on?"

I nodded and grabbed the back of my shirt, hauling it over my head and letting it falling to the floor. I wanted her too damn bad to strip all the way, but I unfastened my belt and jeans before prowling closer to her. Mara backed up, running into the door, but the look in her eyes said she wanted me to catch her, to claim her and ruin her for all other men. Not that I was ever letting someone else touch her. I'd fucking kill anyone who tried.

Mara's hands settled at my waist, shoving my jeans and boxer briefs down far enough my cock sprang out, hard and ready for her. She gripped the shaft with her small hand and stroked it a few times.

"I'm not stopping until I've filled you up in every way possible," I said, my voice mostly a growl. "You want that?"

She stared at me, eyes wide. I leaned in closer, my cock brushing her belly as my lips ghosted along her ear. "You want my cum, sweet girl? Tell me you want it, want my cock in your mouth, thrusting in your pussy, and pounding that tight little ass."

Mara whimpered, and when I pulled away I saw her eyes were closed and her breathing was labored. Yeah, she liked that idea. If her nipples had been any harder, they'd probably slice through the material of her bra. I leaned down and closed my lips around the tip of one breast, the lace rough against my tongue as I laved it through the material. Mara's hand went to my head, pulling me even closer. I snaked a hand down inside her panties, tracing my fingers along her wet slit. She was more than ready for me, but I wasn't in a rush. I wanted her, every inch of her, and I wasn't stopping until I'd fucked her in every way possible. I had a feeling we were both going to be sore tomorrow.

I drew away, taking a step back again. I pointed at the ground. "On your knees."

Mara trembled as she sank down to the floor, her hands braced on her thighs as she waited for my next instruction. She looked so damn beautiful, just waiting for my cock. The look in her eyes was hungry, and I knew she wanted this as much as I did. Mara might have been a virgin when I took her the first time, but she was made for this, made for my cock, for fucking.

"Open," I told her.

Her jaw dropped, and I reached out, gripping a handful of her hair, then dragging her toward my cock. I painted her lips with pre-cum before easing the head inside. I teased her, pushing in just a little, then pulling back. Her tongue flicked against me, then curled around my shaft as I sank farther into her mouth. I held her steady as I thrust in and out of her mouth, each stroke a little deeper than the last until she was taking all of me.

"That's it, sweet girl. Take every fucking inch."

She moaned as I fucked her mouth, slow and steady at first, then a little faster. I could feel my climax coming, my balls drawing up. I took her mouth harder, and with a groan I let loose, spurt after spurt of cum filling her mouth and sliding down her throat.

"Keep sucking, baby. Make me nice and hard again."

She reached up and gripped my hips before putting that talented tongue of hers to good use. She licked, sucked, and teased my shaft until I was ready to go again. Her mouth felt like fucking heaven, but I didn't want to come down her throat again. I wanted in that sweet pussy of hers. I pulled free of her lips and hauled her to her feet, then pressed her against the door.

Her lips were swollen and red, and there was a drop of cum at the corner of her mouth. I flicked it away with my thumb, then took my time looking her over. It seemed a shame such perfect breasts should be confined, even if the packaging was pretty. I pulled the cups down and teased her nipples with my fingers, smiling when I saw her squeezing her thighs together.

"Feel good, baby?" I asked.

Mara bit her lip and nodded.

"Want more?" I asked.

"Please," she said softly. "Please fuck me."

My lips brushed against hers. "You want my cock?"

She moaned, and her eyes fluttered shut as my fingers coasted along the crotch of her panties.

"Want my cock in your pussy?"

She nodded and spread her legs a little, giving me room to play. I eased a finger under the material and stroked her satiny lips. If I'd thought she was wet before, she was beyond soaked now. It seemed my dirty girl had gotten turned on by me using her the way I had, fucking that delicious mouth of hers. I stroked over her clit, and she cried out, grinding against me.

"You want to come?" I asked, leaning forward to nip her bottom lip.

"Make me come, Rocky. I need to so bad."

I rubbed her clit, the little bud slippery from her cream, until her legs trembled and she was hanging onto me like her life depended on it. I kept stroking it until she came, her release flooding her panties. A groan slipped out of me as I thought about fucking her, how amazing she'd feel right now. I pulled my finger free of her panties and lifted her, then pinned her to the door with my body. Reaching between us, I shoved her panties to the side and entered her with one long thrust.

Mara cried out as I filled her, not stopping until every inch of my cock was buried inside her. Her ankles were locked behind my back, and I began stroking in and out of her. Deep. Hard. I didn't have it in me to be gentle right then. I wanted her too fucking bad. The door rattled on its hinges as I pounded into her, driving my cock into her wet little pussy again and again. When she came, she screamed my name and her nails bit into my skin. It was just the right amount of pain to send me over the edge, and I filled her up with my cum, pumping until every drop had been wrung from my balls.

With my dick deep inside her, I gripped her ass and carefully carried her to the bedroom, mindful that my pants could slip at any moment and cause both of us to tumble to the floor. I made it to the bed without incident and finally pulled out of her. Our mingled fluids gushed down her thighs, and I gently nudged her onto the bed, then pulled her panties down her legs. I loved seeing her thighs all wet and sticky, knowing I was the cause.

"I know I've played around with your ass, but I haven't fucked you there yet. Are you up for that today?" I asked. As badly as I wanted to take her there, I wouldn't do it if she didn't feel ready. I wanted the experience to be mind-blowing for both of us. The way her pussy squeezed me, I knew her ass would be ten times better.

"I'm ready," she said, a blush staining her cheeks.

She started to roll over, but I stopped her, just wanting to look for another moment. Her bra was still pushed down under her breasts and her dusky nipples were hard. Her thighs were parted, and her pussy and thighs were covered in cum. Fuck, but that was a gorgeous sight. It was tempting to take a picture, just so I'd remember this moment forever.

"Hands and knees, sweet girl," I said, as I opened the bedside table and pulled out the lube.

She rolled to her belly, then got her knees up under her and presented her ass to me. Her thighs were spread enough that I had a nice view of her pussy as well. I reached for her and popped the cap open on the bottle in my hand. Spreading her ass cheeks wide, I drizzled some lube between them, then used my finger to work it into her. The tight little ring of muscle resisted at first, but it didn't take long before she was taking my finger.

I tossed the lube aside, and while I stretched her ass, I slid my cock back into her pussy. Using slow, shallow strokes, I fucked her while I worked on getting a second and then third finger into her tight little hole. If I were into sharing, I'd be willing to bet that sweet little Mara could handle two cocks at once. But that shit wasn't ever going to happen because she was mine and only mine.

Withdrawing from her pussy and pulling my fingers free, I used my hands to spread her wide-open.

"You ready, sweet girl? Just remember to breathe out and relax. Push out against me when I enter you."

"Yes, Rocky," she said softly.

I lined up my cock and ground my teeth together as I struggled to get inside her. She was so fucking tight, even after me stretching her, but finally I got the head of my cock into her ass. She whimpered and squirmed beneath me. A quick swat to her ass made her grow still, and I rubbed away the sting before sliding a little more of my cock into her.

"You okay, baby?" I asked.

"So full," she murmured.

"Does it hurt?" I asked.

"It burns, but don't stop."

I groaned as I worked more of my dick inside her, as I finally bottomed out, my balls slapping her pussy, I knew I wouldn't last for long. I'd never felt anything so tight, and my eyes damn near crossed from the exquisite pleasure.

"I'll take things slow," I told her.

"No."

"What do you mean 'no'?"

"Don't baby me, Rocky. If you want to fuck me, then do it. I don't need slow. Take me the way you really want to."

My stomach clenched. "Sweet girl, what I want is to ride this ass hard and deep, and I don't think you're anywhere near ready for that."

"So I'll be sore tomorrow," she said. "Wouldn't be the first time."

"Mara…"

"Please," she begged. "I want all of you, Rocky. I don't want you to feel like you have to hold back."

I leaned forward and kissed her spine. "Then hold on, little girl."

She clenched her hands on the bedding, and I gripped her hips tight. I tried to temper my thrusts at first, wanting to be careful with her, despite what she'd said, but soon I was taking her as fast, deep, and hard as I wanted. I groaned as I pounded into her, fucking her the way I'd been wanting since the moment she flashed me back at the cabin. I rode her ass, giving her every inch, again and again.

"Play with your clit," I said, my teeth clenched. "Make yourself come. I'm so damn close."

Mara shifted and obeyed my command, and soon she was crying out and pushing back against me. I felt the gush of moisture from her pussy coating my balls as I slammed into her again and again, filling her ass with my cum. I stayed buried inside her a moment, trying to catch my breath, my cock twitching from the force of my release. As I eased out of her, she moaned and collapsed onto the bed.

I let her rest while I went down the hall to the bathroom and started the shower. She was half-asleep when I went back for her, and I pulled her into my arms, carrying her with ease. I stepped into the shower with her still in my arms, then let her slide down my body until she was standing on her own. She wrapped her arms around my waist and hugged me tight, resting her cheek over my heart.

It was amazing how much my life had changed in such a short amount of time. I hadn't wanted a woman, hadn't wanted a family, but it seemed Fate had other ideas in mind for me, and now I had both, and I couldn't have been fucking happier. I would protect her for the rest of my life, her and our child, and I would make sure they never wanted for anything. She had my heart, owned my soul, and there wasn't a damn thing I wouldn't do for her.

"Thank you," she whispered.

She was thanking me? "For what?"

"For saving me, for protecting me, for loving me."

"I will save you every time you need to be rescued, protect you every day from now until eternity, and love you until I draw my last breath. You're mine, Mara." I tipped her chin up. "And I'm yours."

A soft smile curved her lips and a sense of peace settled over me, something I'd thought I'd never feel again. Maybe I hadn't been the one to save her. Maybe she had been the one to save me. Or perhaps we saved each other.

She might wear a *Property of Rocky* stamp on her body, but my heart was tattooed with *Property of Mara*.

Bull (Dixie Reapers MC 4)
Harley Wylde

Darian: When the guy I'd been seeing turned out to be a rapist sleazeball, I ran… and it led me straight to *him*. They call him Bull, and I can see why. The guy is massive, and I do mean everywhere. He's so much older than me, but I can't seem to care. The way he holds me, murmurs softly to me, I feel safe. No one's ever cared what happened to me, but he does. I can tell he wants me, even though he's fighting himself. But he doesn't have to… because I'm his. I've held onto my virginity all these years, but I want him more than I ever thought I'd want someone. I want his hands on me, his body over mine. And for once, I'm going to get what I want. And I want Bull.

Bull: Darian's younger than my damn daughter, but there's something about the sweet girl that draws me closer. When I look into her eyes, I see that she's a fighter, but I can also see that she's been badly broken, and I want to be the one to put the pieces back together. I have nothing to offer her. There's more than twenty years between us, and I know I need to walk away. I'm just a dirty old man who wants her under me. I'm hard as a damn post anytime she's nearby, and I have to fight the urge to spread those creamy thighs of hers and drive into her, claiming her body and making her mine… until I have no fight left in me. I wanted to be a better man, to walk away, but I can't. She begs me so sweetly, and soon I can't resist anymore. She's mine. And any fucker who tries to take her from me is going to die a slow and painful death.

Prologue

Bull

I downed a shot of whiskey, the amber liquid burning through me. My brothers were cutting up and having a good ol' time while I suffered in silence. Maybe I was getting too old for this shit, but something felt like it was missing these days. My VP had claimed my daughter as his old lady, and I was now a grandpa twice over. Hell, even Torch's old lady had returned, and she'd made him a daddy.

I'd never once thought about taking an old lady, always content with the club pussy. Hell, there were nights I had three or four women. Of course, the older I got, the harder it was to go all damn night like I used to. Or maybe the easy women with their painted lips and fake bodies just didn't do it for me anymore. Forty-nine wasn't exactly over the hill, but I was feeling every one of those years tonight.

I wanted something different. I wanted... a woman. *My* woman. Someone who was just mine and not spreading her legs for anyone who crooked a finger. I wanted an old lady to go home to at the end of the day, someone to hold at night. Maybe in my old age what I was craving was a sense of closeness, that feeling everyone describes when they meet the one person meant for them. That insane instant attraction, the feeling like you can't breathe if they walk away.

Yeah. I wanted that.

The Prospect behind the bar placed the whiskey bottle near my hand, and I poured myself another shot. At least if I kept drinking, the next time a club slut came onto me, I could claim I had whiskey dick and couldn't get it up. They might be whores, but they had feelings too. The last thing I wanted to do was make them feel unattractive, even if they just didn't do a damn thing for me these days.

Hell, I hadn't gotten laid in months. Not for lack of the women trying, but I just wasn't interested anymore. It got tiresome, fucking random women, sometimes being the third or fourth guy to stick my dick in them. Virgins were about as rare as a fucking unicorn, but I'd just be happy with a woman who hadn't slept with more men than I had fingers and toes. I didn't think that was asking too much.

I finished off half the bottle of whiskey before I pried myself off the stool and staggered out to my bike. I stared at it a moment, then realized I'd had far too much to drink. I didn't like driving when I was drunk, so I pocketed my keys and started walking. Home wasn't far away. When I'd become a grandpa, Torch had given me a small house so the kids could visit with me in my own space without me bringing them into the clubhouse. I was grateful, but most nights the house was damn quiet. And too fucking empty.

I stumbled up my steps and let myself in since I never locked the door. After I staggered down the hall, I pushed my way into my bedroom, kicked off my boots, and face-planted on the bed. I felt like a fucking pansy, moping because I was alone. But as I stared across the expanse of my king-size bed, I couldn't help but wish there was a soft warm body cuddled up against me. The sweet scent of a woman wrapped in my arms.

But who the fuck would want an asshole biker like me?

Chapter One

Darian
Two Weeks Later

My lungs felt like they were on fire as my arms pumped and my legs ran as fast as they could go. The *slap slap slap* of my shoes hitting the pavement filled the air around me, along with the huffing of my breath. I didn't dare take a moment to even look over my shoulder as I charged through the darkened streets. I was in Nowhere, Alabama, some small town my supposed boyfriend had brought me to, promising an awesome party. Little had I realized, I was the entertainment. Thank God I hadn't swallowed the pills he'd given me! If I had, I might not have survived what they had planned for me.

I seemed to be on the outskirts of town, with hardly any businesses or homes surrounding me, but I could see lights and a neon sign in the distance, and I prayed that I would find help when I got there. When I'd taken off, I'd heard them running after me, the charge of their steps spurring me on. Thankfully they were too stoned or stupid to realize they'd catch me faster in their cars, and in their bumbling attempts to catch me, I'd managed to get away. Or so I hoped. They could still be there, coming for me in the darkness, waiting until I weakened.

A huge gate came into focus with what looked like a bar behind it. I'd never seen a bar behind a fence topped with barbed wire before, but I didn't much care what the place looked like, as long as they would help me. Maybe let me make a call, even though I didn't know who to reach out to. It wasn't like I had an abundance of friends, and I had no family that I knew of. I collapsed when I reached the gate, my hands sliding down the bars as my knees hit the pavement. My breath sawed in and out of my lungs, and spots danced across my vision.

"What are you doing here, sweet thing?" a male voice drawled from behind the fence.

I tried to look up, but I was too damn exhausted. Whatever adrenaline rush I'd experienced, it was waning, and intense fatigue was settling into my body, making it damn near impossible to stay upright. I didn't know how far I'd run, but it had to have been several miles or more, and for someone who wasn't very athletic, that felt like a ton. My hands slipped from the bars, and I fell onto my back on the pavement of the driveway and stared up at the starry sky. The man cursed, and the gate opened, then booted steps came my way. The face peering down at me was obscured by the darkness, but he'd sounded young. Maybe late teens or early twenties? Old enough his voice had already changed. Whoever he was, he made no move to touch me.

I heard the roar of an engine from down the road, and soon a single headlight washed across me. I turned toward the light, straining to see whoever was there, my eyes squinting at the brightness. The headlight shut off, and I blinked a few times, trying to focus.

"What's going on, Johnny?" a deeper voice asked, sending chills down my spine. There was something about that voice, something I liked. It was powerful, commanding.

"I don't know, Bull. She came running up here like her life depended on it, then just fell on the ground. She won't talk."

I heard an engine shut off then heavy footsteps came toward me. The first thing I saw was long, blond hair, then a darker beard came into view. Piercing eyes peered down at me, with concern etched on the stranger's face. In the dark, I couldn't guess his age very well, could barely make out all his features, but he was close enough I caught his scent -- leather with a hint of something warm and spicy. And what kind of name was Bull?

His touch was gentle as he brushed my hair back from my face, my long locks close in color to his. With infinite care, he scooped me up into his arms and rose to his full height. The world spun a moment, and when I looked around, I realized I was really far off the ground. He was incredibly tall, definitely over six feet. I looked back up at the man holding me, wanting to speak yet not knowing what to say. I should say something. I knew that much. He was a stranger, and for all I knew, I was in more trouble than earlier. His gaze left mine to settle on the guy he'd called Johnny.

I felt bereft without him looking at me, as if something had been taken away that was rightfully mine. Maybe I was losing my mind and going crazy. The run must have scrambled my brains as well as my insides. I definitely wasn't thinking rationally. Never in my life had I reacted to a man like I was reacting to Bull.

"Bring my bike through the gates. I'll come back for it later," Bull said.

So the rumbling engine had been a motorcycle. Wait. Come back for it? Where were we going? I should have panicked, but all I felt was this soothing calm. It was almost like being in his arms was enough to make me feel safe. *That's ridiculous, Darian. He's a stranger. What if he's a rapist or a murderer*? But ridiculous or not, that was how I felt. Even though I didn't know where I was, or who he was, I felt like I could trust him. There was this feeling deep in my gut that the man holding me would never hurt me. I'd trusted that instinct often enough over the years, and had I listened to it when Leo had asked me out, I wouldn't be in this mess now. It had never steered me wrong before.

He didn't say anything more, just started walking down what appeared to be a road. Had they fenced off part of the town? Why was there a road behind that massive gate? The building we passed, the one I'd assumed was a bar, said *Dixie Reapers* across the top in neon lights. That still didn't tell me anything. The road he was walking on wound around the building, and soon I saw houses. There had been a row of motorcycles parked outside the bar, and I saw more in the driveways of the homes we passed. I was getting more and more confused. Why would there be a business and a bunch of houses behind a fence topped with barbed wire? Where the hell was I? Were they some kind of cult? And what was with all the bikes? Did they not believe in vehicles with more than two wheels? It almost like being on a set from that show… what was it called? *Sons of Anarchy*?

We passed quite a few homes before he walked up the steps of a one-story house with a wide front porch. The color looked gray, but without a porch light on, I couldn't tell for certain. He somehow managed to open the door without dropping me, then carried me inside, kicking the door shut behind him. He didn't bother to lock it, but I doubted anyone was getting past their guarded gate. I just didn't know if that gate should make me feel safer or more afraid. Despite Bull's gentle touch, I had no idea who he was or what kind of place I'd landed in.

Bull didn't hesitate when he entered the house but strode into the living room and eased me down onto the couch. He flicked on a lamp, and as the room flooded with light, I was surprised to see that he seemed much older than my twenty-one years. There were lines at the corners of his eyes, but he was a very handsome man. As I took in the details of his face, I felt this intense pull toward him. I'd seen attractive men before. Well, mostly boys. But there was something about him, something different. The look in his eyes said he'd seen shit I couldn't even fathom, and yet the way he watched me... it made me feel all warm and gooey inside.

He pulled off his leather jacket and tossed it onto a chair, and I felt my eyes widen as I took in his broad chest and large biceps. There was some sort of leather vest over his T-shirt, but I couldn't read the writing. Even if the lines on his face hadn't belied his age, there was no mistaking his body for that of a boy. He was definitely all man. The T-shirt he wore was stretched tightly across him, and my fingers itched to see if his chest was as hard as it looked. I could understand now why they called him Bull. The man was huge. My gaze dipped down below his belt, and my cheeks flushed when I saw his cock straining against his zipper. Yeah, he was big. Everywhere.

"What's your name?" he asked, drawing my attention away from what was hidden in his jeans.

"Darlan. Darian Crosse."

"You don't sound like you're from around here."

I shook my head. "I'm from Georgia. The guy I was seeing told me about this awesome party and brought me here."

Bull's eyebrows rose. "And where is he now?"

"Probably still looking for me."

Bull rocked back on his heels, shoving his hands into his pockets. I was too busy admiring him again to say anything more. I couldn't say he was beautiful, but I'd never met anyone like Bull before. I felt like I could look at him all day.

"Is he the one you're running from?" Bull asked.

"Him and the others," I murmured, still admiring him.

His eyes narrowed. "What others?"

I tipped my head back and closed my eyes a moment. Their faces, with their leering smiles, flashed in my mind. Bile rose in my throat as I thought about the words I'd heard, their intentions toward me, and their complete lack of humanity. Fear and revulsion rolled through me, and I knew I was damn lucky to have gotten away.

I focused on him again, trying to shake free from the horror of what had nearly happened to me. "The party Leo took me to expected me to be the entertainment, even though I hadn't known that at the time. I'd confessed to Leo a few days ago that I was a virgin and was waiting for the right guy and the right time. I thought he was understanding and might be the one. I didn't realize he was excited about my virginity for another reason."

"That doesn't explain the others you mentioned. Who were they?"

"Leo tried to drug me earlier, but I didn't take the pills. When we got into town, we drove to some rundown place. I think it's a few miles from here, but I honestly don't know how far I ran. It was a house full of guys. Some looked younger than me and some looked older. Maybe late twenties or early thirties. When we stepped into the house, I realized quickly I was the only girl there. The guys weren't quiet about their plans. They were going to take turns with me. All twelve of them and one said he was willing to pay Leo to be the one to take my virginity. Thankfully, it looked like they'd already been partying pretty hard, and they were either drunk, stoned, or both."

A chill entered his eyes, and his hands clenched at his sides. Suddenly the protective man who had been so tender with me looked more like a Viking warrior about to go off to battle. With his long blond hair and beard, I could easily see him with a sword, or whatever Vikings had used in times of war.

"They were going to gang rape you?" His voice sounded calmer than he looked. Anger poured off him in waves.

My throat tightened, and I swallowed as tears filled my eyes. I hadn't admitted to myself yet that that's what they'd planned. Oh, I'd run the moment I'd realized what they were going to do, but then I'd pushed it to the back of my mind and not used *that* word. Instead, I broke it down into pieces I could stomach instead of looking at the whole picture.

Bull noticed my distress and sank down onto his haunches in front of me. Some of the anger had faded from his eyes, and the tender guy who had picked me up off the pavement was back. He reached for me slowly, brushing tears off my cheeks that I hadn't even realized I'd shed. That was enough to make the dam break, and I started crying in earnest. Bull gathered me in his arms and sat on the couch, settling me in his lap. Cradled against his broad chest, I felt like nothing could harm me. I clung to him, my hands twisted in the fabric of his shirt as I soaked him with my tears. He didn't seem to mind, though, murmuring words of comfort to me.

Despite my distress over what had nearly happened to me, I felt completely safe in his arms. Being held by him was almost like coming home. That sense of rightness, of belonging. I'd never had that before, and it startled me that I would feel it now, with a complete stranger. I'd tried to always trust that inner voice, though, and mine was saying that Bull was different, special.

"If they come here, will that guy at the gate tell them I'm here?" I asked as I got myself under control again.

"No. Johnny won't say a word to anyone about you being here. Except maybe to Torch."

I sniffled. "You all have weird names."

Bull chuckled. "They're road names. I'm part of the Dixie Reapers MC. Bull is what they call me."

"MC. Like in *Sons of Anarchy*?"

He snorted. "Not exactly. Oh, our hands aren't clean, but most of that show was strictly drama meant to entertain people."

"So, if Bull is your road name, what's your real name?" I asked.

I could see the hesitation in his eyes, and I wondered if it was taboo to ask him that. I didn't know anything about the way of life in a MC. I hadn't even been around bikers up close before, except watching them pass by on the freeway. He was the first one I'd ever spoken to.

"Michael. My name is Michael, but outside this house I'm Bull and only Bull."

I nodded. "I understand."

He softly caressed my cheek. "But you can call me Michael if you want. When we're here, by ourselves. No one's used that name in a really long time."

I felt the bulge in his pants pressing against my ass, and I didn't think it was possible, but it felt like it was growing even larger. Holy hell! My breath caught in my throat at the unmistakable desire in his eyes. No one had ever looked at me like that. Oh, boys had told me I was pretty and said they wanted to fuck me. But the way Bull -- Michael? -- looked at me... it was like he wanted to devour me. My nipples pebbled, and as his hands shifted, I felt a sudden jolt in my core.

This is wrong, Darian. What the hell is the matter with you? You were almost raped and now some stranger is turning you on? Are you just going to give it up to some random guy?

Despite my inner pep talk, my body didn't seem to be listening. Desire curled through me, heating the blood in my veins. Even if his arms hadn't been around me, I wouldn't have gotten up and walked away. I'd waited so long to feel like this. Was the timing all wrong? Oh yeah. But I couldn't ignore the way I felt, didn't *want* to ignore it.

There was a reason I was still a virgin. No one had ever turned me on, especially not like this. An ache began to build, and I squeezed my thighs together, but it didn't seem to help. The way Michael looked at me, I could tell that he knew what was happening to me, and that look said he was enjoying the effect he had on me.

"I'm not the right man to deflower a virgin," he said, his voice thick and rough. "But damn if you aren't tempting as hell. I'm probably old enough to be your father. I should take you to Torch, let him assign someone to help you. But I don't want to."

"What do you want?" I asked.

His gaze skimmed over me, resting on my breasts a moment. "I want you in my bed. I want to see you spread open and begging for me, your wet little pussy aching for my cock. I want to fuck you so thoroughly that you'll never want another man ever again."

My breath hitched at his words.

"But what I'm going to do is show you to the guest room and let you get some sleep. We can work on your problem tomorrow."

Disappointment hit me hard. He helped me stand, then led the way down the hall, passing a closed door, a bathroom, then stopping at a bedroom. Michael flipped on the light and motioned for me to step inside. The walls were a pale blue, and there was a full-size bed with a navy comforter taking up most of the space. The room wasn't very big, but it was adequate. It was actually nicer than any room I'd ever had. The furniture looked new, even if it was sparse with just the bed, a nightstand with a clock, and a dresser.

"If you need something to sleep in, there are some shirts in the top drawer. They'll be big on you, but it's the best I can do for tonight," he said.

"Thank you," I said softly. "For everything."

He stared at me a moment, and I wondered if he was going to change his mind about hauling me off to his bed, but he sighed loudly, then turned and walked away, closing the door behind him. I pulled off my shoes and clothes, even removing my panties before I pulled out a soft T-shirt from the dresser. I held it up to my nose and breathed in deeply, smiling because it smelled just like Bull.

I pulled the shirt over my head and turned to look at the bed. If he wasn't going to take me to his room, then I might as well get some sleep. He was probably right. We didn't need to complicate matters, but it didn't stop me from wanting him. It scared me, how intensely I felt about a man I'd just met. But there was an undeniable connection between us. Maybe I had daddy issues, or maybe I was just a woman craving the touch of an incredibly sexy man.

Turning off the light, I padded across the room and pulled down the covers, then slipped into bed. As I stared up at the ceiling, I felt the throbbing between my legs and knew I wasn't going to sleep anytime soon. I wasn't a complete stranger to sex, even if I was a virgin. Oh, I'd never undressed in front of anyone before, but my high school boyfriend had talked me into giving him blowjobs, and he'd tried to stick his hand down my pants a few times. And on my eighteenth birthday, I'd gotten curious enough about sex to buy a small vibrator. I was wishing I had it with me. It was nowhere near the size of Bull, but it had always made me feel good.

With the covers pulled up to my chest, I reached under the blankets and jerked the T-shirt up to my waist, then planted my feet on the mattress and spread my legs. The house was still and quiet, and I bit my lip in hopes I wouldn't make any noise. I would be mortified if Bull caught me masturbating. My hand slid between my legs and over the smooth lips of my pussy. I parted the lips and plunged a finger into my channel, then brought it up to circle my clit.

My eyes closed, and I pictured it was Bull between my legs. If anything, the ache grew worse. I rubbed my clit slowly so I could savor the sensations. The build-up was always the best part. My thighs trembled as I pictured Bull between my spread legs, naked, his hard cock pointed toward me. My finger rubbed faster and a whimper escaped me.

I slid my finger back into my pussy, jerking my hips as I tried to fuck myself, but it wasn't enough, not nearly. I felt so damn empty, and for the first time, I cursed my virginity. If I weren't inexperienced, Bull would likely be in here now fucking me into the mattress. I couldn't stop the sounds that spilled from my lips as I chased after an elusive orgasm that seemed always just out of reach, alternating between plunging my finger inside me and playing with my clit. Normally, I'd have gotten off by now, but I was too wound up from the things Bull had said, and the way his cock had felt pressing against me.

I was getting frustrated and almost stopped what I was doing, thinking it was pointless, when the door flew open. My eyes went wide as I saw Bull standing in the doorway, shirtless, barefoot, and his jeans unfastened. My finger stilled, and my chest rose and fell as I waited to see what he would do. As he stepped into the room, I knew that things were about to change. I just hadn't realized how much.

Chapter Two

Bull

Fucking hell! I could hear her soft little sounds down the hall as she pleasured herself, and it damn near killed me. I was forty-fucking-nine years old, not some wet-behind-the-ears college boy. Pussy had been an everyday occurrence for me, for as long as I could remember, even if I had been in a self-induced dry spell lately. Hell, if I went to the clubhouse now, I could have two or three club sluts doing anything I asked. But I didn't want them. I wanted the sweet girl down the hall, the girl with the haunted eyes and broken soul.

I growled in frustration and jerked my jeans back up my legs, not bothering to fasten them. I might not be good enough for her, but it didn't mean I had to let her suffer. It was obvious she was just as wound up as I was, maybe more so. I stomped down the hall and threw open her bedroom door. Even though she was completely covered, I could tell her legs were bent and open. My cock hardened to the point of pain, and I knew it was peeking out of the top of my jeans. Randy bastard.

Moving farther into the room, I waited, almost hoping she'd scream at me to leave. This was wrong on so many levels, but I wanted to taste her. I'd never had anyone as sweet as Darian, and for just once in my life, I wanted to know what that was like. What innocence would feel like, taste like. I reached for the bedding and jerked the covers to the foot of the bed. Her eyes went wide and she gasped, and even though she didn't try to cover herself, her hand jerked from between her legs and her cheeks flushed a bright pink.

With her knees parted, I had a clear view of her pretty pussy. The bare lips glistened in the moonlight, dewy with her juices. Crawling onto the bed, I moved closer to her, my gaze fastened between her legs. I slid my hands up her calves, and when I reached her knees, I pressed against the inside of them, making her spread even farther. The lips of her pussy parted until I had a clear view of everything, even that tight virgin hole that I wanted desperately to fill with my cock, to pump full of my cum.

"Tell me to stop," I said harshly. "Make me leave."

I felt her gaze on me and looked up to meet her eyes.

"Stay," she said softly. "I want it to be you."

With a growl, I lowered myself to the mattress, her legs pressing against my shoulders. Her scent was overwhelming and so fucking sexy. I licked my lips, knowing before I'd even had a taste that she would be the best I'd ever had. She was all pink and soft, the silky wet lips of her pussy just begging for my mouth.

I placed one forearm across her belly holding her down, leaving her at my mercy, and I spread her pussy even wider with my other. Unable to hold back another moment, I leaned forward and lapped at her sweetness. Her taste exploded on my tongue as I licked the soft lips before sliding my tongue the length of her pussy.

Darian cried out and I felt her tense under my arm. She squirmed or tried to. I held her down as I went back for more, ravaging her with my mouth. I thrust my tongue into her channel and groaned at how tight she felt. My dick would likely split her wide open, but fuck if the thought of seeing her stretched wide around my cock didn't turn me on even more.

I could feel pre-cum soaking the bedding under me, but I wasn't done with my sweet girl just yet. I tongue-fucked her, driving her crazy, then sucked her little clit into my mouth. She made a keening sound, and I could tell she was close to coming. I wanted that, wanted her cream coating me. I sucked, nibbled, and teased until her release left her in a gush that coated my lips. I drank her down, relishing every drop.

Darian panted as her body trembled. I could walk away now. She was satisfied. I could cover her back up and go back to my room to take my cock in my hand and fuck my fist to the image of her spread open like this. I rose to my knees, intent on doing just that when she stopped me.

"Don't go," she said.

"I'm no good for you."

"Isn't that for me to decide? I'm not some child. Just because I'm a virgin doesn't mean I'm not a woman who knows what she wants."

I stared down at her, indecision warring inside me.

"Take off the shirt," I said. "Show me those perky breasts of yours. I want to see just how hard those nipples are."

She sat up, tugging the shirt off and tossing it aside. Her breasts bounced when she flopped back onto the bed again. Not overly large, but a handful. Her pink nipples were pebbled and looked damn near perfect. *She* was perfect.

"If we do this, I don't know that I'll be able to let you walk away," I told her. Although, I had a feeling Torch and Venom wouldn't let me keep her. Not after the fuss I made over Venom and Ridley getting together.

I'd never been one for a long-term commitment. Never cared if a woman left my bed and then warmed ten more, even if I had been wanting more recently. But then, I'd never met anyone like Darian before. The moment I'd looked into those troubled blue eyes, she'd had me. I'd seen the fight in her, but I'd also seen so much more. I didn't know her full story, and I didn't need to. She was broken, but not damaged beyond repair. For some reason, I wanted to be the one to put her back together.

"I don't understand," she said. "It's just sex."

I shook my head. "Not this time. Not with you."

I reached out and lightly stroked her between her legs, making her moan.

"Has anyone ever touched you? Anyone ever put their mouth on you like I just did?"

She shook her head.

I hesitated. "Have you ever even seen a cock? Not on TV but up close?"

Her cheeks flushed. "My high school boyfriend sometimes made me suck him off."

I growled, not liking the thought of a cock, other than mine, being in her mouth. And fuck if I didn't want that really damn bad all of a sudden. If I took the edge off, then maybe I wouldn't want her so much. Maybe then I could walk away.

I braced my hands on either side of her and leaned down until my face was close to hers. "You good at sucking cock, baby?"

Her eyes dilated, and she nodded slowly. "My boyfriend said I was."

"Prove it."

Her body flushed, and I could tell she wanted this as much as I did.

"I'm clean," I told her, in case she was worried. "I've always insisted on condoms, even for a blowjob. I only screwed that up once, but that was over twenty years ago, and I've been tested since then. I don't want anything between us, not even a thin piece of latex."

She licked her lips, and I took that as agreement. I crawled up her body until I straddled her chest.

"Part those lips, baby. Let me fuck your mouth."

I felt her body shift under me, and I reached back, grabbing her leg. "Keep those open too. Every time my cock thrusts into your mouth, imagine me pounding that sweet pussy."

Darian whimpered, and her lips parted, as did her legs. I pushed my jeans down enough that my cock and balls were free. Then I gripped the headboard with one hand and fisted her hair with the other, tilting her head back. My cock strained toward her, and flexing my hips, I painted her lips with pre-cum before sliding inside.

"Fuck!" I couldn't remember anything feeling so damn good before. Her tongue swirled around me before I plunged deeper into her mouth. She felt like fucking heaven.

"Take it all, baby girl," I said. "Every damn inch. Open that throat up."

With every stroke, I went a little deeper until she was taking all of me. I nearly cracked the headboard with my iron grip as I fucked her mouth. I watched as my cock disappeared between her lips again and again, and I felt my balls brushing against her chin.

"Such a good girl," I crooned. "You're going to swallow, aren't you?"

She hummed around my cock, and it was enough to set me off. I growled as I thrust harder, cum spurting out of my cock and filling her mouth, splashing the back of her throat. Even after the last drop had been wrung from me, I kept fucking that hot, wet mouth, not ready for the pleasure to end just yet. My cock, still hard and now coated with saliva, slipped free of her mouth, and I eased back down her body.

Darian trembled and licked the cum from her lips.

"You good now?" I asked. "We can stop right here and now."

"Are you going to make me beg?" she asked.

Fuck if the thought of her begging didn't make me even harder.

"I want to feel you inside me," she said. "I want you to claim my innocence. I want…"

"You want what?"

Her cheeks burned bright pink. "I want your cum. I want to feel it inside me, down there."

My heart pounded. "Are you on the pill?"

She hesitated, then nodded. Something about that hesitation made me want to back away, but she was offering herself up on a silver platter. I might be an asshole on the best of days, but even a saint would have trouble walking out the door right now. A fucking virgin and she wanted me. I'd be stupid to give up this once-in-a-lifetime chance. She was giving me something special.

"Last chance to change your mind," I said.

"I want you, Michael."

The soft way she said my name was the final nail in my coffin. I gripped her hips and pulled her closer. Her pussy was still slick and wide open as if she were begging for my cock. I lined up with that tight little virgin hole and made myself go slow as I eased into her. Her silken walls clasped me like a glove, pulling me in. Sweat coated my body as I fought for control.

Darian's expression was pinched, but there was a determination in her eyes.

"Just do it," she said.

Tightening my hold on her, I thrust forward, fast and deep. She cried out, pain etched on her features, and I held still, waiting for her body to adjust to me. As I felt the tension ease in her, I started a slow and steady thrust. I couldn't help but watch as I fucked her, my shaft shiny with a smear of blood. The proof that no one had been inside her but me.

She stretched tight around my cock, and I wished I had a picture of how perfectly we fit together. The next time I took my cock in hand, this was the sight I'd see in my mind. Darian spread open, her pussy greedily sucking me in as I fucked her.

"Play with your nipples, baby. Make yourself feel good," I said.

The sight of her hands cupping her breasts, her fingers rolling and pinching her nipples, made my balls draw up, and I knew I wouldn't last much longer. I'd never come so fast in my life, and here I was, ready to blow a second time, and I'd barely been inside her. She would be sore tomorrow, but I couldn't hold back. I pounded into her little pussy, taking her hard and fast, giving her every inch of my cock. I wasn't a small man, and some couldn't handle me. But she could. Almost like she was fucking made to take my cock. The bed rocked against the wall as I fucked a load of cum into her. I groaned as spurt after spurt filled her up.

I was a fucking asshole, finishing before her. It was her first time, and I was fucking it up. My cock still twitched and unbelievably was still hard. I reached for her pussy, rubbing her clit as I began stroking in and out again. It wasn't long before she was screaming out my name, her body tightening, her back arching. I felt the gush of her release but kept rubbing and fucking my cock into her until the last of the aftershocks had stopped.

I didn't want to pull out, even though I knew I should. Darian lay panting and spent, looking well-fucked.

"You're fucking beautiful," I murmured.

She gave me a tired smile and held her arms open. Keeping us joined, I braced my weight and leaned over her. The look in her eyes was soft and dreamy, and I couldn't resist kissing her. No one had ever looked at me like that before. When I pulled back, she gripped my shoulders and locked her legs around my waist.

"You're still hard," she said.

I chuckled a little. "Yeah, you seem to have that effect on me."

"Just me?" she asked, seeming insecure for a moment.

"Just you."

"Are you leaving now? Going back to your room?"

"Is that what you want?" I asked, pressing my cock a little deeper.

"Only if you take me with you."

I pulled out and stood next to the bed, then scooped her up into my arms. By some miracle, I didn't lose my pants and trip before I made it to my bedroom, where I eased her down on the bed, then stripped out of my jeans. A shower would have been a good idea, but seeing her pussy smeared with my cum made me feel like a fucking caveman. I liked that she was marked that way.

"I wasn't too rough, was I?" I asked as I settled next to her on the bed, my hand caressing her belly.

"No. I liked it." Her cheeks warmed. "I especially liked it when you fucked my mouth. I think I like you being in control like that."

I kissed her and pulled her tight against my body. "Then you're in luck because I'm a dominant asshole, in and out of the bedroom. It gets me off when I tell you what to do when I fuck you the way I did. But that doesn't mean I won't listen to you. You say stop and I stop. You tell me it's too much, and I'll slow down."

"I know," she said. "I could tell that about you."

"What's that?"

"Despite your blustering about not being a nice man, I could tell you were honorable. It might be some outlaw code that you follow, but I sensed that you wouldn't hurt me."

I stroked her softly. "It's hard to imagine anyone wanting to hurt an angel like you."

"Can we… can we do that again?" she asked.

"Which part?" I pressed a kiss to her lips, then along her jaw.

"Everything," she said, her voice breathy. "I want to do everything."

I groaned, knowing she didn't understand what she was saying. But as her soft body pressed against me, her small hands stroking me, I knew that I'd give her anything she asked for. Somehow this slip of a woman had wrapped me around her finger with one damn look.

Now I knew how Venom felt.

Shit. Ridley. My daughter wasn't going to understand. She might be with a guy older than her, but I didn't think she'd like her daddy being with someone who seemed to be around her age.

"I should have asked before, but you are legal, right, baby?" The last thing I needed was to have just fucked some kid who wasn't even old enough yet.

She smiled. "I'm twenty-one."

Well, thank fuck for that, but I still inwardly winced. She was younger than my daughter, and I knew Ridley was going to give me hell. So was my VP once he found out. I'd pitched a goddamn fit when they'd gotten together, and here I was, ready to claim a girl even younger than my daughter. Fuck.

If I was going to hell, I might as well enjoy the ride.

Slipping between her legs again, I entered her with one sure thrust, making both of us groan. I fucked Darian until the sun started to rise, coming in her pussy, down her throat, across those perky breasts. I gave her anything and everything she asked for.

And when morning came, I watched her sleep, looking all sweet and innocent as she curled herself against me. Yeah, I was fucked. No way I'd get to keep her, but fuck if I wanted anyone else to have her.

Mine!

My cock twitched in agreement. I'd fucked her. Marked her with my cum inside and out. As far as I was concerned, she belonged to me. But I had this sinking suspicion my Pres and VP might not agree with me, and I was not looking forward to that conversation. If they forbade me from claiming Darian, then I'd have to let her go, as much as that would pain me. Now that I'd had her, I knew I would never want anyone else.

Chapter Three

Darian

The smell of coffee and bacon woke me from the most delicious dream. I couldn't remember the last time I'd slept so hard, and for once I felt almost refreshed. I stretched and winced at the aches and twinges I normally didn't feel. As I slowly opened my eyes, my surroundings came into focus, and panic welled inside me when I didn't recognize anything. Where the hell was I? And why was I naked? My heart raced as horrible scenarios sped through my mind, then slowly bits and pieces of the previous night came to me until everything slammed into me at once. Leaving Georgia. The party. The leering men. Running. Finding Bull. My cheeks flushed as I thought about what happened after that, and why my body felt the way it did now, and why I was definitely naked and in his bed.

A smile lifted the corners of my lips as I stretched again, tossed off the covers, and went into the adjoining bathroom. Thankfully, we'd showered after that last round, or I'd have been a sticky mess right now. Not that I had minded getting messy, not in the least. Even now his scent clung to me, and I loved it. I used the bathroom and washed my hands, then squeezed a little toothpaste onto my finger and ran it over my teeth to freshen my breath. When I was finished, I snatched Bull's discarded shirt off the floor and pulled it over my head. It fell to mid-thigh, and I lifted the collar to my nose, breathing him in. I couldn't remember a time I was happier than I was right this minute, even if I knew it wouldn't last.

Following the smells coming from the kitchen, I made my way through his home until I found Bull standing over the stove. He was shirtless with his jeans slung low. His long, blond hair hung down his back in a tangled mess, and I blushed as I remembered grabbing handfuls of it as he'd thrust into me. Damn, but the man was sexy, even first thing in the morning. I squinted out the window over the sink. Yeah, morning. The sun wasn't quite high enough for it to be noon just yet, even though I felt like I'd slept the day away.

"Morning," he said without turning around.

"How did you know I was here?" I asked.

He glanced at me, a smile on his face. "You aren't exactly quiet. I hope you like scrambled eggs. It's the only kind I know how to make. Every time I try over easy, they end up scrambled."

I bit my lip so I wouldn't laugh. "Scrambled is fine."

He tipped his head toward the small table and four chairs. "Have a seat. It's pretty much done. Salt and pepper on your eggs?"

"And cheese, if you have it."

"Now you sound like my daughter."

I stilled and looked around, half expecting a small child to wander in at any moment. "Daughter?"

"Yeah. She always asked to have eggs made with cheese too."

"She doesn't anymore?" I asked.

He grew quiet for a moment. "I'm sure she does. She just doesn't ask me for them anymore."

Since he didn't seem to be married -- thank God! -- I had to wonder if his ex got his daughter in the divorce. Or were they ever married? It had to suck not getting to see your kid all the time. He carried two plates to the table, and I smiled up at him, hoping to ease the tension I noticed in his shoulders at the mention of his daughter.

"Her name's Ridley," he said. "And I'm going to hear an earful about you."

"You're going to tell your daughter about me?" I asked, my eyes wide. I'd figured it was just a one-time thing, no matter how incredible last night was. Yeah, he'd said he wanted to keep me, but he hadn't really meant it, right? I'd figured it was just one of those heat of the moment kind of things that guys said. Was he really wanting more?

Bull sighed. "Sooner or later someone is going to tell my club President that you're here in my house, and then he's going to have questions. Which means the VP will be there too, and Venom will tell Ridley."

My brow furrowed. I didn't understand what his club VP had to do with his daughter. "Why would your VP tell your daughter anything about us?"

He took a bite of egg and stared at me a moment. "Because they're together."

My fork clattered to the table. What the… What kind of sick man would be with a little girl? Had I traded one nightmare for another? He'd seemed normal enough, but was the man I'd slept with really a monster? My heart kicked in my chest, and my palms started to sweat. If I bolted out of here now, how far would I get?

A half smile tipped the corner of Bull's lips as if he could read my thoughts, but I didn't know what he found so funny about the situation. "I should have probably prefaced that with the fact my daughter is older than you."

She was… Oh. My heart began to slow, and then his words sank in.

"Your daughter is *older* than me?" I asked.

He nodded. "Not by much, but yeah. I kicked up a fuss when she wanted to be with Venom, and here I am sleeping with someone almost thirty years younger than me."

I snorted. "Yeah, right. There's no way you're that much older than me. I mean, have you seen you?"

"I'm forty-nine, Darian."

My mouth opened and shut a few times, but I couldn't think of anything to say. He certainly didn't *look* forty-nine. I'd figured he was in his mid-thirties. I didn't see so much as one gray hair on his head, not even a glimmer of what I'd heard women refer to as their glitter streaks. Not that a big badass like Bull would call them any such thing.

"How old did you think I was?" he asked, seeming genuinely curious.

I shrugged. "Thirties."

He smiled and shook his head a little. "You're good for my ego."

I ate a few more bites, glancing at him every now and then. He had to have known about the age difference last night when I'd told him I was twenty-one, and yet he'd still slept with me. If he was worried how people would react, I had to wonder if maybe he wouldn't have touched me if I hadn't begged him to. My cheeks flushed as I thought about how brazen and wanton I'd been last night. That was definitely not like me. For one, I'd never desired anyone in my life, until him. But there was just something about the man sitting next to me that made me want things I shouldn't. Girls like me didn't get to be with guys like him.

There was a pounding on the front door, and Bull sighed, hung his head a moment, then pushed his chair back and went to answer it. After a minute I heard raised voices and wondered if I should stay put or go investigate. If he was being yelled at because of me, it only seemed right that I go give him my support. The way he'd talked about his VP and President, I didn't think they would really want me here in Bull's house, even though I didn't understand why. When it sounded like things were escalating, I pushed back my chair, gathered my courage, and went to find Bull.

He was blocking the entrance of his house, and as big as he was, I couldn't see around him. But I did hear a man's voice, full of anger, telling him in no certain terms that I was to be brought to the clubhouse. Whatever that was.

"I don't want her around all that shit," Bull said. "She's an innocent and shouldn't have to see any of that."

Torch snorted. "My wife is in the clubhouse with my daughter, and Ridley is there with your grandkids. Do you think I'd let the club sluts anywhere near that place with our families around?"

Bull's posture relaxed a little. "She's been through enough already."

I stepped closer and placed a hand on his bicep. "If they need to talk to me, I'll go. I just need to get dressed first."

Bull turned, and I saw a silver-haired man on the front porch. His gaze was assessing as he scanned me from head to toe, and I felt my cheeks flush when I remembered I wasn't wearing panties. Not that he seemed the least bit interested in me. But then he'd said he was married and had a daughter.

"Darian…"

I shushed him the only way I could think of. I pulled him down and placed my lips on his. He stiffened for a moment before kissing me back. A look of resignation crossed his face as he pulled away, but I didn't understand. It was just a talk, right? Besides, our night of fun was over, and I should probably figure out how to get back home. I obviously wasn't going to get back the same way I'd gotten here.

"I'll talk to him," I said. Then I turned my gaze toward the other man. "Can I finish my breakfast and get dressed first?"

He nodded. "Of course. Bull can bring you to the clubhouse when you're ready."

"Thank you," I said softly, then tugged my massive man away from the door. He shut it in the other man's face, and I winced as I led Bull back to the kitchen. He was living up to his name at the moment, acting like an enraged bull, and I had no doubt he'd pay for that later. I didn't know who that man was, but I was betting he was someone important.

I sat back down and started on my breakfast again, but Bull was staring at me with his jaw clenched. I just wasn't certain if he was pissed at me or the man who was on the porch. He watched me intently, his hands fisted on the table. After I was finished eating, I carried my plate to the sink and rinsed it, then turned to face him, crossing my arms over my belly.

"Say something."

"What do you want me to say?" he asked.

"I'm sorry I interrupted you. And I'm sorry I kissed you."

He closed his eyes and his shoulders relaxed, then his head dropped almost in defeat. When he turned to face me, all the anger I'd felt coming off him was gone. Slowly, he stood and came toward me, wrapping an arm around my waist and pulling me closer.

"I'm not upset you kissed me. I'm not mad at you at all, angel. I'm upset that I've been commanded to take you to the clubhouse. I knew they'd try to take you from me, but I'd hoped to have more time with you first."

"I don't understand," I said, lifting my hands to rest them on his chest. "Why will they take me away? And you sound like you want to keep me or something. I figured last night was just… well, a one-time deal."

His gaze darkened. "I told you that if I claimed your innocence that you were mine. Did you think I was lying?"

My breath caught in my throat. "N-no. I just… I figured it was the heat of the moment and you didn't really mean it. I've never been with anyone before, obviously, so I thought it was just something guys said when they wanted sex."

"I don't make it a habit to say things that I don't mean, Darian. Do you not want to stay with me? I'd understand. I'm a lot older than you, and I'm sure you could have any guy you wanted."

"It's not that. Please don't ever think that."

"Then what?" he asked. "Make me understand."

I took a deep breath and let it out slowly. I didn't often talk about my past, and I didn't know that I was ready to do that now. But I needed to tell him something so he didn't think my hesitance to believe him had anything to do with him and had everything to do with me.

"No one's ever wanted me. I don't mean sexually. I've had guys want in my pants before, obviously since I was running from some last night, but no one's ever wanted me to stick around. I've never had anyone want me in any other capacity. They wanted to take a virgin or sleep with the new girl… but they haven't cared about me as a person at all. And with you --"

"You thought I was just like them?" he asked.

"I guess I didn't think someone like you could possibly want to keep me. You're insanely good-looking, and I'm sure you have women ready to fall into your bed with a snap of your fingers. I don't... I don't know why you'd want to keep me."

He cupped my cheek and leaned down closer so that his lips were a whisper away from mine. "If I could, I would keep you with me forever. In my bed every night, in my arms every morning. You're strong, Darian, a fighter, and maybe a little bit broken. But when I look into your eyes, I see someone of worth, someone I want to know better. Someone I want to keep for myself. I've been around long enough to know that a woman like you doesn't come around very often. Yeah, I could have any club slut I want, but I don't want them. I don't want easy."

I blinked as tears pricked my eyes. No one had ever said something so sweet to me before.

"You don't even know me," I protested. I wasn't anything wonderful, wasn't special in the least. If he knew... but I didn't want to tell him. I didn't want him to look at me the way everyone else did.

"Have you lied to me about anything?" he asked.

I hesitated a moment. Perhaps a moment too long.

His gaze narrowed. "What did you lie about? Are you really twenty-one?"

"I'm really twenty-one," I assured him. That wasn't what I'd lied about. He'd be furious if he found out, though.

"Darian --"

"We should go. They're waiting, right?"

He released me and stepped back, a look of disappointment clouding his face. I hated that I'd put that look there, but if he knew I wasn't on the pill like I'd said… No, I didn't want to think about the consequences. How likely was it I'd end up pregnant on my first night of sex anyway? Maybe I should have paid more attention in health class when I was younger. I should have just told him, but I'd been worried that he would back away, and I'd wanted him too damn much.

I skirted around him and went to the guestroom to get my clothes. Bull stormed down the hallway and slammed his bedroom door. I winced as it rattled on the hinges and hated that I'd been the one to make him so angry. It wouldn't matter much longer anyway. Once I talked to his President and VP and told them my story, he'd ask me to leave anyway. No one wanted to keep trash around.

Dressing quickly, I waited for him by the front door. He appeared about ten minutes later, in a fresh pair of jeans, another black T-shirt, and that leather vest thing he'd had on last night. He didn't touch me and didn't speak to me as he stepped out onto the porch. My throat burned and so did my eyes as I realized just how much I'd screwed up by not being completely honest with him. Not that I'd expected our time together to last past this morning anyway.

I followed him outside, closing the door behind me, then stayed a few steps behind as we went to the building near the gates with the neon sign on top. I didn't think he wanted to look at me right now. We entered the building, and my eyes took a moment to adjust the dimly lit room. The interior wasn't what I was expecting, and I saw a handful of people, including two women who looked to be around my age sitting at a table in the corner. One of them had a toddler on her right knee and a baby in her arms, the other had an even smaller bundle in her arms. I didn't know if I was supposed to sit with them or follow Bull, so I stayed close to him, but I felt the eyes of everyone in the room on me.

We walked down a hall, and he pushed open two wooden double doors that had Church carved into the frame over them. I stayed on his heels and came to an abrupt stop when I saw the man from this morning and another man sitting next to him at a long conference table. Bull approached and sank into a seat next to the gray-haired man, but I hovered near the doors, uncertain what I should do.

"She fucking lied to me," Bull said.

I swallowed hard and watched as the other two men turned accusing gazes my way. The man I'd thought was tender and sweet last night turned to face me with anger blazing in his eyes.

"So which part did you lie about, Darian? The men being after you? Was it all a game to get to one of us? Did someone send you here?" Bull demanded.

"Wh-what? No. No! I didn't lie about that."

"Then what did you lie about?" he asked, his voice harsh and unforgiving.

My cheeks flushed, and I dropped my gaze to the floor. "I lied about being on birth control," I said in a near whisper.

I heard a chair crash to the floor and looked up to find Bull staring at me.

"What?" he asked.

"I said I lied about being on birth control. I'm not, but I didn't want you to stop."

It seemed like all the anger drained out of him as he approached me, reaching for me slowly and setting his hands on my waist.

"Baby girl, I already knew you lied about that. You hesitated last night when I asked. I knew I should stop but I didn't want to, so I ignored the fact you were most likely not telling me the truth."

"You're not mad that I lied about that?" I asked.

"No, angel. I'm not mad about that. I wish you'd have just told me that at the house. I'm sorry I lost my temper with you. I thought you were hiding something more serious, something that could turn deadly for me and the club."

I leaned my cheek against his chest and wrapped my arms around his waist. I hadn't liked him being angry with me. Plenty of people had lost their tempers with me before; knowing I'd made Bull mad at me hurt more than I'd thought possible.

"Why don't we back up a little?" the gray-haired man said. "What men?"

Bull turned and took my hand, leading me over to the table. He righted his chair, then sat and pulled me down onto his lap.

"Darian, this is my President, Torch, and the VP, Venom. Neither of them will hurt you."

"What men?" Torch asked again.

"A guy I was seeing brought me here from Georgia. He told me we were going to a party, but when I got here, I found out I was the entertainment." I told them exactly what I'd heard and about running into the night with no direction. My cheeks flushed when I talked about Bull taking me to his home, but I didn't think it was any of their business what happened after that.

"Who was guarding the gate last night?" Venom asked.

"Johnny," Bull answered.

"We'll have to find out if anyone came here looking for her." Venom swung his gaze my way. "Who at home is going to miss you? How much time do we have before the authorities are alerted that you're a missing person?"

"No one," I said softly. "No one will miss me."

"Friends? Family?" Torch asked.

"I don't have any," I admitted. Shame burned through me, having to tell these powerful men that I had nothing and no one to return to.

"Darian," Bull said, his voice pitched low. "Honey, where do you live in Georgia? You have to have someone in your life."

"I'm just a waitress at a diner. My boss lets me rent the studio apartment upstairs for a few hundred a month. I don't even own the furniture there, just a backpack full of clothes and some books I got at a sale the library was having," I said.

Bull's arms tightened around my waist.

"How did you meet the guy you came here with?" Venom asked.

"He was a customer at the diner. He had flirted with me when he'd come in, and one day he asked me out. We went on a few dates, but he kept pressuring me to have sex, and I recently confided that I was a virgin and that's why I was holding out. I thought he understood, but he just wanted to use me."

"Do you need to call your boss?" Torch asked.

"I had yesterday and today off, but if I'm not there for my shift tomorrow, he'll assume I skipped out and replace me. Turnover is pretty high at the diner. I didn't have much in the apartment to lose, but it was everything I owned."

Bull nuzzled the side of my neck. "I'll take you shopping for some new things. Angel, why did you have so little?"

My cheeks flushed again. "I was a foster kid, and I never finished high school. Most places I applied never even called for an interview, so it was hard to find a job sometimes. There would be weeks or months that I wouldn't have a place to stay, which meant going to the shelters. People steal stuff there all the time, so what little I had was taken from me."

Venom looked from me to Bull, then back again. "How old are you, Darian?"

"Twenty-one."

Venom raised a brow at Bull, who growled softly.

"Shut it," Bull said. "I knew when you found out her age that I'd never hear the fucking end of it. I'm sorry I gave you such a hard time about Ridley. You've spent the last three years proving that I was wrong. She adores you."

Venom smirked. "We make cute babies too."

Bull snorted. "Like I'm going to say my grandkids are ugly regardless of who the daddy is?"

"So, what's the deal, Bull?" Torch asked. "Are you requesting a property patch?"

"Property patch?" I asked. What the hell was that?

"We haven't had the full talk about how things are with a MC, even though I did tell her I'm part of one. She didn't know where she was or who we are," Bull said. "We didn't have the discussion about old ladies."

"Old ladies?" I asked.

"It's just a term," Torch said. "Doesn't mean the women are actually old. It's what we call the women in our lives, the ones we claim."

My brow furrowed. "But you referred to your wife earlier."

Torch smiled a little. "That's because I married the woman I claimed as my old lady. Took me three years to get her here to do it, though."

"And you're married to Bull's daughter?" I asked Venom.

Both his eyebrows went up.

"Um, no," he said.

"But you have kids together? And you didn't think she'd want to marry you?" I asked.

Bull chuckled a little. "Yes, Venom, don't you think my daughter, the mother of your children, might want a ring on her finger?"

"Fuck you," Venom growled at Bull. "Ridley's perfectly content as an old lady and doesn't need a fucking ring to know that I love her."

Torch pointed to the leather vest he was wearing. "This is called a cut. The patch on my chest shows I'm the president of the club, and our logo is on the back with Dixie Reapers across the top and a rocker on the bottom that says where our chapter is from. Our women receive a cut that has *Property of* and whoever they belong to on the bottom rocker on the back, as well as a smaller property patch on the front."

"And I'd have to wear that if he claimed me? Like all the time?" I asked.

Torch smiled. "Isabella doesn't wear hers unless she's going beyond the gates or when she comes to the clubhouse. Although, when her pregnancy advanced, she had to leave it at home because it didn't fit anymore."

"So, are you?" Venom asked. "Claiming her?"

I turned wide eyes toward Bull, who was looking at me thoughtfully.

"You don't have to do that," I told him. "Just because we slept together… I can still walk out of here, and you can go back to your life the way it was before."

"Is that what you want?" he asked. "Do you want to walk out of here and never see me again? Or do you want to stay?"

I wanted to stay, more than anything, but there was still so much I didn't understand about being part of a MC. Was I expected to act a certain way? Were there rituals or something I'd have to learn? It was like being part of a completely different world, and I didn't know if I was strong enough to survive.

Bull waited patiently for my answer, and I felt Torch and Venom watching me too. I really didn't have anything to return to back home. My apartment was a joke, and I hadn't lied about my meager possessions. If I didn't go back, I wasn't missing out on anything. But if I did… if I did return and I walked away from Bull, I had a feeling I would regret it for the rest of my life.

"Not to try to force your decision," Torch said. "But if the two of you slept together last night and you're not on birth control, it's possible you could be pregnant."

The breath stalled in my lungs as I thought about that a moment.

"Would you be okay with that?" I asked Bull. "You already have a daughter and grandchildren. Do you want to start over again with a baby in the house? If it's too much, if that isn't something you want, then I'll walk away, and you won't ever have to hear from me again. I mean, there's a chance I'm not even pregnant, but I don't want you to feel cornered."

Bull gave me the most tender look ever before softly brushing his lips against mine. "Having a baby with you wouldn't be a bad thing, Darian. Yes, I already have a grown daughter and two small granddaughters, but if you decide to stay, then I'd really like to have a family with you. I didn't get to do things the right way with Ridley, but I'd make sure any kids we had would have both their parents and would know they were loved."

"Ridley always knew you loved her," Venom said. "It's why she came here when she was in trouble."

"Yeah, but I made a lot of mistakes," Bull said. "I can't claim any part of raising Ridley. It's a miracle her mother didn't fuck her up."

I winced. "No love lost between you?"

Bull snorted. "No. I fucking hated her mother, and that bitch did everything she could to keep Ridley from me, even moved to another damn state. Then she tried to sell my fucking daughter."

My eyes went wide. Obviously, there was a huge story there, and I wanted to hear it sometime. The rage I saw in Venom's eyes said now wasn't the right time. It was apparent that he loved Ridley and didn't like the reminder of what had nearly happened to her.

"So, are you staying?" Torch asked.

"I'll stay," I said looking at Bull. "If that's really what you want."

He stared at me thoughtfully. "Before, when you said no one had ever wanted you… you meant as in ever, didn't you? Not even your parents?"

I slowly shook my head. No, no one had ever wanted me.

"I want you," he said softly. "I want you to be mine, but I'm not an easy man to live with. This life can sometimes be hard, and it can be dangerous, but I will protect you with my life."

"We need to figure out what happened to the men looking for her," Venom said. "They could be a problem."

"You write down any names you know or remember hearing," Torch said, sliding a pad and pen over to me. "I'll have Wire see if he can find anything on these assholes, and we'll handle it."

I only knew my supposed boyfriend's name but as I struggled to think about last night, I realized I'd heard mention of two others, at least their first names, so I wrote them down too. I didn't remember the street the house had been on, but I did recall the house number and jotted that down, along with a description of the decrepit structure. I didn't know if anything I gave them would help in the slightest, but it was nice to know they wanted to find the guys who had wanted to hurt me.

"Are we done?" Bull asked.

Torch nodded. "I'll order the property patch for her. You know Isabella and Ridley are going to want to meet her. Isabella just turned twenty-one a few months ago, and Ridley's only two years older. I'm sure they'll have a lot to talk about."

"That's what I'm afraid of," Bull muttered.

Venom smirked at him, and Bull flipped him off.

"If I'm staying, I'll need to get a few things," I said. "I had to borrow your hairbrush this morning, and I brushed my teeth with my finger. A change of clothes would be nice too."

Bull kissed my cheek. "We'll go out and get everything you need."

"I don't need a lot," I assured him.

"Angel, I'm going to take care of you. You don't have to struggle anymore, all right? I'm not an overly rich man, but I have enough in the bank to make sure my woman has everything she needs."

"You're actually a little richer than you thought," Torch said. "Wire was depositing funds into everyone's account this morning. That shipment we spoke about last week found a new home, and since you were a big part of gathering those items, you're getting a decent chunk of change from it."

I didn't think I wanted to know what they were talking about. He'd told me their hands weren't exactly clean, and if something illegal was going on, I'd prefer to remain ignorant of the details. I'd never been in trouble with the law before, and I didn't plan to start now.

Bull tapped my hip and I stood up. He rose to his rather impressive height, then escorted me out of the room. I noticed he quickly bypassed the table with Isabella and Ridley and only stopped at the bar long enough to bark at the guy behind it that he needed the truck keys.

"We aren't taking your motorcycle?" I asked as he hustled me out the door.

"Need room for your new things. I'll take you for a ride soon, though." He gave me a warm smile, then boosted me into the truck.

I'd never been shopping before, not at a real store anyway, not even when I was in foster care. None of my foster parents had cared if my clothes fit properly, so I was both excited and a little anxious. What exactly would it be like to shop with a guy like Bull?

Chapter Four

Bull

I couldn't remember a time I'd ever gone shopping with a woman before. I'd never had the chance to take my daughter shopping since she'd been a tiny thing when her mother took her to Florida. When Ridley had come back into my life, she'd been fully grown and immediately attached herself to Venom. I'd never been married, never even had anyone steady in my life. I'd figured I would hate going from store to store, expecting to shell out a wad of cash to get the stuff Darian needed. Nope, not my woman. No, she wanted the 24-hour store where you could get everything from food to shoes and gardening supplies. I don't think she even looked at anything that cost more than twenty dollars, and I'd had to fight with her to even get that far. Hell, she hadn't even wanted to come here. She'd wanted the damn thrift store.

She put back a pair of jeans that I could tell she really loved, and I fought not to growl at her.

"What's wrong with those?" I asked.

"They cost too much. I was serious, Bull. Just take me to the thrift store. I can find tons of stuff there for a fraction of the cost."

I pinched the bridge of my nose. I'd used the app on my phone to check my bank account before we'd even come through the front door of the store. Torch had not only paid me for the last shipment of guns, but he'd paid me *very* well. I could have easily taken her to some upscale stores, but the stubborn woman wouldn't budge on the issue. So we'd compromised and were in this store.

"Darian, if you like the jeans, buy the damn jeans. Hell, if you like them as much as I suspect you do, buy several pairs. You're not going to put a dent in my bank account, sweetheart. I promise I can afford anything you want in this store."

She looked up at me with uncertainty in her eyes. I knew she wanted them, but I also knew from what she'd said earlier she wasn't used to owning much of anything. It sounded like she'd had to fight for anything she'd had, and it hadn't been much. I wanted to beat the hell out of the parents who had given her up, and I wasn't too pleased with the foster parents who had let her drop out of school either. Not that I thought any less of her for not finishing high school, but I could tell from the way she'd said it that it bothered her. Just another way for her to feel inferior. While she had been rather bold last night, asking me to stay with her, I could tell that she was still insecure in some ways.

A myriad of expressions crossed her face, and I moved in closer, placing my hand on her hip. Hope. Fear. Indecision. Vulnerability. Gently, I pressed my lips to hers in a soft, brief kiss. Nothing like I wanted to give her, but I didn't want to be asked to leave the store either.

"Angel, I want you to have everything you need, and that includes getting you the things you want. You deserve nice things, even nicer than what this store has to offer. And I want to give them to you."

"The things here are nicer than anything I've ever owned," she said in a near whisper. "I've never had anything new before."

"I want to take care of you, Darian. Stop fighting me and buy the things you like. Will those jeans make you feel pretty? Will they make you happy?" I asked.

She hesitantly nodded.

"Then as far as I'm concerned, you need them. So buy them. Buy three or four. Hell, buy every pair in your size. I promise I can afford it."

"All right," she agreed, then picked the jeans back up and placed them in the shopping cart before selecting three other similar pairs.

She started to walk off, but I snagged a few more pair of jeans in her size that were priced a little higher and tossed them into the cart too. She gave me the side-eye but kept going. Some shorts were added to the pile along the way, but I noticed she picked the cheapest ones she could find. I noted the size of the shirts she was putting into the cart and added more of those too. I had no idea if she'd actually like any of the things I put in there, but I figured she could try everything on and see what worked and what didn't. Women did that kind of thing, didn't they? I personally just grabbed whatever was my size and ran to the nearest checkout.

On the way to shoes, she stopped in the intimates department, and her cheeks flushed bright pink as she browsed the panties, bras, and sleepwear. Picking up a purple thong, I waved it under her nose.

"I think these would be hot."

She snatched them from my hand, hung them back up, and kept moving. "I'd prefer not to have things up my butt all day."

"But on occasion is all right?" I couldn't help but ask since she'd left herself wide open for that one.

She gasped and stared at me wide-eyed. "I can't believe you just said that in here," she said in a loud whisper.

She was cute when she was all flustered and blushing. I decided not to tease her anymore as she finished making her selections, but I did toss in some sexy nightgowns we had passed. I'd actually prefer it if she just went to bed naked, but since she was tossing in matching pajama sets I was going to assume she'd prefer to be clothed.

When we reached the shoes, I insisted she try on at least a dozen pair, and even then I could only convince her to buy four. I didn't know much about women's shoes, but if the movies were to be believed, then shoes and purses were a necessity. But then I led her over to the selection of purses, and she stared at them like she'd never seen anything like it before.

I frowned. "You do have a purse, right? I don't remember you arriving with one."

She froze and stared at me, fear flashing in her eyes. "I left it at the party. They have my license and my bank card. Not that there's much in my account, but they could overdraw it, and then I'd be stuck with tons of fees."

"We'll take care of it when we get back. You can call your bank and tell them you haven't seen your wallet since last night. Maybe they'll reverse any charges if there have been any. Do we need to arrange for your things to come from Georgia? Birth certificate or social security card?"

"Both of those things are in my apartment."

I nodded. "We can call your boss when we get back to the truck. Maybe he'll be willing to ship them to you."

It took her damn near an hour to try on all the clothes we'd shoved into the cart, and I didn't like that I couldn't see them on her, but I waited patiently outside the dressing room. When she came out, she tried to only put a handful of outfits back into the cart and I held out a hand for the rest.

"It's too much," she insisted. "I don't need all this."

"Yes," I said. "You do. Stop arguing, woman, and let me do something nice for you."

Her cheeks flushed, and she dropped her gaze before nodding. I stuffed everything back into the cart and then pushed it to the furniture department. Nothing in my bedroom matched, but it didn't seem to bother Darian. It's possible she hadn't gotten a good look, but from what I'd learned of her past, I figured just having something new that was just hers would be exciting. She didn't seem like the type to care if things matched or not. I found a five-drawer chest that was in stock and close in color to the furniture I already had, then tossed it onto the bottom of the cart. She gave me a questioning glance, but I knew she'd need someplace to put all this new stuff.

I headed to the front of the store, hunting for a checkout line that wasn't ten people deep. When it was our turn, I did my best to distract Darian so she wouldn't freak out over the total, especially as it climbed into the hundreds. I had a feeling that was probably more she'd spent on clothes for an entire year before.

I paid and placed the sacks into the cart, then pushed it out to the parking lot. Once everything was loaded in the backseat, I helped Darian into the truck and handed her my cell phone. While she called her boss, I headed back to the compound. I hoped her bank would still be open by the time we got to the house.

Another Prospect was manning the gate when we got back, and he waved us through. I drove straight to the house and sent Darian inside to take care of her bank situation while I hauled all her bags into the house. I carried everything to the master bedroom and placed the sacks on the floor. Then I hauled the chest of drawers into the bedroom too and pulled out my toolbox so I could put the damn thing together. I had the back and sides screwed together when Darian came into the room, her face paler than usual.

"What's wrong, angel?" I asked, rising from the floor.

"They not only emptied my account, I'm overdrawn by several thousand dollars, and that's before the fees. The bank said they can't help me until I file a police report since I told them my purse was stolen. So I looked up the non-emergency number for your police department, and they said they'd take my report but asked me to bring my ID, except I don't have any now."

I wrapped my arms around her and hugged her tight. "We'll get it figured out. If I have to, I'll get Wire to hack into the Georgia DMV and have a new license mailed to you here. I'm sure that's something he could do. In Alabama, it's pretty easy to get a replacement, but I've heard other states can be difficult. I think Georgia might be one of them."

"You have someone who's going to hack into…" She shook her head. "I don't think I want to know."

I smiled and kissed her. "We'll get everything figured out. Your boss is mailing your stuff, right?"

"Yeah, but he's taking the shipping fees out of my last paycheck."

I bit the inside of my cheek, wanting to offer to add her to my account, but I didn't think she'd go for that. Especially not if she knew how much was in there. Which meant I'd just have to resolve her current banking issue.

"Does your bank have branches here?" I asked.

She shook her head. "It was just a small local bank."

"Then we'll work on getting your issue resolved and close out your account, and when you get your ID, we'll open a new one for you here. Until then, I'll give you some cash in case there's anything you need when I'm not around."

"I can't take more of your money," she said. "You've already bought me all that stuff today, and you're letting me stay here."

"Baby, I'm not anywhere near done yet."

As much as I wanted to shower her with gifts, I knew I'd have to take things slow. She'd need a car, for one, but that could wait while we sorted out the other stuff, like her bank and identification problems. Even though I was getting to use one of the trucks, the vehicle wasn't just mine to use all the time. I had every intention of putting money into an account for her each month, whether she protested or not. While I'd kept her from meeting Ridley and Isabella earlier, I knew it wouldn't be long before they showed up on my doorstep. And I had a feeling they would welcome Darian and befriend her. I was counting on it.

My house wasn't as large as some of the ones in the compound, but it was a three-bedroom, two bath, with room to grow. The way it was set up, it would be easy to add another room or two if we ever needed to. I had an unfinished attic that had windows already in place. It would just be a matter of putting sheetrock on the walls and completing the flooring, then adding some walls. Nothing I couldn't handle, especially with some help from my brothers. It had a full staircase off the closed-in porch off the kitchen. I smiled a little, thinking about Darian pregnant with my baby.

Right now, I had a guest room, and the other bedroom was set up for my grandkids when they visited. I usually kept Farrah overnight once a week, and after Mariah was a little older, she'd come stay with me too. It gave Ridley some time to breathe, and I loved getting to spend time with my sweet girls. But if Darian was pregnant, I'd have to either get started on those extra rooms upstairs or change the guest room into a nursery.

I pulled away from those thoughts and focused on the woman in my arms. Even though I was so much taller than she, she felt perfect in my arms. Darian snuggled against me, rubbing her cheek against my shirt, and she sighed a little. I wanted to give her the world, and it was an odd feeling since I'd never really cared about a woman before, except my daughter and my granddaughters, but that was different. They were blood. Although I knew that didn't always mean something. Ridley's mother had tried to sell her, and Darian's parents had tossed her away.

"Do you know anything about your parents?" I asked.

Darian shook her head.

"Have you always lived in Georgia?"

"I think so. My social worker said I was put into the system when I was three, and the woman who left me claimed to be my mother. She was living outside Atlanta at the time. I don't really remember anything before foster care, though."

"What about your dad?" I asked.

"He was never mentioned. My birth certificate says his name was Damon Crosse. My mom was Lilian Porter."

That name triggered something in my memories, but I couldn't place it. Had I met a Damon Crosse at some point? The club had some dealings with other MCs in the nearby states, but I'd never personally been to Georgia before. If that's where Darian was from, it was doubtful I'd ever met her dad.

"If Wire can do a little digging and get some information on your parents, would you want to know more about them? Even if your mom gave you up, maybe your dad didn't know anything about it. He could be looking for you," I said. I know if Ridley had vanished I'd have gone looking.

"What if... what if we find him but he never wanted me?" Darian asked, a tremor in her voice.

"Angel, if you don't want to look for your parents, then we won't."

She bit her lip. "I think... I think my mother was a, um, working girl. I don't know for sure, but it was just the way my social worker spoke about her one time."

"Only one way to know for sure, honey. But it's up to you. I won't put in the request if you don't want me to."

"Do you really think he looked for me?" she asked softly.

"If I didn't know what had happened to my daughter, I'd have torn the world apart trying to find her. There's also the possibility that he never knew your mom was pregnant. The man might like to know he has a daughter as sweet as you." He winked. "And gorgeous too."

"I'm nothing special," she muttered.

I lifted her chin with my finger and stared down into her eyes. "To me you are."

She looked up at me a few minutes before nodding. "Okay. Ask Wire to find them. If I understood why my mother got rid of me, then maybe…"

"Maybe you wouldn't feel so abandoned?" I asked.

She nodded again.

"I'll send him a text, then finish putting your furniture together. When I'm done, we can get some lunch, and then you can put your things away."

"I could… make lunch?"

"Are you asking me if you can make lunch, or do you want to make lunch?" I asked.

"I want to," she said.

"Honey, this is your home now. You can do whatever you want. The kitchen is fairly well-stocked. I'll eat whatever you make. Just don't ever try to feed me raw fish."

Her nose crinkled. "That sounds gross."

"Then we're agreed. No sushi. Ever."

I swatted her ass as she turned to walk away, and she gave me a saucy smile over her shoulder. Pulling my phone from my pocket, I shot off a message to Wire with her parents' names and asked him to check into things. I also asked if he could do something about getting her another license, without me having to drive her into Georgia to get one. I'd asked her on the way home if she remembered her license number, and the look she'd cast my way had been kind of cute.

"Seriously? You think I memorized my driver's license number?" she'd asked.

Maybe it was only guys who did that sort of thing? Heck if I knew. I'd never really bothered to get to know a woman before. Hadn't ever been tempted to know them longer than it took to fuck them, until now.

With that task done, I focused on the furniture again. I even had to put the drawers together, which was a bitch. It definitely wasn't a quality piece but it would work for now. Maybe with all that money sitting in my account, I'd buy a new bedroom set for us. Something that matched. Someone at the compound would be happy to take the used items. One of the Prospects would probably jump at the chance to get their hands on my king-size bed and mattress. I'd seen the way the duplexes were furnished, and they didn't have much. Torch may have set aside two duplexes for the Prospects to share at the back of the compound, so they would be nearby whenever we needed them, but he hadn't given them much in the way of comfort.

Hell, with more and more of the patched members moving into homes on the compound, there wasn't a reason the Prospects couldn't use the rooms in the clubhouse. Torch, Venom, and several others, myself included, had given up our rooms there. Maybe I'd bring that up at the next meeting. They were small rooms with just a dresser, bed, and tiny-ass bathroom. They hadn't been used for much except sleeping or fucking club sluts anyway. Until we'd started moving into the homes on the property, none of us had spent much time alone. The Prospects wouldn't really need more space than the rooms provided. Not until they'd earned it. To me, the duplexes should be reserved for patched members who wanted their own space. But what the hell did I know? I wasn't in charge of shit, and that was fine with me.

The smell of tomatoes hit my nose as I set the finished chest of drawers against the wall, and I headed for the kitchen to see what Darian was making. She looked cute as a damn pixie standing in front of the stove stirring some red sauce in a pot. She'd pulled her hair up on top of her head in some sort of messy knot with little, escaped strands clinging to her neck. At some point she'd kicked off her shoes and rolled up the hems of her jeans until they were partway up her calves. One strap of her tank top had fallen down her shoulder. Pulling my phone from my pocket, I snapped a picture of her before making my presence known.

"Baby, if you were hot, you could have changed into one of your new outfits," I said as I moved closer and settled my hands at her waist.

She smiled at me over her shoulder. "I'm fine. I didn't want to get in the way while you were putting that chest together."

"That doesn't smell anything like the jar of sauce I usually buy," I told her, sniffing the air.

"Because I added some chopped garlic and onion I found in your pantry, then I browned the ground chicken I saw in the fridge and added it too. The noodles are already finished, so if you're done working, we can eat," she said. "If you'd had tomatoes, paste, and some other herbs, I could have made the sauce."

I kissed the side of her neck. "Sounds good, honey. I'll get some drinks for us."

While she dished up the food, I took two sodas out of the fridge and grabbed two forks from the drawer near the sink. I didn't have fancy napkins, but I did pull some paper towels off the roll and put them on the table. Darian set the plates down, then started digging through the fridge.

"What are you looking for?" I asked.

"Parmesan. I thought maybe you'd have some since you had like four jars of sauce and half a dozen pasta boxes in your pantry."

"It's in a plastic container on the second shelf."

She pulled it out and stared at it. "This is like... real grated parmesan?"

"Yeah. It costs more than the canned stuff, but it tastes a lot better."

She got out a spoon, then sprinkled some over both our plates before returning the cheese to the fridge. If she hadn't ever had real parmesan before, I wondered what else she'd been missing out on. I should have known with the way she was living that she probably had eaten cheap meals if she'd eaten at all. My stomach knotted as I thought of her homeless and starving.

I took a bite and winked at her. "This is really good, angel."

"It's not much."

"You know how to cook from scratch?" I asked.

She bit her lip then hesitantly nodded. "I can do a little. In theory. At one of my foster homes, they had three kids who were their actual children. The grandma would come over and cook with them sometimes, and I'd watch. She made her own pasta and everything. I've never actually tried to cook anything but boxed meals before, or ramen, but I think I could cook something if I tried."

"Next time we buy groceries, you pick out whatever you want. Experiment as much as you want, and if something doesn't turn out quite right, we can always order pizza or something that night. Would you like some cookbooks?"

Her eyes lit up, and she flashed me a smile. "I'd love that."

"My daughter goes to the bookstore every chance she gets. Sometimes Isabella goes with her. I can either ask them to pick up something for you or..."

"Or?" she asked.

"Or you can go with them. You'll have to meet them sooner or later."

Panic flashed across her face, and I smiled a little. "Honey, they don't bite. And I can't think of a single reason they won't love you. If anyone is going to get a hard time from Ridley, it will be me, and I admittedly deserve it. I told you I wasn't very nice when she wanted to be with Venom. But that's my problem and not yours."

"All right. I'll meet them."

I winked at her. "I'll make sure it's painless. Maybe we can all go out to dinner together. You'll love the kids. Farrah is a little hyper because of her age, but she's a sweetheart, and Mariah already has everyone wrapped around her little finger."

Her brow furrowed a little.

"You do like kids, don't you?" I asked.

"It's not that. I mean, I was around kids of all ages when I was in the system. I've just not really been around many since then. But…"

"But what, angel?"

"If you're their grandfather… and we're together… they're not going to call me Grandma, are they?"

I nearly choked on my bite of pasta and burst out laughing. I'd never even thought of that. Oh yeah, my daughter was going to give me grief for sure. And judging the narrow-eyed glare Darian was casting my way now, she wasn't much happier about the situation.

"Honey, you can ask them to call you whatever you want." I fought a smile. "But I'd love to see the look on my daughter's face if her kids call you Grandma."

She snorted and went back to eating, but I caught the little smile lurking at the corners of her lips. I had a feeling with Darian in my life there would never be a dull moment.

Chapter Five

Darian

We'd barely finished lunch before we were summoned to the clubhouse again. I didn't know what was going on, and I didn't think Bull did either. He looked concerned but held my hand tightly as we walked down the narrow hall to the room at the far end. The door stood ajar, and I saw a bank of computer monitors before we stepped inside. Torch and Venom were already there, along with two other guys I hadn't met before.

"Close the door," Torch said.

Bull pushed it shut, then wrapped his arm around me, as if he were trying to shield me from whatever was about to happen.

"Why the fucking hell didn't either of you say a word about her daddy being Damon Crosse?" Torch asked, anger blazing in his eyes.

My heart pounded in my chest. Who the hell was my dad that just hearing his name had put that look on the President's face?

Bull looked from one man to another. "I just found out right before I sent that text to Wire. Why? Who the fuck is Damon Crosse?"

Torch lifted a brow and looked at the man next to him. The giant, nearly as big as Bull, folded his arms over his chest. Venom didn't look pleased with the situation either, and the guy sitting in front of all those screens looked… worried?

"You might know him by the name Scratch," Venom said.

"Oh, shit," Bull muttered. "He helped Ridley, so he can't be all bad, right?"

"You willing to take that chance?" one of the unknown men asked.

"Tank, what the fuck should I do about it? I can't change who her daddy is," Bull said.

"Ink her. Tonight," the man at the computer said. "Devil's Boneyard has their own hacker. Shade. He's not as good as me, but he's good enough that he'll be able to figure out who was just searching for his VP. We might not have long before they show up on our doorstep. I should have talked to Torch before running my search, but I hadn't known he already knew who the man was. I figured her dad was just someone average, and not part of a MC. If I'd known I was looking up the VP of Devil's Boneyard, I'd have taken a different route."

"Shit, Wire," Bull mumbled.

"He's right," Torch said. "If you're set on keeping her, she needs to be inked tonight. There's no guarantee even that will stop her daddy from dragging her out of here, but it's your best shot."

"Um, who's Scratch, and what's the Devil's Boneyard?" I asked.

"Scratch is your daddy's road name. He's the VP of a club in the Florida Panhandle called Devil's Boneyard, and he runs a chop shop there. From what little I know of that club, none of them are married or have old ladies, and none have children. Or at least, that's the rumor," Torch said. "Something about not having any weak links."

"Which makes your woman rather rare," Venom said. "If those rumors are true. And it likely means Scratch doesn't know he has a daughter, or at least he doesn't know she's alive."

"Fuck me," Bull muttered.

"What do you mean by inked?" I asked.

Bull winced. "We kind of forgot that step in explaining things. The old ladies of the Dixie Reapers get a property tattoo. Ridley and Isabella both opted to get theirs on their forearm just above their wrist. But it can go on your back, or I guess anywhere else you want it."

"You mean like a tattoo?" I asked, my voice coming out as a squeak. I was deathly afraid of needles.

"Yeah, a tattoo," Bull said. "We can make it as plain or as pretty as you want."

"But I…" I swallowed hard. "That's the only way to keep me safe?"

"There are no guarantees," Wire said. "But yeah, it's your best shot at staying with Bull when your daddy dearest shows up. Assuming you want to stay."

"I want to stay," I blurted then looked up at Bull. "I want to stay with you. If I have to get a tattoo, then I will, but I'll need you to hold my hand. I can't stand needles."

"Zipper's already here," Tank said. "We called him when we called you. Figured you'd want to get this over with."

Bull nodded. He led me from the room and through another door. I was surprised that the space had been set up like a mini tattoo shop. Another man wearing one of those leather cuts was sitting on a stool and pulled out different bottles of ink and prepped some sort of machine.

"Zipper, this is Darian," Bull said, pushing the door shut behind us.

Zipper smiled at me. "Nice to meet you, Darian. Ever had a tattoo before?"

"No, and um… I should probably tell you I'm scared of needles."

He nodded, then motioned to the chair. "Have a seat."

I eased onto the black leather, and Bull took my hand. Zipper explained how the tattooing process worked, talked to me about aftercare, and even showed me how the tattoo gun operated. I wasn't quite so nervous by the time he was finished with this spiel, but I still held tight to Bull's hand.

"Do you know what you want?" Zipper asked, looking at Bull.

"She needs something delicate, like her, but she's strong too," Bull said.

"Got it. Strong but pretty." Zipper winked at me. "Any color preferences?"

"I like every color of the rainbow," I said. "Except orange."

"Where are you from, darlin'? I detect an accent that isn't from around here," Zipper said.

"Georgia," I answered.

Zipper got a thoughtful look on his face, then pulled out his phone. He tapped and scrolled the screen, but I didn't know what he was searching for. After a moment, he turned it toward me. There was a beautiful butterfly on the screen. It was mostly a pale yellow and black but the bottom of the wings was a brilliant blue.

"It's the Tiger Swallowtail," Zipper said. "And according to Google, it's the state butterfly for Georgia. I could work that into your tattoo if you want."

"It's beautiful," I said.

"I was thinking of maybe a Magnolia blossom too, depending on where you want this. If it's going on your arm, there won't be much room."

"Why a Magnolia blossom?" Bull asked.

"Because they're beautiful trees, but they're also pretty damn strong. Like your woman. But I can ink whatever the two of you want."

"I like the idea of the flower and the butterfly," I said. "But it needs to be somewhere that I can show to other people without having to get naked."

Zipper chuckled. "Well, there's your lower back, or across your ribs. Both would give me enough room to work. But I have to tell you, the rib area hurts like a bitch compared to getting it on your back. Lots of bones to ink across."

I tightened my grip on Bull's hand. I didn't like the idea of pain, but I wanted the tattoo somewhere I could see it and enjoy it. If I was going to do this, and I had no doubt it would be my only tattoo, then I might as well go all out.

"Ribs," I said.

Admiration shone in Zipper's eyes as he nodded. "I'll get the inks set up. You'll have to either take off your shirt or at least pull it up to the bottom of your bra. I promise to remain a gentleman either way."

There was something in his eyes, a flash of pain, and I wondered what caused it. Was there maybe someone special in his life, and he just wasn't interested in any other females? Or perhaps someone he wished was part of his life. Maybe someone he'd lost? I readjusted on the chair, and Bull helped arrange my shirt, and then I said a prayer that I wouldn't embarrass the both of us by screaming my damn head off while Zipper inked me.

I tried to take calming breaths and relax as much as possible, but the moment the tattoo gun touched my skin I tensed. I focused on Bull, staring into his eyes, and tried not to think about the pain. Tears pricked my eyes, but I refused to let them fall. He thought I was strong, and I was going to prove him right.

It felt like the tattoo took forever, and my stomach was rumbling by the time Zipper was finished. He put some ointment over my newly inked ribs, then let me look in a mirror before he covered the tattoo. I remembered his words from earlier, about how to care for it, and promised to follow his instructions carefully. Bull helped me stand and pulled my shirt down to hide my exposed torso.

I paused as I started to follow Bull out of the room and turned back to Zipper. "Whoever she is, maybe she misses you too," I said.

His eyebrows rose, and a half-smile tipped up the corner of his lips. "Maybe."

Without another word, I followed Bull from the room. My ribs ached, and I tried not to wince with every step I took. Even though it had probably been the most painful thing I'd ever done, I wasn't sorry. Even though it looked raw and angry right now, the artwork was beautiful. Who'd have ever guessed a rough and tough biker could be so artistic? I wondered if he'd done Bull's tattoos. Some of them were really gorgeous, and one was on the scary side with creepy skulls hanging on a tree filled with ravens. Whoever had done it was talented, but the image freaked me out a little. I hadn't had the nerve to ask Bull the meaning behind it.

"Where are we going now?" I asked.

"I thought we'd sit at the bar and have a burger and fries, then head home to take care of your new ink. I'll text Venom and set up something for dinnertime with Ridley and the girls."

My stomach flipped and flopped at the thought of meeting his daughter and grandchildren. What was

Ridley going to think about her dad being with me? He'd said I was younger than her. If our roles were reversed, I probably wouldn't be too happy about the situation. Oh hell. Dad. That word. I'd never much thought about my dad once I'd reached my teen years, figuring he'd forgotten me just like my mother had. But what if I'd been wrong all this time? I didn't know what to think about him being a biker in another club, and I really hoped he didn't cause trouble for me now. I'd been without him for this long. I'd survive fifty years without his presence in my life.

It worried me that Torch seemed concerned, though. I didn't really know the guy, but he didn't seem like the type to be apprehensive over nothing. If he thought my dad might come for me, then I had to wonder if that might really happen. I wasn't sure how I felt about meeting the man after all these years. To me, he was just a sperm donor and likely an unwilling one. Oh, I had no doubt he'd fucked my mother, but then so had half the state of Georgia if the social worker could be believed. Not that the woman knew I'd overheard her telling a coworker about the type of person my mother was.

Bull gripped my hips and lifted me onto a barstool, then claimed the seat next to me. A young guy wearing one of those cuts came over. I noticed his said *Prospect* on it, not that I had any idea what that meant. I might have watched an episode or two of *Sons of Anarchy*, but I'd never really gotten into the show or understood what was going on. I was more of a *Buffy the Vampire Slayer* kind of TV watcher. Even though the show had been before my time, I'd stumbled across some episodes on TV one day and had gotten hooked. Who didn't love a kickass girl who killed vampires and demons?

Bull ordered our food, which probably should have bothered me. I'd often enough heard women bitch when their men ordered for them, but honestly, it was kind of nice having someone take care of me. I'd been struggling for so long that I finally felt like I could breathe. Even though I had a possible confrontation with my dad hanging over my head, all things considered, life was pretty good right now. The best it had ever been, in fact.

"Ivan," Bull said. "This is Darian, my old lady as of today."

It still felt weird getting called that when I was only twenty-one. Maybe I'd get used to it at some point. I still didn't understand the concept of old ladies. I was his, but we weren't married, and yet I was more than a girlfriend. At least, I thought that's how it worked? There was definitely a learning curve.

Ivan flashed me a smile. "Welcome to the Dixie Reapers."

He was cute, in a boyish way. Not that he was a boy. If I had to guess, he was probably older than me, but he didn't have anything on Bull. But then, I'd never met anyone I found as attractive as the man sitting next to me. Probably a good thing since I'd just agreed to be his forever.

Ivan wandered off, calling out our order to someone on the other side of a small serving window. With my back to the room, I couldn't really observe anyone. On the way to the bar, I'd noticed a few women who were barely dressed, and I wondered who they were. Did they belong to someone like I belonged to Bull? Was I expected to dress that way? Bull hadn't said anything about my clothing choices when we'd gone shopping. There was still so much I didn't know about this way of life, and I had a feeling I needed to learn fast. Everything had happened so suddenly, and I felt a little like Dorothy being dropped into Oz by the twister.

Our food was delivered, and as I picked up my burger to take a bite, the cloying scent of perfume filled my nose, making me gag. I turned toward the scent, and my eyes widened at the blonde with long, red nails currently plastered to Bull's side. She was batting her eyes at him and practically shoving her cleavage into his face, but Bull didn't look the least bit happy with the situation. The woman was everything I wasn't. Sexy, definitely older than me, and she had this aura that screamed she knew exactly what she was doing in the bedroom.

I stared, not certain how I was supposed to react. Technically, he was mine, but was I supposed to smack the shit out of her and demand she take her hands off my man? Or was I supposed to let Bull handle it? I didn't like the look she was giving him, and as her hand slid down to his thigh, then crept closer to his crotch, I felt a spark of something deep inside.

"Hey! Keep your bitch-ass hands off him," I yelled at her.

Bull slowly turned his head my way, a slight smile on his face. I gulped and blinked, not knowing where my outburst had come from. I'd never felt possessive of someone before, or ever been prone to violence, but I suddenly wanted to drag the woman away by her platinum strands of perfect hair and toss her out on her ass, which was probably perfect too.

The woman sneered at me. "You stay out of this, little girl. I know what Bull likes. There's history between us, and you can never please him the way I do."

My eyes widened as I looked from her to him. There was a flash of something in his eyes, almost like shame, and I knew that what she said was true. Whoever she was, they'd obviously slept together, possibly lots of times. If he'd had someone like her, what the hell was he doing with me? I could never look like this woman, no matter how much makeup I put on, or how tight my clothes were. I'd never have a body like that.

"Darian," he said softly, but I held up a hand and slid off the barstool.

Insecurities hounded me as I stared at the perfect woman. I knew that Bull hadn't given me any reason to feel inferior to her, but I did just the same. Maybe it was because no one had ever wanted me. Abandonment issues or something. Maybe it was growing up without hugs and praise from an adult for my entire life. Or maybe I was just fucked up all on my own.

"I'm not that hungry." Skirting around them, I headed outside.

He called out to me, but I just moved faster. I remembered the direction of Bull's house and started doing this half-walk, half-jog that I hoped would put some distance between us. Bull hadn't locked the door when we'd left earlier so getting inside shouldn't be an issue. I should have stayed to fight for him, deep down I knew that, but I still didn't feel confident with my place in his life. Yes, he'd inked me and said I was his, but what exactly did that mean in his world? Would I have to deal with women like that one all the time? Were there a lot of them he'd slept with that still hung around? I didn't know how I felt about that. And even worse, even though he said I was his, did that mean he was really mine? Or would I have to share him?

I knew part of my worries had to do with my upbringing or lack of one, but it also had a great deal to do with the fact I didn't know the man I'd let claim me. Oh, he made me feel things no one else ever had before, and I felt safe and cherished when his arms were around me. But I honestly didn't know much about him. I didn't know his past, how he came to be part of the Dixie Reapers, or anything else. Maybe we'd moved too fast, but I didn't regret my decision. I'd just have to learn to grow a thicker skin.

My entire world had changed so suddenly, and I wasn't even sure which way was up right now. It didn't take me long to realize I was lost somewhere in the compound. The houses I passed didn't look the least bit familiar, and I wondered if I'd missed a turn. I had no idea how big this place was, but I felt a sudden spike of fear that I'd be wandering around out here all day and night. The farther I walked, the fewer homes I saw. Maybe I should have just knocked on someone's door? But I hadn't met many people since coming here, and I didn't know what kind of reception I would get. Yeah, I now had ink saying I was Bull's, but would they really care?

After a bit more walking, my feet started to ache and my ribs were hurting from the tattoo. A line of trees nearby drew my attention and I went to sit under one. I remembered in elementary school a teacher once told us if we were lost and we couldn't find an adult, the best thing to do was remain still until someone found us. This probably wasn't what she'd had in mind, but maybe the same principle would work. I tipped my head back against the trunk of the tree after I'd settled at the base and closed my eyes. How long before someone would find me? Would Bull even care that I was missing? Would he notice? He seemed to want me, but I still didn't understand how he could want someone like me when he could have that sexy woman who'd tried to lay claim to him in the clubhouse. Was she with him even now?

My gut clenched at the thought. He'd made me feel special, something no one else had ever done before. I couldn't remember a time in my life anyone had given a shit about me. For some reason, I'd thought he might be different. The way he touched me, kissed me... I'd never felt something like that before. Maybe I'd just read too much into things.

I didn't know how long I stayed under the tree, but slowly, the sun began lowering in the sky. The horizon was awash with pinks and oranges before I heard the rumble of a motorcycle. A blond man I hadn't seen before stopped his bike at the edge of the grass, put down the kickstand, and shut off the engine. He approached me slowly and knelt a foot away, almost as if he were afraid he'd spook me.

"Darian?" he asked.

I nodded.

"I'm Flicker. You scared the shit out of Bull. He's been yelling at everyone and was about to tear the damn compound apart. He didn't realize you'd left the front porch, and by the time he got away from the grabby club slut, you'd disappeared. How long have you been out here, honey?"

I shrugged. "A while. I got lost."

He smiled a little and held out a hand. "Come on. Let's get you home so that man of yours can settle the fuck down. I think Torch is about ready to tranquilize him."

"He wouldn't really do that, would he?" I asked, accepting his hand and standing up.

"Your man didn't exactly get his name because he's subtle. And yeah, if Torch thought it would be best for everyone, he would have no trouble doing something like that, or knocking him the fuck out," Flicker said. He helped me onto the back of the bike, and then we were off.

It felt awkward holding onto a man I didn't even know, and I tried to keep some distance between us without me falling off. That would just be a perfect ending to my crappy afternoon. Flicker had barely pulled into the driveway before Bull was charging down the steps toward me. The bike hadn't even come to a complete stop before Bull had pulled me off and into his arms. His embrace was tight as he breathed me in, and I winced and bit my lip to stop from crying out as he squeezed my tattoo. I felt a tremor run through him and realized that he must have been really concerned. Had I really worried him that much?

"I'm fine," I said softly. "I just got lost."

"I'll let everyone know she's safe," Flicker said, then I heard his bike take off down the road.

"I'm sorry if I scared you," I mumbled against Bull's chest. "I was trying to come home, but I guess I got turned around."

"I thought you were gone, but Johnny was at the gate and said no one had left," Bull said. "Then I thought maybe your dad was already here and had found a way to get to you."

He pulled back and cupped my cheek. The tenderness and concern in his eyes made my eyes prick with tears. I'd never known anyone before who cared what happened to me. While I didn't like that I'd worried him, it was nice to know that someone actually felt something for me, strongly enough that they would miss me if I were gone.

"Come on, sweet girl," Bull said. "Let's take care of that tattoo and get you something to eat. I brought your burger home. We can heat it up, or I can take you somewhere for dinner if you want."

"I'm… I'm sorry for running off. I know I should have stayed and put her in her place but…"

He tipped my chin up and lightly pressed his lips to mine. "She's not going to be a problem anymore. All right? I won't lie. There are others, but I think the message has been delivered that the club sluts are to give me a wide berth from now on. I think I got to be something of a challenge for them because I haven't touched them for a while."

He led me into the house and straight back to our bathroom. While I stripped out of my clothes, he started the shower, then undressed. He tested the water before taking my hand and pulling me into the glassed-in stall. Bull shut the door, then washed me with the lightest touch, almost as if he were afraid I'd break. He crowded me against the tiled wall and cupped my jaw. The intensity of his gaze nearly took my breath away.

"No more running. If you don't like something, you tell me. If someone says or does something they shouldn't, you tell me. It's my job to take care of you, Darian, and I know I should have put that slut in her place a lot faster than I did, and for that I'm sorry. When you told her to keep her hands off me, I thought you were going to take care of her."

"I guess that's what an old lady would have done, huh?" I asked.

"Yeah. But you've been my old lady for not even a day." He smiled a little. "Once you settle in a little more, I'm sure you'll be kicking all their asses."

I hoped he was right. I'd never been around a bunch of bikers before, and I really wanted to fit in. Having friends and being part of a family would be a new experience for me. We finished washing each other, then Bull gently dried me and tended to my tattoo. Part of me was disappointed he hadn't tried to do more. While he got dressed, in what seemed to be his standard T-shirt, jeans, boots, and his leather cut, I stared at all the clothes he'd bought for me.

"Are we still meeting your daughter and her family for dinner?" I asked. Ridley might have caught a quick look at me as I'd run through the clubhouse that first time, but if I was going to actually meet her, I wanted to look nice.

"You've probably had enough excitement for one day. We can get together with Ridley and the girls anytime. If you're up for going out somewhere, there's a good steak place not too far from here. Nothing fancy, but the food is really good," Bull said.

"Steak?" I looked away from my clothes and stared at him.

"What?" His brow furrowed. "You don't eat steak?"

"I've never tried it."

He rubbed a hand through his beard, then nodded his head. "Then we're going to eat steak tonight. Anything else you want to try, you let me know, and I'll make it happen. But if you want anchovies on your pizza, I'm ordering you one of your own. That shit's nasty."

I giggled and went back to looking at my new wardrobe. He'd said the place was casual so I pulled out one of my new pair of jeans and a fitted black top with a cutout pattern down the short sleeves. It was cute without being dressy. The back of my neck warmed, and I glanced toward Bull to find him watching me intently as I pulled out a pretty lace bra and matching panties. My cheeks flushed, and the garments fell to the floor as he prowled closer.

"You're wearing those?" he asked, his lips brushing along my neck.

"Y-yes."

"Maybe we have a little more time than I thought, because I damn sure won't be able to keep my hands to myself knowing what you have on under your clothes."

"Michael," I moaned.

"It's going to be quick."

"I don't care. I know you'll make it up to me later."

"You better fucking believe I will. I'm going to taste every inch of you tonight and fuck you until both of us pass out."

I squeezed my thighs together as an ache began to build. Would I always get so turned on just from him talking dirty to me? I loved the filthy things that came out of his mouth, especially when he was deep inside me. I didn't think I'd ever mind sleepless nights if it meant that I got to feel his hands and lips on me.

I heard the rasp of his zipper, then he kicked my feet farther apart. I braced my hands on the top of the chest and pushed my ass out. His hand went from my hip, down my belly, and between my splayed legs. The first brush of his fingers over my clit and I cried out, feeling like sparks were shooting through me. His touch was magic, and nothing would ever convince me otherwise.

He worked my clit as he rubbed his cock against my ass. If he kept it up, I was going to come before he even got inside me, but that may have been exactly what he wanted.

"Michael, please," I begged.

"Not yet, baby. I want you nice and wet."

He kept teasing me, alternating between stroking my clit and lightly pinching it. I was a quivering mess, whimpers and more pleading words escaping my lips, but he wouldn't relent. I wanted his cock inside me, and I wasn't above grinding against him in an effort to make his iron-clad control snap.

He pulled his hips back, and I felt a sharp sting as he swatted my ass. "Be a good girl," he said. "You'll get my cock when I'm good and ready to give it to you."

"Michael, I need you. I need your cock so badly."

"Soon, baby."

The next time he pinched my clit, I came, screaming out his name as waves of pleasure rolled over me. His beard tickled my shoulder as he kissed his way up to my neck and then nipped my ear.

"Don't move," he said.

I felt him move away and heard a drawer opening. A moment later, I heard the snick of a bottle opening and I tried to look over my shoulder but received another swat to my ass.

"Face forward," he said.

The demanding tone of his voice had me biting my lip.

I didn't know what he was doing, and when he parted the cheeks of my ass, I tensed for a moment. My body was drawn tight and yet he didn't make a move. Other than holding me open, he didn't touch me, didn't speak. Not knowing what would happen next was making my heart race.

"Do you know what I thought that first night when I found you in the bedroom?" he asked.

"No, what?"

"I thought about how much I wanted your lips around my cock, wanted to fuck your pussy until you couldn't walk… and I thought about how much I wanted to pound into this tight little ass of yours."

I gasped and tensed more. "You're… you're going to…"

"Oh yeah, baby. And I'm willing to bet that you're going to like it."

I felt his finger, slick with lube, brush against a place I'd always thought of as forbidden. My cheeks flamed as I realized that it actually felt pretty damn good, even if it was a little weird. His beard tickled me as he kissed along my upper back and slowly worked his finger inside me.

"That's it, baby. Relax and let me in," he murmured.

Relaxing was easier said than done, but I was trying. I wanted to please him, and if he thought this was something I would enjoy, then I was willing to listen. I knew that if it hurt, or if I didn't like it, that he'd stop. He might be a big, tough biker, but he also cared about me, and I knew Michael would never hurt me.

"Fuck, Darian. So damn tight."

His finger slowly fucked me, and soon I felt that growing ache between my legs again. I tried to spread farther, wanting his cock so damn bad. I could feel my juices trickling down my legs I was so fucking wet.

"Let's see if you can take two," he said.

I gasped at the pinch of a second finger being added, but after a few strokes, I was moaning and wanting more. It burned a little, but there was something building inside me. I didn't even get a warning before he added a third finger, and I felt like I was stretched to the max, but I knew his cock was even bigger. I didn't know if I could handle him fucking my ass, and I wasn't sure if that shiver that raked over me was from fear or excitement. Or maybe it was both.

"Still want my cock?" he asked, his lips brushing against my ear.

"Yes. So much."

"I could never deny you something you wanted," he said.

I felt his cock brush my pussy and then he was thrusting inside, deep and hard as his fingers kept working my ass. I cried out from the overwhelming sensations. He didn't slow down, didn't stop, just fucked me with an intensity I'd never felt before. His cock plunged into my pussy again and again as those fingers nearly drove me mad. It didn't take long before I was coming again, and I heard him grunt as his release splashed inside me.

"Christ, Darian. The things you do to me."

I whimpered as he drove into me again and again. Even when his cock was twitching and he'd stilled inside me, he still felt hard as a damn post. His cock slid free of my body, but his fingers were still working my ass. I trembled, wanting more and yet not knowing if I could handle it.

"I'll stop if you want me to, but I really want to fuck this ass of yours," he murmured.

"Keep going."

His fingers slid free of me, and then I felt the head of his cock press against that tight hole. It took everything in me to relax enough to let him in, and it burned way more than his fingers had. He was fucking huge, and I didn't know if I could take him, but he took his time working his cock into me. Once he was buried deep inside me, he began playing with my clit again. I felt more turned on than I ever had before, and it didn't take much before I was pushing back against him. He seemed to take that as some sort of sign, and soon his cock was driving into me, harder and deeper with every stroke.

"Michael!" I cried out as I felt another orgasm drawing close.

"Come for me, baby," he said. "Let me feel that ass squeeze my cock."

His words alone triggered my release, and as stars burst behind my closed eyelids, I felt the heat of his release as he came again. When it was over and both of us were breathing hard, he wrapped an arm around my waist, keeping his cock inside me.

"You're fucking incredible," he said, pressing a kiss to my cheek.

"I think… I think it would be okay for us to do that again sometime."

He chuckled and slowly slid out of my body. I felt thoroughly used, my clit throbbing and my pussy and ass a little on the sore side, but it was the good kind of achiness. He led me into the bathroom and cleaned us both up.

When we stepped back into the bedroom, I couldn't help but stare at him as I hurried into my clothes.

I didn't know how I'd lucked out to find a man like him, but I couldn't have been more thankful. I grabbed some no-show socks from the drawer and the black ankle boots out of the closet. I was glad now that he'd insisted I get them since they went so well with this outfit.

He headed out of the bedroom, but I wasn't quite ready. I ducked into the bathroom to finish up. I'd never been much for wearing makeup, but I had grabbed some blush, mascara, and lip gloss at the store, so I quickly put some on, then blew my hair dry. When I was finished, I found Bull reclining on the couch, flipping through channels on the TV. I worried my bottom lip and danced from foot to foot. I'd never made a guy wait on me before. He didn't seem irritated but…

"I didn't take too long, did I?" I asked.

He turned to face me, and a slow smile spread across his lips. "You're well worth the wait."

"Are we taking your bike?"

"I'd rather wait until I can get a helmet for you. Torch offered to let me continue using one of the club trucks until I can get some other transportation sorted out. You should have a car so you can get around on your own, once this thing with your dad is settled."

"You don't have to buy me a car. That's too much. The clothes already cost a lot."

Bull stood and came toward me, gripping my waist. "Darian, you're mine. Remember what we talked about?"

"You're going to take care of me," I said softly.

"Right. And that means if you need a car, I'm going to get you a car. Although…"

"What?" I asked.

"Your daddy runs a chop shop. He may decide he wants to provide you with one since he hasn't done shit for you all your life." He winced. "Sorry. I shouldn't have said that."

"It's fine. You're right. I never even knew who he was, other than a name on my birth certificate. It's not like he ever tried to find me."

"I still shouldn't have said that, and I'm sorry. I wasn't trying to be an insensitive asshole, although admittedly, I probably am one most days. Not intentionally, though."

I smiled and pulled him down for a kiss. "It's fine, Bull."

"I thought we agreed you'd call me Michael," he said. "As long as it's just us. I'm Bull to everyone else, but then, you're not like them. You're mine."

I toyed with his hair as I fought for courage. "Does that mean you're mine too? Or will I have to share you with those other women?"

His eyes darkened, and he growled before his grip tightened on me. "I don't want anyone but you, Darian. Those women were fun for a while, but they didn't mean anything to me. Half the time, I didn't even know what their names were. I know that doesn't paint me in the best light, but I don't want to lie to you."

"They're so much more... well, more. I'll never look like that woman from earlier or have her sexiness or confidence."

His hand cupped my cheek. "Baby, to me, you're far sexier than she could ever be. And confidence can grow over time. From what you've told me of your life, it hasn't been all that spectacular so far, but that's going to change. Everyone in your life has let you down in some way, but I refuse to do that. I already screwed up earlier, and I'll likely mess up again in the future. But never doubt for a moment that you're who I want to be with."

"She probably knows all the things you like in the bedroom," I said. "You were my first. I don't even know what the hell I'm doing when we're in bed together."

He smiled and kissed me again. "You're doing more than fine in that department. You get me harder than anyone ever has before, and I'm not just saying that. If I wanted one of the club sluts, I'd have kept screwing them, but you are exactly what I've been wanting. Do you have any idea how hot it is that I got to be your first and that I'll be your only? Those women have fucked countless men, and while they may have learned some skills along the way, being with them is... passionless. They're just a place to stick your dick when you want to get laid, as bad as that sounds, but they aren't the kind of women you make your forever girl."

"I just don't want you to wake up one morning and regret claiming me," I said.

"Baby, I'm not going anywhere and neither are you. This is our home. Mine and yours. And if there's a baby," he said, placing his hand on my belly, "it will be loved. I'm not going to abandon you, Darian, neither of you."

"I'll try to do better. I know I have some issues to work through, and it might take some time, but I'll eventually get there."

He winked. "Let's go eat. You have to be starving by now."

He took me by the hand and led me out to the truck that was parked in the driveway. I hadn't noticed it earlier, but then I'd been focused on the man rushing toward me. If he wanted to buy me a car, I wouldn't argue, but I hated that he was spending so much money on me.

Maybe I could at least talk him into something used. I'd never owned a brand-new car, or really a brand-new anything, and I didn't see a reason to start now. Pre-loved was just as good. For a short time, I'd had a car that I'd bought for five hundred dollars, and it had been so old that it had fallen apart within a year. After having to walk everywhere for the last year, any transportation would be better than none.

Chapter Six

Bull

Being with Darian was going to be an adventure. There were so many things she hadn't experienced, and I wanted to make sure she had the chance to really live her life. It was hard for me to imagine never having had steak, or new clothes. What else had she missed out on all these years? If I could track down her mother, I might be tempted to beat the bitch. I still wanted to know how her dad was going to justify not looking for her all this time, unless he really hadn't known about her. But unless Darian's mom had kept her pregnancy a complete secret, I didn't know how that was possible. If the Devil's Boneyard hacker was as good as Wire claimed, then Darian would have been easy enough for him to locate. Something wasn't right about the entire thing, and I only hoped it didn't blow up in our faces. I did know one thing, though. I'd fight for her. She was mine, and no way was I going to let someone take her away.

Her face was flushed with pleasure as she took in the atmosphere of the restaurant. There was a bucket of peanuts in the center of the table and the empty shells littered the floor. Dim lighting made the place feel cozy, and she seemed to like the red checkered tablecloth since she kept running her fingers over it. She'd said she'd never had steak, but I hadn't thought to ask if she'd ever been out to eat somewhere before. At least, someplace that didn't have a drive-thru.

A waitress stopped at our table, flashing a bright smile at us. The fact she included Darian in that smile and didn't focus just on me already guaranteed she would get a nice tip. She set down the drinks we'd ordered from the hostess who had seated us and then placed two straws on the table.

"My name is Marney, and I'll be your server tonight. Have you had a chance to look over the menu?"

"I think she's still deciding, but for now let's order the appetizer sampler," I said. "We should be ready in a few minutes."

Marney nodded. "I'll go place that order and check back in a bit."

Darian kept worrying at her lower lip as she looked over the menu. I had a feeling it wasn't so much that she couldn't choose but that she was worried about the cost. We'd stopped at the bank on the way here, and I probably should have let her see how much I'd withdrawn so she'd stop stressing. Hell, I should just show her my account balance, but I wasn't certain that wouldn't freak her the fuck out. It was likely more money than she'd seen in her entire life. Probably more than she would have made in twenty years waitressing.

"Angel, just order whatever you want. If you want the twenty-five-dollar filet, then order it. Hell, get the steak and lobster if that's what you want to try. You're not going to put me in the poorhouse even if you ordered every expensive thing on the menu."

Her eyes widened a little.

I might regret it later, but I pulled out my wallet and retrieved the bank slip that had my balance printed on it, then I slid it across the table toward her. I tapped the paper to make her look down. When she saw the amount, her face blanched, and she swayed a moment. Leaping out of my chair, I grabbed her before she passed out.

"Hell, darlin'. That wasn't how I planned for that to go. I just wanted you to stop worrying about money."

"That's a lot of money," she whispered, a tiny bit of color coming back to her cheeks. "That's more than I could make in a lifetime."

"Torch takes care of us, and truthfully, I haven't really spent a lot of what I've earned over the years. My house is property of the Dixie Reapers and doesn't cost me a dime except for maintenance. My bike is paid for and is several years old. I've lived a simple life, Darian."

"I think I'm okay," she said, shooing me back to my seat.

"I meant what I said. Order anything you want. Have you ever had lobster or shrimp?"

"No."

"Then why don't you get the six-ounce steak, with the lobster tail, and fried shrimp? Whatever you don't like, you don't have to eat. I've never cared for lobster myself, but Ridley loves it."

She smiled a little. "You know, I don't have to try *everything* that I've missed out on all at one time. We can spread things out. I think I'll save the seafood for another day. But thank you for encouraging me to try new things and letting me order whatever I want."

The waitress returned and took our order, promising the appetizer would be out in a few minutes. She did leave a basket of rolls on the table with honey butter, and two small plates. Darian stared at them, and I picked one up, set it on a plate and passed it to her. The look on her face as she accepted it nearly broke my heart. Had no one ever done anything for her in her entire life? It had sounded bleak, what little she'd shared with me. It bothered me that she'd done without so many things most of her life, and I wasn't too pleased with either of her parents. Ridley had spoken of Scratch a few times and thought he'd been nice. I did owe him for making sure my daughter made it to the Dixie Reapers compound when she'd run from her mother and stepdad.

I didn't know anything about Scratch, not really, but if Darian was his daughter, then he had to be close to my age. I had a feeling he wasn't going to be overly thrilled that I'd claimed his daughter. With some luck, the ink on her ribs would keep him from trying to walk off with her. But if things went bad, it could mean all-out war between the Dixie Reapers and Devil's Boneyard. I really hoped it didn't go that way. If anything, maybe Darian could bring the two clubs together. We could always use more allies. It wasn't that Devil's Boneyard were enemies, but I wouldn't call them friends either. More like we knew about each other and kept to our own areas.

"How long have you been part of the Dixie Reapers?" Darian asked.

"Almost thirty years. I was just a cocky kid when I started prospecting. When I was growing up, my dad had a bike that he was always tinkering with, and he'd let me help. Learned everything I know about bikes from him. I saved up my money and bought my own when I was seventeen and started prospecting shortly after. Dad wasn't sure what to think about the Dixie Reapers, but he never tried to hold me back. He died around the time Ridley was born, and my mom sold his bike to pay for the funeral."

"Where's your mom now?" Darian asked.

"She died about twenty years ago. Drunk driver."

"I'm sorry. So all you have now are Ridley and her family?" Darian asked.

"And you."

Her cheeks flushed.

When our food arrived, Darian just stared at the appetizer a moment. Sensing her hesitation, I filled a small plate for her with a little of everything, then did the same for myself, making sure to leave plenty on the platter in case she wanted more. I could easily demolish the entire thing on my own, but I was going to make sure my woman was taken care of first.

The look of pleasure on her face, with her flushed cheeks and sparkling eyes, made me wonder if she'd ever tried any of this stuff before. Surely she'd at least had mozzarella sticks before? As she dipped her quesadilla into sour cream, then took a bite she hummed in appreciation.

"So good," she murmured before taking another bite.

I smiled a little, watching her eat. Something as simple as a quesadilla filled her with joy. I'd always taken for granted getting to eat out at places like this, but for Darian it was a new experience, and something she'd been denied her entire life. I wanted to see that look on her face all the time, and I liked being the one to put it there. All right, so the food technically was making her happy, but I was providing the food for her. I'd never really given a lot of thought to the providing aspect of a relationship. I'd wanted a woman in my bed and in my life, but I hadn't really thought about everything that would entail.

We ate the entire appetizer, then waited patiently for our dinner to arrive. Darian spoke a little more about her childhood, but I could tell she was glossing over things. I'd known a few kids in the foster system when I'd been a kid myself, and I'd heard some horror stories. It made me wonder if Darian had some of those herself, and just didn't want to share, or more likely, just wanted to forget. The thought of anyone harming her was enough to make me want to pound the shit out of something.

"How many foster families did you have?" I asked.

"A lot," she answered, tracing a pattern on the table with her finger. "Some weren't so bad. I mean, I was mostly ignored, but I preferred that over…"

"Over what?"

She shrugged and wouldn't make eye contact.

"Baby, I know you were a virgin, but did something happen while you were in foster care?"

"Sometimes the dads would get a little grabby once I turned thirteen. It never took long for the moms to catch on, and then I'd be off to another home. Nothing really bad happened to me, not like some of the stories I've heard. Maybe a boob grab here and there, or a slap on my ass. Inappropriate for sure, but I was never raped or made to do anything horrible."

That eased my mind a little, but I didn't like the thought of men touching her when they shouldn't have. No one should ever have to go through that. If I could rid the world of all the rapists and child molesters, I'd gladly do so. Our club might be into some illegal shit, but we didn't deal in women or children, and never would. At least, not under Torch's watch. If that ever changed, my ass was out of here. I didn't see Torch passing on the gavel to anyone he didn't trust, though. If he ever stepped down, the job of Pres would likely go to Venom, unless Torch had a son at some point who was old enough to take over. As often as he cornered that wife of his, it wouldn't surprise me if another baby was on the way before too long.

Speaking of… I needed to do a little research and find out just how soon we'd know whether or not Darian was pregnant. Was there a set timetable? You'd think I'd already know this shit since I had a daughter, but I hadn't had much contact with Ridley's mom after I'd fucked her, other than to make sure my little girl was taken care of once she arrived in this world. The thought of having a kid with Darian filled me with longing. I wanted that. I never thought I'd want more kids, but I do. Ridley disappeared from my life when she was just a tiny thing, even though I traveled to Florida to spend as much time with her as I could over the years. Having a kid with Darian would mean I'd have a chance to do the parenting thing the right way, and I'd get to enjoy every second of my kid's life this time.

"You just got this weird look on your face," she said, as the waitress set our plates on the table.

"Need anything else?" the waitress asked.

"I think we're good, thanks," Darian said, then focused on me again. "What were you thinking?"

"Just imagining you pregnant."

Her jaw dropped a little, and she stared at me. "I know we discussed that it was possible, but I didn't realize it was something you really wanted."

"I want it. With you. Only with you."

She smiled a little and ate a few more bites. I could tell by the look of rapture crossing her face that steak was definitely a big hit. I might not make one as tasty as these, but I'd have to keep some on hand to grill for her whenever she wanted another one. Or we could just come back here.

"When will we know if my dad is coming?" she asked.

"I don't think he'll warn us. I have a feeling he'll just show up. He's probably going to want some answers once he finds out who was checking into him, especially since Wire was searching for Scratch's real name. That's going to likely make warning bells go off in the man's head."

"How could he not know about me? We have the same last name. How could he have been put on my birth certificate without knowing I exist?"

"I don't know, Darian. I think each state is different when it comes to that kind of thing. But it's possible he did know about you, and maybe he and your mom just weren't compatible. I can't imagine him willingly walking away from you, though."

I hadn't known her that long, but I honestly couldn't see someone meeting her and not wanting to spend more time with her. She was sweet, and even though she'd led a hard life, there was still an innocence about her, and not just because she'd been a virgin. Ever since I'd laid eyes on her, I'd felt this urge to protect her. And that's exactly what I'd do, even if I had to protect her from her daddy. Getting on the bad side of Devil's Boneyard wasn't overly smart, but no one was going to hurt Darian on my watch.

We finished our meal, and I paid the check. When we stepped outside she reached for my hand, her slender fingers sliding against my palm. She was so much smaller than I was, and her hand felt delicate in mine. I looked up at the stars for a moment and just breathed in the fresh air. Darian leaned her head against my arm, and I smiled down at her. I'd done some really fucked-up things in my lifetime, and I had no idea what I'd ever done to deserve an angel like her, but I was going to hold tight and never let her go.

"What are you thinking?" she asked softly.

"That I don't deserve you."

She gave me a startled look. "You don't deserve me? Are you kidding me? I'm the one who doesn't deserve you."

I kissed her softly. "We'll just have to agree to disagree on this one. Come on, baby. Let's go home."

"Home. I like the sound of that."

I did too. I helped her into the truck before walking around to the driver's side. My phone chirped in my pocket, and I pulled it out, swiping the screen and opening a text from Wire.

They're still here.

What the fuck did that mean? I dialed his cell and waited for him to answer.

"Who the fuck is still here?" I asked when he picked up.

"The guy who brought Darian and some of the thugs who were going to harm her. Thought you'd want to know. I was able to track them down. For whatever reason, the asshole didn't leave town. I could be wrong, but I think they're looking for another girl to, um, party with."

I growled into the phone. "Not on my watch."

"Want me to send some guys to round them up? I can have them delivered to our special place at the back of the property."

"Yeah. Do that, then call me. I'd like to have a conversation with them."

Although, I didn't plan to use my voice for most of it. Wire disconnected the call ,and I climbed into the truck. Darian gave me a worried look, but I smiled and winked, hoping to set her at ease. That last thing she needed to know was that the garbage hadn't left town yet. I didn't want her more worried than she already was. While I didn't know for certain she was pregnant, I remembered Venom being concerned about stressing Ridley out during her pregnancies. I didn't want to do anything that would harm Darian or a child she might be carrying.

"Everything okay?" she asked as I pulled out onto the street.

"Everything's fine. I just need to take care of some business later on, but we can go home right now. Wire said he'd call when I'm needed."

"Is it dangerous?" she asked softly.

"No, baby. I'll be perfectly fine."

She seemed to take me at my word and didn't say anything else the rest of the way home. The silence between us wasn't awkward, though. I pulled through the gate, waving to one of our newer Prospects. He held up a hand, making me pull to a stop.

"What's up, Gabe?" I asked.

I hadn't had many dealings with the man just yet. He'd only asked to prospect a few weeks ago, when he'd returned home from the military. Seemed like a good enough guy, even if he did have that haunted look in his eyes. I knew what that look meant. He'd seen too much shit, and probably done too much shit, things that would likely fester inside him until he figured out how to deal with it.

"Heard about your job later," Gabe said, glancing toward Darian. "If you need someone to watch over her while you take care of business, I'm finished here in another half hour. Johnny's taking over after that."

"Thanks, Gabe. I appreciate it."

"Anytime, Bull."

I drove down the winding road through the compound until I reached the house, then parked in the driveway. Darian got out and went straight inside the house, leaving the door open for me. I couldn't remember ever really locking my doors around here, but I didn't want anyone to disturb us, so after I shut the front door, I twisted the deadbolt into place before following my woman through the house.

Wasn't hard to find her since she'd left a trail of breadcrumbs for me to follow. First were her shoes and socks, then her shirt. A few more steps and I came across her jeans. By the time I reached the bedroom, I'd found her bra and panties too, and my woman was lounging on the bed, naked as could be. Just the way I liked her. I smiled and started stripping out of my clothes.

"Does my baby need some extra attention?" I asked as I prowled closer.

She licked her lips as her gaze zeroed in on my cock. I was already hard, but fuck if that didn't turn me on even more. Reaching out, I grabbed her ankles and dragged her across the bed. She gave a little squeak and bit her lip in a way that drove me wild. As much as I loved seeing her wrap those lips around my cock, I didn't have enough patience right now. My palms pushed at her inner thighs until her legs parted, and I groaned as the scent of her arousal teased me.

"Fuck, baby. You're already soaking wet."

"Only you can do that to me. It only takes a look, or just sharing the same air with you," she admitted. "I can pretty much just think about you and get all hot and bothered."

"I am one lucky, lucky man." My finger trailed along the lips of her pussy. "All this cream for me?"

"Uh-huh."

I licked her juices from my finger and loved the way her eyes darkened as she watched me. As much as I would love to play all night with her, I knew Wire would be calling before long, and I'd have work to take care of. She deserved more than a fast, hard fuck, but that was about all I could do right now.

"I don't have time for slow right now, baby."

"I don't care. I just want you, Michael."

I hesitated only a moment before gripping her hips and slowly sinking into her. Christ, but she was so fucking tight! I didn't stop until I was buried deep in her pussy. Darian moaned, and I felt her silken walls clench me even tighter. She was going to fucking kill me, but it was the best damn way to go. I tried to be slow and easy, wanting to prolong the moment. I thrust hard and deep again and again, loving the way her body accepted me. We fit together so perfectly, as if we were made for one another.

"More," she begged. "Don't hold back."

"Darian." I growled a little, then tightened my grip on her hips and drove into her. I fucked her so damn hard that she'd have scooted across the mattress if I hadn't been holding onto her. She cried out as her cheeks flushed, and a look of pure bliss crossed her face.

I heard my phone going off in the pocket of my jeans, discarded near the bedroom door, but hell if I was stopping to answer it. I was close, so fucking close, but I wasn't going to come until she did. No way I would do that to her. I released one hip and brushed my thumb across her clit. Darian gasped, and I felt her body tighten.

"That's it, baby. Come for me."

She whimpered as I teased her little nub, and soon I felt her release coating my cock as she screamed out my name.

"Michael! Don't stop. God, don't stop!" Her hands clawed at the bedding as her back bowed.

I kept thrusting until the last of her orgasm began to ebb, and then I finally let go, roaring out my release as I filled her tight little pussy full of cum. My cock pulsed inside her as I fought to catch my breath. She lay limp and sated, a slight smile curving her lips. As much as I hated to cut our time short, my phone was going off again, and I knew I couldn't put things off any longer.

Leaning down, I claimed her lips, my arm curving under her back to press her tight against my chest. God, but I loved the way she felt in my arms! If I hadn't asked for the particular job waiting for me, I'd have blown it off and stayed right where I was.

"Gotta go, baby. I'll be back soon as I can."

I kissed her once more, then eased out of her sweet pussy. Since I was likely going to get messy anyway, I didn't bother with a shower and just pulled my clothes back on. I winked at her before I disappeared out the door, hoping to ease the worried look in her eyes. Part of me wanted to tell her what was going on, but I didn't know how she'd react. Even though they'd tried to hurt her, I wasn't sure if she'd want me to retaliate or not. She was such a sweetheart; she could be the type to forgive them. And that I wasn't going to allow. They were going to pay, and pay dearly.

When I stepped out of my house, Gabe was already lounging against his bike in the driveway. He nodded to me, and I knew he'd keep an eye on Darian. He wouldn't let anyone into my home while I was away, and if my woman needed something, someone was here to help her. I only hoped she remembered that Gabe was stopping by and didn't go wandering past any windows without clothes on.

I took my bike and drove through the compound. The houses and duplexes disappeared and soon the road was only banked by trees. When I reached the back of the property, an old barn loomed against the skyline. Thanks to Wire, I knew what I'd find inside. One Leo Martin, and three of his cohorts. Men who had thought to harm the precious woman lying in my bed right now. Rage built inside me as I dismounted my bike and pushed open the barn doors.

Four men, who looked like they were a range of ages from early twenties to early thirties, were tied to chairs. Each held a defiant look, as if they thought there was actually an escape from this situation. Oh, there was an escape, but not the one they were hoping for. Two Prospects shut the barn doors behind me, and I advanced into the space. I stopped a few feet from the men and studied each one.

"Which one of you is Leo?" I asked.

"Far left," Ivan said.

I looked at the man who had sold out my woman to his friends. He didn't look like much to me, and I honestly didn't know what Darian had seen in him. His hair looked like it hadn't been washed in a few days, and there was just a slimy appearance to him overall. He reminded me of a used car salesman from those small lots where you just knew the cars were going to fall apart the moment you pulled off the lot, but they still managed to talk you into buying something. Slick. That's what he was.

"Do you know why you're here?" I asked Leo.

He snorted. "I already told your goons. I don't owe no one nothin'. So whatever you think you have on me, you're wrong."

"Those aren't goons. They're my brothers," I said. "And I don't recall saying anything about you owing me something."

Some of Leo's attitude melted away, and there was uncertainty in his eyes. I waited, knowing eventually he'd ask why he was here. The other three were looking his way, probably wondering what the hell he'd gotten them into. They were every bit as much to blame, though. Not one of them had tried to help Darian, and likely they would have raped her. Bile rose in my throat as I thought about any of them putting their hands on her, hurting her that way. No woman deserved such treatment, no man or child either. Animals like these needed to be put down because they would never change. They were sick, twisted, and got off on hurting and degrading others.

"Does the name Darian Crosse mean anything to the four of you?" I asked, watching for a reaction. Three of them didn't so much as blink, but Leo flinched.

"What does that bitch have to do with anything?" he asked.

"That bitch, as you call her, is under my protection. I wasn't at all pleased to hear the story of how she ended up at our front gates. We may have only found four of you, but I know there were others. And eventually, we'll find them too. There's nowhere they can run, nowhere they can hide. They'll slither out of hiding sooner or later, then they'll end up right where you are now. Even if I have to wait months to make it happen."

Leo snorted. "Like you're gonna do anything."

"Shut up," one of the others muttered.

Leo glared at him. "What? He's a pussy."

"He's a fucking Dixie Reaper," the man said. "If he's claimed that girl, none of us are getting out of here."

"Oh, you'll leave this barn," I said. "You just won't be breathing anymore."

Three of my brothers stepped forward. Zipper, Tank, and Flicker lined up beside me, each in front of an asshole tied to a chair. Leo was mine, though. The Prospects stood near the doors, not that we needed a lookout. We were on our own turf, and no one was going to stop what was about to happen.

I pulled off my cut and my shirt, not wanting to get blood on either, handing them off to Ivan. With grim determination, I whaled on Leo, trying to put my fist through his damn face over and over again, before moving down to his ribs and stomach. I beat the hell out of him, leaving him bloody and almost unrecognizable. I didn't stop, not even when his eyes swelled shut, not when he began spitting out teeth. It was like all the fires of hell were burning in my veins as I unleashed my rage on him. I could feel bones give way, and still I went after him.

A hand landed on my shoulder and I glared at Coyote. I hadn't heard him come in and didn't much care when he'd decided to show up. He'd once been known as Pete, while he was prospecting, but he'd been patched in shortly after my daughter arrived. He was a good man, a good brother. But I didn't much like being interrupted right now. I wouldn't be satisfied until the little worm in front of me was six feet under. Maybe we'd even bury him alive, let him choke on dirt.

"You should clean up and get home to your woman," Coyote said. "Word on the street is that

Devil's Boneyard will be here by morning, maybe sooner. Darian needs you. I can finish this up."

"Make sure he's still alive when you remove his fingers and what's left of his teeth. I don't expect the body will ever be found, but let's make sure they can't identify him if it is. I want him to suffer for the vile things he wanted to do to Darian. Make them all fucking suffer."

Coyote nodded. "It will be done. Now leave that shit at the door. Don't take it home to Darian."

I used a utility sink on the far wall to wash as much of the blood off me as I could. If we kept this shit up, we'd need to install a shower out here. Now that more of us were settling down, we tried not to walk around covered in the blood of our enemies. The women tended to get squeamish around such things, not to mention we didn't want the kids to see us this way.

After I pulled on my shirt and my cut, I stopped at the barn doors, taking a deep breath, before I stepped out into the moonlight. The sweet air was refreshing, and like Coyote had suggested, I left all my anger in the barn. It didn't take me long to return home, and with a nod to Gabe, I got off my bike and went into the house to find my woman. If what Coyote said was true, it wouldn't be long before all hell broke loose. I didn't know whether Scratch was coming for Darian, or just because we'd run a search on him. Maybe not knowing was the worst. Was he going to arrive pissed off that we'd been digging through his personal life? Or was he coming for his daughter?

I stopped just inside the bedroom doorway and stared at her a moment. Darian was curled up in the middle of our bed, one of her new pajama sets on, and she looked fucking adorable. I stripped out of my clothes, dumping them in the hamper and hanging up my cut, then quickly showered. I didn't want to take even the slightest chance of having anything of Leo on me when I crawled into bed with her. When I was finished and had towel dried my hair, I slid into bed and pulled her tight against my chest. She murmured in her sleep, then breathed out a sigh, as she settled against me.

"I've got you, baby," I murmured before kissing the top of her head. "And I'm never letting you go."

I only hoped those words didn't come back to bite me in the ass once daddy dearest showed up.

Chapter Seven

Darian

Something was going on, but I didn't know what. Bull was tense, and he'd spent the morning slamming things around in the kitchen while he made breakfast. Now he was brooding over a cup of coffee which, if my nose didn't deceive me, had a splash of rum in it. I wanted him to talk to me, to tell me what was coming, but I was worried that I already knew. The way he was behaving... Damon Crosse was coming. Maybe he was already in town.

I didn't know how to feel about meeting my dad for the first time. Until now, he'd just been a name on a piece of paper. I didn't care who he was, or what MC he was part of, if he thought for one moment that I would walk out the door with him, then he was sadly mistaken. My life was finally turning down a better path, and now that I had Bull, I didn't want to go anywhere. In some ways, we barely knew one another, and in others... it felt like I'd known him forever. When I looked into his eyes, I felt like I'd come home.

His phone chirped with an incoming text, and his expression grew grim as he read it. "We're needed at the clubhouse."

I rubbed my hands against my denim clad thighs. This was it. For the first time in my life, I was going to meet my dad. *Oh, God. I think I may throw up.* Nausea welled inside me, and I bolted out of my seat and ran for the bathroom, losing the breakfast I'd just eaten. I felt Bull rubbing my back in soothing strokes.

"It's okay, baby. I'm not going to let anything happen to you."

"What if he tries to take me away?" I asked as I closed the lid and flushed.

"He won't."

I gave a slight nod, then brushed my teeth and splashed some cool water on my face. I was thankful I hadn't bothered with makeup or it might have run down my face. Bull gripped my hand tightly and led me outside. I was trembling so hard I knew I'd never be able to hold onto him if we took the bike, so I tugged him toward the truck. He helped me onto the passenger seat, then walked around to the driver's side. The ride to the clubhouse was quiet, with not even the radio playing for background noise. A line of bikes was stretched across the front of the building when we arrived, and I started to panic again.

Bull got out of the truck, but when he opened my door, he just cupped my cheek and brushed a kiss against my forehead. "Deep, slow breaths, baby. I promise that I won't let anything happen to you. And neither will any of the other Dixie Reapers. You're part of our family now."

"All right," I said softly.

I gripped his hand tightly as we entered the clubhouse, my eyes adjusting to dim lighting. None of the party girls were around, and for that I was thankful. What I was about to do was hard enough already without dealing with their drama. There were four men at the bar who wore a different cut than everyone else. A horned devil decorated the back, standing on a pile of human bones. *Devil's Boneyard MC* was stitched across the top. When they turned to face us, it only took me a moment to figure out which one was my father. I recognized his eyes, because I saw the same shade of blue every morning when I looked in the mirror.

He looked momentarily startled, then slowly stood. The others followed his lead, and I cowered a little closer to Bull. It was a shit thing to do, and I should have had more backbone, but I didn't know these men, didn't know what they were capable of, and I didn't think I wanted to find out. I saw the front of his cut said *Scratch -- VP*, and I quickly read the others. *Havoc. Shade. Jackal*. One had a title attached to his name, but it was the VP who held my attention.

"I think someone needs to start explaining," Scratch said.

Torch moved closer, as did Venom and several other Dixie Reapers. Bull's hand tightened on mine. I noticed I was the only female in the clubhouse, and I suddenly wondered if that was on purpose. Torch and Venom had made sure their women, and their kids, were nowhere near this mess. And I wished I was in hiding right along with them. I couldn't decipher the look in Scratch's eyes, but I didn't think he was going to be pleased that I was standing here.

"Scratch, this is Darian Crosse. She's Bull's old lady… and your daughter," Torch said.

"My…" Scratch ran a hand through his hair, then fury flashed across his face. "That bitch!"

I flinched and tried to hide behind Bull, but he wouldn't let me. He didn't let go by any means, but he also didn't shield me from Scratch. Maybe he thought I was safe enough, surrounded by the Dixie Reapers, or maybe he just wanted me to face my fear. Scratch noticed, and his gaze softened a moment. He didn't look quite so much like a badass biker when he looked at me like that, and a little of my apprehension faded.

"I'm sorry, Darian. I didn't mean to scare you," he said. "Your momma…"

"I didn't know my mother," I said. Which was mostly true. I'd lived with her, as far as I knew, for the first few years of my life. But I didn't remember anything about her.

"What do you mean you didn't know her?" Scratch asked.

"She gave me up when I was a toddler. I don't remember anything about her."

If we were in a cartoon, I think steam would have billowed out of his ears as his face flushed a bright red. The man looked ready to commit murder, and maybe he was.

"She gave you up?" he asked. "What exactly does that mean?"

"Darian spent her life in foster care," Bull answered for me. "Are you saying you didn't know anything about it? Your name was on her birth certificate, so you must have known she existed."

"Oh, I knew that bitch was pregnant with my daughter, and I was even there for the birth. I didn't stick around, though, and maybe I should have. Once she'd found out she was pregnant, she'd taken off to Georgia. I tracked her down and filled out all the proper paperwork to make sure my daughter had my name. I'd never have done it, but I didn't trust the slut who gave birth to her. Being my daughter was a double-edged sword for Darian. If people knew about her, they could use her against me. But there was also the chance that it could save her. Then that woman called me about two years later and told me Darian had died," Scratch said.

"You never thought to check?" Torch asked.

Scratch shrugged. "I didn't think I had any reason to doubt her. I'd always figured she'd try to get as much money out of me as she could. I paid child support, and even got to see Darian a few times."

"So you wanted me?" I asked. "You didn't abandon me?"

He took a step closer, but Bull growled at him, freezing the man in his tracks. "No, sweetheart. I didn't abandon you. I have no idea how she managed to give you up without me knowing about it."

"I think I can answer that," Wire said. "There's a paper trail on Darian, and it includes a waiver from you, stating you were waiving your rights to your daughter. It's dated the month before Darian was put into the system."

"I'm gonna kill that bitch," Scratch said.

"You'd have to bring her back from the dead first," Wire said. "She overdosed."

"Good riddance," my father muttered. He looked like he wanted to get closer to me, and I slowly released Bull's hand and took a few steps toward Scratch.

"I know you're my dad, but I don't know you." I bit my lip. "But I'd like to."

He smiled a little. "I'd like that too, sweetheart."

"So much for the Devil's Boneyard being all child-free bachelors," one of the Dixie Reapers snorted.

Darkness entered Scratch's eyes. "People are going to try to use you against me, Darian. I can't change that. It's just part of this way of life. The club was into some bad shit a while back. We got rid of the rotten apples, so to speak, but there are still enemies out there who would do anything to hurt us. Including taking you."

"They'll never get their hands on her," Bull said. "She might be your daughter, but she's part of the Dixie Reapers family too. And we take care of our own."

Scratch narrowed his eyes. "And how exactly did my precious daughter end up shackled to you?"

"That's a story that's going to require some alcohol," Torch said. "Why don't you claim a table and get to know your daughter a little, then we'll talk."

Scratch nodded, and I followed him to a nearby round table. I sank onto a chair, and Bull sat beside me. Scratch kept eyeing him, like he didn't quite trust the man in my life. I remembered something that had been said once we'd learned just who my daddy was. He'd helped Bull's daughter, Ridley.

I nudged Bull. "Shouldn't you thank him?"

"For what?" Bull muttered.

"Ridley," I said simply.

He sighed and nodded.

"Ridley?" Scratch asked.

"My daughter got into some trouble a few years ago. She stopped at your chop shop on her way here. You gave her a bike and destroyed her phone," Bull said.

Scratch's eyebrow went up. "Are you telling me that sweet girl that was escaping that Benton asshole is your daughter?"

"Yeah, that was my daughter you helped."

"Isn't she older than Darian? And yet you've claimed *my* daughter as your old lady? You don't think that's a little fucked up?" Scratch asked.

"He didn't force me to be with him," I said, wanting to defuse the situation. "Bull makes me feel safe, and I know he cares about me. I care about him too. And…"

"And what?" Scratch asked.

My cheeks flushed. "I could be pregnant. It's too soon to tell yet."

- 245 -

Scratch shook his head before focusing on Bull again. "You hurt her, and I will end you. If I'd known she was still alive, you'd have never gotten your hands on her. She's fucking Devil's Boneyard royalty, and you don't deserve her."

"I'm the one who doesn't deserve him," I told my father. "You have no idea what my life has been like, or what he's saved me from. You don't get to sit there and judge him."

Scratch seemed amused by my outburst. "Very well. You're all grown up, and despite what your mother did, you seem to have turned out pretty good. If he's what you want, I won't stand in the way. But I'm also not going anywhere. You ever need me, I'll be here. And I better damn sure get to see any grandkids you give me."

"I can agree to that," I said.

"I'm sure the Devil's Boneyard has their own holiday celebrations, but you're welcome to stay with us at Christmas. I'd imagine you'd want to spend this one with your daughter, now that you know she's still alive," Bull said.

Scratch opened his mouth to respond just as the clubhouse door flew open and slammed against the wall. A petite redhead stormed inside with a Prospect hot on her heels.

"I'm sorry, Tank. I tried to stop her," the Prospect said as he reached for the redhead's arm.

"Don't you fucking touch me!" she said, snapping her teeth at him.

Tank groaned and met the redhead in the middle of the room. "What the fuck are you doing here, Josephine?"

"It's Josie," she said. "I hate that fucking name, and you damn well know it."

"Fine. What the fuck are you doing here, Josie?" Tank asked.

"Mom has gone too damn far this time. Either you do something or I won't be held responsible for my actions."

I leaned closer to Bull and whispered, "Who's Josie?"

"Tank's little sister," he muttered. "Half-sister. She's a little younger than you, and quite the handful."

Scratch chuckled as he watched his guys. "I'm thinking Jackal might like to attempt taming her. I haven't seen him with quite that look on his face before."

I looked toward the man called Jackal and realized my daddy was right. There was a gleam in his eyes that said he'd love to get his hands on Josie. He wasn't bad looking, but he was closer to Tank's age than Josie's, and something told me her big brother wasn't going to like that.

"You know your whore mother doesn't listen to a fucking thing I say," Tank said. "You're nineteen, Josie. Move the fuck out."

"And go where?"

Tank shrugged.

Josie screeched and stomped her foot before marching over to the bar. The Prospect handing out drinks stared at her wide-eyed, and I couldn't really blame him. She looked like she would be a force to be reckoned with. I didn't think I'd ever met anyone quite like her before.

"Whiskey," she snapped at the Prospect.

"You're underage," Tank said.

"Since when do you obey the law?" she sneered.

Tank tossed his hands into the air and turned away from her. "Someone else can deal with this shit."

Jackal moved a little closer to Josie, but the redhead seemed oblivious as she threatened the Prospect if he didn't serve her a damn whiskey.

"Are they always like that?" I asked.

Bull snorted. "Pretty much."

"I think Jackal's about to make a move on her," I said.

"He won't hurt her," Scratch said. "Can't promise he won't make her scream his name, though."

"Daddy!" I hadn't meant to call him that, but it felt good. I'd always wondered what it was like to have a father, and now I found out I had one who actually wanted me.

His gaze jerked to mine, surprise flashing in their blue depths.

"Can you please *not* talk about sex in front of me? You may not be a saint, and obviously you got it on with my mom at some point, but I'd like to pretend that I was delivered by a stork. A girl should *never* have to think about sex and her parents," I said.

"I won't talk about sex around you ever again… as long as you keep calling me daddy."

I smiled at him softly. "You're not what I was expecting. I thought you'd storm in here and try to take me away from Bull. I was so scared about meeting you that I threw up this morning."

"If you weren't already claimed, then I would have taken you with me." His gaze flashed to Bull's. "But I don't see a property patch on her."

"It's being made," Bull said. "She's inked, though."

Scratch nodded.

Bull pulled out his phone and frowned at it. "Isabella and Ridley are out front."

"They can come in, can't they?" I asked. Now that I'd faced the fear of meeting my dad, I was ready to meet Bull's daughter.

"We're still an unknown to Torch," Scratch said. "He's not going to want his woman in here. Not that we'd hurt any of you. Now that my baby is part of the Dixie Reapers, maybe we should talk about some sort of agreement between our two clubs."

Bull nodded. "I'm sure Venom and Torch would be agreeable to that. Can't ever have too many allies."

"If they aren't coming in, why are they here?" I asked, pulling Bull's attention back to the fact his daughter was outside.

"They want to take you somewhere, but you don't have to go if you don't want to," Bull said.

"Go on, sweetheart," Scratch said. "As long as it's okay with your old man. I'll stick around for a day or two, and we'll catch up."

Bull kissed my cheek, then helped me stand, giving me a nudge toward the clubhouse door. I glanced back once, happy to see they were getting along, and then stepped out into the sunshine. Ridley and Isabella were leaning against an SUV, both dressed similarly to me.

"I'm so not calling you Mom," Ridley said.

I faltered for a moment and nearly tripped before I burst out laughing.

She grinned and so did Isabella.

"Where are the kids?" I asked.

"We left them with Johnny," Isabella said. "They adore him."

Ridley nodded. "Sometimes I think my kids like Johnny better than they like me."

"So, your dad said you wanted to take me somewhere?" I asked.

Ridley nodded. "Get in. We're having a girls' day."

"A girls' day?" I asked, my brow furrowed. I'd never had one of those before. What exactly did someone do on a girls' day? Was it like in the movies with spa trips and shopping? Then again, these women were Dixie Reapers. Wouldn't surprise me if a girls' day for them included going to the shooting range or something.

"Did you have breakfast?" Isabella asked.

"Um, sort of."

"Sort of?" Ridley asked.

"I ate, but then I was so stressed about meeting my dad for the first time that I threw it back up."

Isabella's gaze dropped to my stomach, and I folded my arms across myself.

"I'm not pregnant," I said. "Or rather, I don't know if I am. It's way too soon to tell."

"Just in case, better not be doing anything that would be bad for a pregnant woman," Isabella said.

Ridley's cheeks flamed and my jaw dropped. "You're pregnant!"

She shrugged. "It wasn't planned, and no one but Venom knows right now. I mean, Mariah is still so little and we'd hoped to wait another year or so before we talked about having a third baby."

Isabella snorted. "You know, just because there was a gap between Farrah and Mariah, it didn't mean that you would have trouble getting pregnant. You should have used protection if you didn't want another one so soon."

Ridley arched a brow. "Really? Does that mean you and Torch are practicing safe sex? Because I hardly see our President not doing his damnedest to knock you up again."

Isabella just grinned. "I'm still making him wait. When I had Lyssa, I made the doctor tell him it would be at least eight weeks before we could have sex again."

"You're terrible," Ridley said with a giggle. "Come on, Darian. We'll go get breakfast and who knows what mischief we'll get into after that. I'm going to enjoy my kid-free day. I love my little monsters, but good Lord, they're exhausting."

We all climbed into the SUV, and as I settled in the backseat, I realized that I'd been worried for nothing. I liked these women, and maybe for once in my life, I'd have some friends. They chattered away the entire car ride, making sure to include me. After fifteen minutes, we pulled to a stop outside a cute white stucco building with a black-and-white striped awning over the red front door. It looked quaint with flower boxes spilling over with brightly colored blossoms along the front.

"Where are we?" I asked.

"It's this little French place we discovered. They have the best breakfast," Isabella said.

I bit my lip, suddenly remembering I didn't have my purse, or any money. Isabella seemed to understand my hesitance of getting out of the car and reached back to grab my hand.

"Hey, today is my treat as a welcome to the Dixie Reapers, okay? Just make sure Bull sets up an account for you before too long. We escape for shopping trips or lunch whenever we can. Besides, you'll feel like you have more freedom if you have your own money."

Would it really be mine, though, if Bull gave it to me? I'd always worked for what I had, and it seemed almost lazy to just sit around and not do anything. Not that I would presume to think that of either Isabella or

Ridley. I was certain their kids kept them busy, and maybe one day I'd have a baby with Bull. It would be fun, getting all the kids together for play dates and stuff, all the things I never got to do as a kid.

The inside of the restaurant was nice, but not so nice that I felt out of place. Comfortable. That was a good word for it. The hostess seated us on a patio out back and left menus with us before wandering off. The area was covered in more fragrant blossoms, and I thought it was probably the most charming place I'd ever seen. I wondered if I could talk Bull into coming here with me, then giggled as I thought about my big badass biker in a place like this.

Ridley grinned. "You just pictured my dad in this place, didn't you? We had the same reaction when we first discovered this place. Torch and Venom would be so out of place, but they'd come if we asked them to."

"Do either of your guys ask you to call them anything other than their club names?" I asked, wondering if that was just something Bull had asked of me.

Isabella smiled. "I call Torch by his given name, but only when it's just the two of us. Although, I occasionally slip. He just gives me a mock glare and swats my ass when it happens."

"Do you know that Venom and I were together long enough for our first daughter to be born before he even told me his name? I've called him Venom for so long I just keep doing it. But his legal name is on the girls' birth certificates," Ridley said. "I think at this point, it would feel weird to call him anything other than Venom."

Isabella winked at me. "Bull asked you to call him something else, didn't he?"

I nodded. "He asked me to call him Michael."

Ridley's eyes went wide. "He actually told you his name? Hell, I spent most of my childhood thinking Bull was his real name. The man's like a damn vault when it comes to his identity."

I snickered. "He seemed rather adamant that I use his given name when it's just the two of us. He said everyone else calls him Bull, but that I'm special."

Ridley smiled softly. "Sounds like maybe my dad is finally going to be happy. I'm glad he found you, Darian. It's a little weird that we're about the same age, and if you have a baby, then my little brother or sister is going to be the same age as my kids, but I think you're going to be good for my dad. And maybe he'll be good for you too."

"Torch wouldn't tell me how you met Bull," Isabella said.

"He saved me," I said, then told them a little about how I'd ended up in Alabama and what my life had been like. I didn't want their sympathy, but I didn't want to feel like I was hiding things from them either.

Isabella and Ridley shared their stories with me of how they'd come to be with the Dixie Reapers. By the time we'd finished eating and had drunk our weight in sweet tea, they'd talked me into going to a movie with them. I'd never hung out with women my age before, or hung out with anyone ever really. I was loving every minute of it, and I hoped we'd have many more days like this in the future.

Chapter Eight

Bull

Scratch rubbed a hand over his jaw. "So you took care of the assholes who were going to hurt my baby girl?"

I nodded. "I beat the hell out of the main guy, but my brothers finished them off. There are still some out there, but we'll get them eventually. I haven't had a chance to speak to anyone yet, but I'm hoping those four gave up some more names before they died."

Torch nodded at Zipper. "Tell him what you know."

"Two of them sang like canaries, in hopes we'd end their lives painlessly. We have the name of every person who was at the party, and Wire is already working on tracking them down. Any financial accounts he finds along the way he's hacked into and diverted the funds into an account for Darian. Seems only fair."

"Any of them still in town?" Scratch asked. "My brothers and I would love to have a chat with them."

Torch looked at me with raised eyebrows. Since Darian was my woman, it was up to me who dealt the justice to those assholes. I shrugged, not really caring. Leo was the main one I had wanted, and I'd let loose on him already. As long as everyone paid the price, I didn't much care who took care of it. And as a father, I understood Scratch's need to protect Darian, even if he hadn't known she was still alive until today.

"Let Devil's Boneyard have them," I said.

Torch nodded. "I'll make sure Wire hands them any info he finds. He seems familiar with Shade, so maybe the two can work together on it. Now, on to other matters."

"An alliance," Scratch said. "I called Cinder before we came in here, and he's given his permission for me to make an agreement on behalf of Devil's Boneyard."

"You're far enough away we won't be able to work together on a regular basis, but if you need our aid, we'll answer," Torch said. "And I hope you'll do the same when we require assistance."

"We can do that," Scratch said. "We won't encroach on your territory if you stay out of ours, as far as business goes. You're welcome to visit anytime you want."

There was a knock on the door, making Torch frown.

"Enter," he barked.

One of the Devil's Boneyard members stepped into the room and looked uncertainly at Scratch. "I didn't want to interrupt, but we have a problem. Maybe a big one."

"What's that?" Scratch asked.

"Jackal took off with that redhead," he said. "And I don't think he's stopping until he reaches the Devil's Boneyard compound."

"Fuck," I muttered.

Tank groaned and banged his head on the table. "Fuck my life."

I snickered, knowing that his baby sister had been a pain in his ass since he'd found out about her. Tank's daddy had liked getting around, so there was no telling how many other siblings might be out there somewhere. I felt a little sorry for the guy, but I knew he was fond of Josie in his own way.

Torch chuckled. "It's not a problem. Our agreement stands. But you might want to give Cinder a heads-up. Josie can be quite the handful, and she isn't opposed to causing chaos everywhere she goes. Wouldn't surprise me if the two of them taking off wasn't her idea."

Tank snorted. "She can wrap just about any guy around her finger just by batting her eyes. Your guy didn't stand a chance."

Scratch looked at Tank with raised eyebrows. "So if he were to claim her, you wouldn't be opposed?"

"His funeral," Tank muttered. "No one in their right mind would volunteer to spend more than an hour in Josie's presence. She's like a squirrel on speed."

He wasn't wrong. The few times I'd encountered Josie, she'd arrived ready to party. And I knew that Tank had gone to rescue her more times than I could count because she was in one scrape or another. But maybe what she needed was a steady man in her life, someone to calm her ass down, or spank it whenever she got out of hand. Jackal looked young, well younger than me by at least a decade, but I had a feeling he wouldn't have much trouble keeping Josie in hand. Maybe they'd be good for each other.

"We have some rooms here in the clubhouse that aren't being used," Torch said. "You're welcome to them during your stay. I try to keep things fairly tame during the day in case our families drop by, but by dinner this place will start to get lively, and the club sluts will pour through the doors. You're welcome to join us for as long as you'd like."

Scratch nodded. "It's appreciated. I know I'd like to stay a few days so I can get to know my daughter, but the others are free to go whenever they want. Or whenever Cinder calls for them."

"In that case," Torch said, slamming the gavel on the table. "Meeting adjourned. Get the fuck out of here."

"Anyone know where those women and my daughter went?" Scratch asked.

"They'll take care of her, but I wouldn't expect them back for a few hours," Torch said. "They love to shop."

Scratch nodded, then looked at me. "Then I guess that gives us some time to get to know one another. Seeing as how we're family now."

Ah hell. I hadn't thought about that aspect of things. Yep, I was now tied to the Devil's Boneyard, through Darian. The Dixie Reapers might have an agreement with them now, but I had a feeling that Scratch would be calling especially on me for any future issues. Not that I had a problem with that. Family looked out for one another, or they were supposed to. I wanted Darian to have the family she'd missed out on her entire life, and for that to happen, I needed to get along with her dad.

I followed Scratch out to the bar, where he asked for two beers from Robby, another fairly new Prospect. I couldn't remember a time we'd had so many. Although, more Prospects meant the patched members didn't have to do all the shit jobs that popped up, so it was nice having so many around. They'd either make the cut and patch in, or they'd wander off and more would replace them.

"I never wanted this way of life for my little girl," Scratch said. "But I figured, if she'd lived, that one day she'd end up with a biker. Of course, I'd thought it would be a Devil's Boneyard member. I can't believe her fucking mother gave her up."

I took a swallow of my beer before answering. "She had a hard life in the system, and even afterward. But I think the hardest thing was that she thought no one wanted her. I know you believed her bitch of a mom when she said Darian died, but why the hell didn't you check up on it? From what I've gathered, her mom wasn't exactly the truth-telling type. Didn't you wonder about a funeral?"

"Truth be told, as much as I was heartbroken over my daughter dying, I was relieved not to be tied to her mom anymore. That woman was a financial drain, and now I'm thinking Darian probably didn't see a penny of that money. It likely went to partying and drugs for her mom, which seriously pisses me the fuck off. The few times I got to see her, she seemed all right. Looked healthy enough and was dressed decently, but now I think her mom was just putting on an act for me so I wouldn't take away her cash cow."

"You have a chance to do right by your daughter now, and I'm not talking financially. I've got her covered. But she'd probably be thrilled if you called every now and then to check on her, once you go back home."

He nodded. "I can do that. Is there anything she needs, though? I don't doubt that you can provide for her, but I feel like I owe her something."

"She could use a car. I was thinking about getting her a SUV sometime this week. I know you have a chop shop, though, so if you have something she might like, I won't stand in your way," I said.

Scratch snorted. "I'm not giving my daughter a hot car. But I will make sure she has a new set of wheels before I leave town."

"So, you said that Devil's Boneyard remained single and kid-free because of some shit that went down. Do I need to worry about your past sins coming knocking on my door?" I asked. "You didn't want kids so they couldn't be used as leverage, and now you have a grown daughter. I just need to know how vigilant I need to be. Are we talking regular type club shit, or something worse?"

"I honestly don't know. I think all that shit is settled now, most of it was dead and buried with our last Pres, but you know how all that works. Just because you think something is over, doesn't always make it so. It's been pretty quiet for the last few years, though." Scratch ran a hand through his hair. "Truth be told, the club sluts are getting tiresome, and I wouldn't mind settling down. I know quite a few of my brothers feel the same way. Finding out about Darian may be the catalyst to really change things within my club."

"Guess that means you aren't pissed anymore that we went digging through your personal shit," I said with a grin.

He gave a bark of laughter. "I guess I actually owe you one. I thought we were coming here to kick some ass, but instead I got knocked on mine."

"When Darian came into the clubhouse, you looked like you'd seen a ghost."

"She looks like a young version of my mother. She has my damn eyes for sure, but the rest of her is all Marian Crosse. Mom would have been thrilled, but she's been gone a long time now. Dad too. I'm afraid the only family Darian has now is me, you, and our clubs. Unless you have other family?" Scratch asked.

"No, just me, my daughter and grandkids, and the Dixie Reapers. My parents are long gone. I think that will be enough for Darian, though. She's been without friends and family for so long, I think being part of the club is a little overwhelming for her. She'll adjust in time, and I'm hoping Isabella and my daughter are helping with that right now, but going from barely scraping by on your own to all this is probably a lot to take in."

Scratch nodded. "I wish I'd known that she needed me all these years. I'd have fought for custody if I thought her mom wouldn't take care of her. I should have known better."

"How'd you meet Darian's mom?" I asked.

"She was a club slut. I was never going to make her my old lady, but she latched onto me the last few months she was with the Devil's Boneyard. When she said she was pregnant, I knew it was mine just because the woman had barely left my bed. And I haven't made that mistake since."

"I wouldn't use the word mistake around Darian," I said. "Not if you're talking about the pregnancy part of that equation."

"Hell, my daughter looks like a fucking angel. She's not the mistake, just her whore mother was. I'll try not speak badly about her mom around her, though. I'm sure there's no love lost there, since she gave up Darian, but I don't want her to think I'm talking trash about the woman. Seems wrong."

Yeah, Scratch was a decent guy, and I was willing to bet he'd have been an awesome dad for Darian. Still could be.

"I know Torch offered you a room here at the clubhouse, but if you want to stay with us, we have a spare room," I said. The thought of having sex with Darian while her dad was just a room away wasn't overly pleasing, but I'd invite the man into our home for her. She needed time with him.

"I appreciate the offer, but I think I'll stay at the clubhouse, at least this time. When I come back, I may take you up on that. Hell, seems like Jackal may have found himself a woman on this visit. Maybe mine will walk through the door too."

I grinned and slapped him on the back. "Just be prepared for awkward family gatherings if you tie yourself to a woman Darian's age. I'm sure my daughter will give me an earful for a while, even though I have no doubt the two will get along great."

Scratch snorted. "Hell, I don't know what kind of woman would settle for a cranky bastard like me. She'd have to be either desperate or something really special. I seem to be in short supply of both types of women these days."

Scratch's phone jingled, and he pulled it out of his pocket, his face going tense as he read the incoming text.

"Christ," he muttered. "Your brother, Tank, may change his mind about killing Jackal."

"What did Josie do now?" I asked.

"Got herself kidnapped," Scratch said. "As much as I want to stick around and spend time with my daughter, I'm being ordered to handle this. I better go talk to Torch and see if any of your brothers want in on this, since Josie is technically Dixie Reapers' property."

I wasn't sure if I wanted to laugh or groan. Not that Josie getting kidnapped was funny, but because that could seriously end badly. That woman got into more trouble than anyone I knew, and knowing her, she likely walked right up to her kidnappers, said something smart, and they nabbed her. Tank would likely join the hunt for her, and maybe a few others, but my ass was staying right here with my woman. Things were still so new between Darian and me that I didn't want to run off to parts unknown for a rescue mission.

"Good luck, man," I said. "Come back and see Darian anytime you want. Door's always open."

He nodded and went to find the Pres. Darian wasn't going to be happy with this turn of events, but I hoped she'd understand. The MC way of life was going to be an adjustment for her, but since her daddy was the VP, he had more responsibility than most. I'd have to explain things to her and hope that Scratch returned before too long. Now that she knew her daddy wanted her, she'd want a relationship with him. And I wanted to make sure that happened. Even if it meant I had to haul her ass to Devil's Boneyard territory.

I finished my beer, then decided to head home until Darian returned. I hoped she was having an amazing time with the girls. The fact I couldn't reach her reminded me that she needed a cell phone. When I stepped out onto the clubhouse porch, instead of heading for home, I went to my local cell phone provider and decided to get Darian a little present. Although, it was more for my peace of mind than anything else. I wanted her to be able to reach me whenever she left the house, and I damn sure didn't like the idea of not being able to call her.

The fact Josie had been kidnapped made me worry that something bad would happen to Darian and I'd never know. While I didn't want to be a controlling asshole, maybe downloading one of those tracker apps to her phone wouldn't be such a horrible idea. I didn't think she'd care too much for it, being as independent as she was, but it could damn well save her life one day. I wouldn't apologize for wanting to protect her.

It took me damn near an hour to get service at the phone store, then select a phone for Darian and get her line activated. A nearby shop caught my eye. *Sinful Pleasures*. I grinned as I headed that way, knowing I would find plenty of things inside for later use with my sexy woman. By the time I got back home, Venom was sitting on my porch with my granddaughters. I loved those little girls with all my heart, but the last thing I wanted to do right now was babysit. I had plans for Darian when she got home, and they didn't involve being quiet with two little girls in the house.

"Is this a family call or are you here as my VP?" I asked as I walked up the steps.

"Farrah was asking for her grandpa," Venom said. "I thought while we waited on Ridley and Darian to return, we could order some pizza and watch movies with the girls."

"Is this a sneaky way for them to meet Darian?" I asked.

He grinned. "Maybe. They really do miss you, though."

"Fine." I sighed. "But after introductions are over, I have plans for my woman… and they don't include two little girls."

"Fair enough."

We went inside, and after I'd put my purchases away, I set up Farrah's favorite DVD while Venom called in our lunch. By the third time the movie played, I was starting to wonder if the women had skipped town and left us with baby duty. The way Venom kept checking his phone he was likely feeling the same way. When the sound of a car pulling into the driveway reached my ears, I moved Farrah from my lap to the couch and met Darian on the front porch.

She melted against me, holding me tight.

"Missed you," she murmured.

"Missed you too, baby. Venom's here with the girls."

"And my dad?" she asked.

"He had to leave on a business matter, but he said he'd return when he could." Her face fell, and I could see the disappointment in her eyes. "If he can't come to us, then we'll go to him, okay? I'll make sure the two of you get some time together."

Darian kissed me, long and deep, before Ridley clomped up the steps and loudly cleared her throat.

"Still adjusting," Ridley said. "Let's not scar me for life, though, okay?"

Darian giggled, and I let the two of them into the house. And just like I'd predicted, both my granddaughters adored Darian. Seeing her hold baby Mariah made me want a family with her in the worst way. I'd always heard that practice makes perfect, and I had no problem practicing all night long every night.

The heated looks she kept casting my way said she felt the same, and I suddenly couldn't wait to get everyone out of my house so I could have some alone time with my woman.

Chapter Nine

Darian

I stood on the porch next to Bull and waved bye to the kids. Not that Mariah could wave yet, but Farrah was waving hard enough to take flight. Ridley and Venom climbed into their SUV and then pulled down the driveway. When all we could see was the glow of their taillights, Bull tugged me into the house and shut the door. He twisted the lock and then gave me a look that nearly melted me.

"You know, I'm suddenly really hungry," I said, retreating a step.

"So am I." He growled and advanced on me.

I bit my lip so I wouldn't smile, then spun and ran for the bedroom. I couldn't help but giggle when he slammed into me, and we both toppled to the bed. I hadn't really wanted to get away from him, but he'd seemed like the type of guy to enjoy a good chase. The hard ridge poking into me said I was one hundred percent correct with that assessment.

"Do you know what happens to naughty girls?" he asked, his breath tickling my ear.

My thighs clenched at his tone. Whatever he had planned, I was up for it. I'd loved everything we'd done together so far, and I was up for exploring a bit more. His body lifted off mine, and he hauled me to my feet, then began stripping my clothes off. When he was finished, he pointed to the bed.

"Hands and knees, facing the headboard. As a matter of fact, why don't you grab hold of the wooden slats?"

I felt myself growing wetter by the minute as I scrambled to obey. I planted my knees in the middle of the bed and grabbed onto the headboard. Michael opened a drawer, and I heard some rustling, and then the clink of metal on metal. I didn't know what he was up to, but my body was tingling in anticipation.

A strip of cloth covered my eyes, and I gasped as he tied it behind my head. I heard the clinking sound again, and a moment later, both my hands were cuffed to the bed. He flattened his hand in the center of my back and pressed until my breasts were flat against the mattress and my ass was in the air. Bull trailed his fingers down my spine, and I felt a sharp sting as he cracked his hand against my ass.

He rubbed away the sting, then he swatted me again. I could feel my ass cheeks burning with every blow, and my pussy started to throb. He placed his hands on the insides of my thighs and spread my legs farther apart, a groan rumbling out of him as the lips of my pussy parted.

"So fucking beautiful," he said, then he nipped me on the ass. "And mine. Completely mine."

"Yes, yours," I murmured.

He swatted me twice more. "I'm taking this ass again. I'm going to fuck it hard and deep, and you're going to beg me for more, aren't you?"

I whimpered getting more and more turned on.

"You don't get to come tonight, until I say you can. Think you can do that for me, baby?"

"I can try," I said.

He spanked me again. "You better more than try, sweet girl. You're not going to get my cock where you want it most if you don't follow directions."

His fingers trailed between the crack of my ass.

"Or maybe you want me to take this ass all night and deprive that sweet pussy."

"No, please."

I heard the lid pop open on the lube. His fingers slid between my ass cheeks, and I fought not to tense up, knowing that he could make me feel really good. Bull scattered kisses across my back as he worked first one finger, then two into my ass, using slow, deep strokes as he prepared me to take his cock. I'd barely started taking three fingers before he withdrew and moved away.

"Wait. Where are you going?"

He chuckled. "Don't worry, pet. I'm coming right back. Just need to get rid of my clothes and get something."

My cheeks flushed, and I worried at my lip. While I loved seeing him naked, it felt extra naughty when he fucked me with his clothes still on.

"Can you... can you leave your clothes on?" I asked softly.

He stopped moving across the room, and everything went so silent it sounded like my heartbeat was echoing in the room.

"Michael?"

"I'm still here. You want me to fuck you with my clothes on?" he asked.

"It... it feels naughtier."

"Well, aren't you just full of surprises. Yeah, baby. If you want my clothes on, I'll keep them on. This time."

I felt the bed dip as he returned, and something bounced on the mattress. My ears strained to hear his every movement since I couldn't rely on my sight. His belt clinked as he unfastened it, then I heard the rasp of his zipper. I thought I heard the bottle of lube being opened again, then his hands stroked my ass. He spread the cheeks wide, and I felt his cock press against me.

"Let me in that tight ass, baby," he murmured. "I'll make it so good for you."

I groaned as he slowly sank into me, his cock making me burn.

"I wish you could see how fucking incredible your ass looks, stretched around my cock. Watching you take me is fucking beautiful."

"More," I begged.

He started stroking in and out of me, each thrust a little harder, a little deeper, until he was almost pounding into me. I cried out in both pleasure and pain. It hurt, but somehow felt so damn good at the same time. One of his hands left me, and I heard a whirring sound.

"Remember what I said. You don't come until I tell you, or you're going to have a very sore ass tomorrow."

He touched a vibrator to my clit, and my hips slammed back against him as I cried out from the shock of pleasure that zipped through me. His cock drove into me as he teased me with the toy. I couldn't help but spread my legs wider, wanting to give him more room to play. It didn't take long for my orgasm to start building, and I didn't know if I'd be able to hold it back or not. It felt stronger than any I'd had before.

"Don't you dare come yet, Darian," he said, his voice holding a hint of growl.

Two more swipes of the toy against my clit, and I couldn't hold on. I started coming, and it felt like I was never going to stop. The pleasure was so intense, with him fucking my ass hard and deep, and the toy buzzing unmercifully, that I thought I might black out. Michael growled as cum shot into my ass, but he didn't stop thrusting. If anything, he seemed to completely lose control and became almost wild in the way he took me.

The toy stayed pressed against me, and one orgasm turned into another. By the time he switched it off and let it fall to the bed, I didn't think I had anything left to give, but he didn't seem anywhere near done with me.

"You came before you were given permission," he said, cracking his hand against my ass.

"I'm sorry."

"I'm not stopping until I fill this sweet ass up with my cum again. And every time you sit down tomorrow, you're going to remember that you disobeyed me. Do you know why?" he asked.

"Why?" I asked, whimpering as his hand cracked against my ass cheek again.

"Because I'm going to fuck this ass hard, and I'm going to spank it until it's red."

His words should have scared me, or at least made me apprehensive. But no, not my traitorous body. If anything, I got even wetter. He drove into me again and again, until he finally came again. His cock twitched and jerked inside me as he panted for breath.

"Christ, woman. I'm getting too damn old to come more than once."

I snorted. "You're not old."

He thrust twice more and smacked my ass again before pulling out. "Guess we'll see how long it takes me to recover."

He removed the blindfold and the handcuffs, then rubbed my wrists. I winced as I rolled onto my back. Yeah, my ass was going to hurt, but I didn't regret a second of what we'd just done. I might be inexperienced, but he was fucking incredible in bed. It was like all he had to do was touch me, and I was ready to take him.

"You okay, baby?" he asked. "I didn't hurt you, did I?"

"I'm good."

He rolled out of bed, and I heard the water running in the bathroom sink. When he came back, he was completely naked. I didn't know why he'd cleaned himself up and not me, unless…

He smirked and reached for the toy. "Feet on the bed and spread those legs, sweet girl. Spread them really fucking wide."

I moaned. Oh God, he wasn't done with me yet. I didn't think I could handle another orgasm, but I did as he said. He clicked the toy on and went straight for my clit. I was still sensitive from coming twice, and if he hadn't splayed a hand across my belly, I may have squirmed away from the touch of the vibrator. It was almost too intense.

"I love it when you spread those legs so damn wide your pussy opens like this. I get to see all of you and see how much you like what I do to you."

The man was going to kill me with all his dirty talking. I was almost certain that if he ever pinned me down and just whispered filthy things in my ear, I'd probably come just from his words alone. Not that I would ever tell him that, or he might actually try it.

"So damn wet," he said, almost reverently.

The toy pressed just a little harder against my clit, and I screamed out his name as I started coming. Michael moved faster than I'd thought possible and before my orgasm had stopped, he was driving his cock into my pussy. He slid a hand under my ass and lifted me, going in deeper with every thrust. He fucked me even after one orgasm turned into two, then he slowly eased from my body.

"You didn't come," I protested.

Michael chuckled. "Sweet girl, I already came twice. I don't think I can come again so fast. But we'll get cleaned up and get something to eat, then maybe you'll let me handcuff you to the bed again."

I licked my lips. "If it's as good as last time, you can handcuff me anytime you want."

"Sassy girl." He leaned down and nipped my lip before kissing me long and hard. "I like it when you're sassy."

"I like it when you're bossy. In the bedroom anyway."

He grinned and kissed me again before leading me into the bathroom and starting the shower. He was so tender and sweet as he washed me, then helped me dry off and get dressed. It sometimes amazed me that the man who was so careful with me, who wanted to make sure I was taken care of, was a badass biker who was probably into things I didn't even want to know about.

I admired the way his muscles flexed as he got dressed, then he gently took my hand and led me out to the truck. I didn't know where he was taking me this time, and I didn't care. As long as I got to spend time with him, then it didn't matter where we went or what we were doing. All that mattered was that we were together.

He snapped my belt buckle into place and as he started to draw away, I reached up and wrapped my hand in his hair, pulling him close again. I pressed my lips to his in a soft kiss.

"I love you."

His eyes widened, and he froze for a moment, then a smile spread across his lips. "Love you too, Darian. I'm one lucky bastard that you came into my life. And that you wanted to stay with me."

"I'm the lucky one."

He winked. "We'll have to agree to disagree."

I knew there was a goofy smile on my face as he closed the door, then walked around to the driver's side, a smile that stayed firmly in place for the entire ride, and even after the hostess seated us. He was mine, and I was his. And nothing else mattered.

Epilogue

Darian
Two Months Later

My dad and Bull were sitting on the couch, sipping beer and watching some show about customizing bikes. They'd gotten along really well during the three days my dad had been with us, and I was grateful for that, even if my sex life had taken a nosedive. I'd tried to get Bull to make love to me that first night my dad was here, and he'd groaned and said he couldn't get hard knowing my daddy was right next door. It had made me giggle at the time, but now I was getting damn frustrated.

I slowly entered the room and stopped in front of my sexy badass. He looked up at me, both eyebrows raised as he waited for me to say whatever was on my mind. A quick glance at my dad showed I had his attention too. Which was perfect.

"You know how you talked about fixing the attic? Adding some bedrooms and maybe a bathroom up there?" I asked.

"Yeah. I figured if we ever had kids we'd need more space," he said.

"Right. So… you have about eight months to get it finished."

My dad snickered, and Bull's jaw dropped.

"Baby, are you trying to say… you're having a baby?" Bull asked.

I nodded.

His beer fell to the floor, spilling across the wood as he grabbed me into his arms and whooped for joy. He spun me in a circle until I became so dizzy I didn't think I could stand upright.

"How long have you known?" my dad asked.

"A few days, but I didn't know how to tell either of you," I said.

"Days?" Bull asked.

"Ridley and I booked a double appointment with her doctor, so I rode with her to see Dr. Myron. They just did a blood test to confirm my pregnancy, but I have another appointment in a few weeks, if you'd like to go with me."

"I'm going to be there every step of the way," he promised.

"If the two of you don't mind, I think I'll just come for the birth," my dad said. "And every major holiday. And all my grandkids' birthdays."

Bull whipped his head around to face my dad. "Was that grandkids plural?"

My dad shrugged. "As fast as you knocked her up, I'm sure there will be others. Might want to build three bedrooms up in the attic."

I hugged Bull tight and made him focus on me again. He looked a little dazed at the thought of having so many kids, and honestly, I didn't care if we had one or four. As long as he was happy, and our kids were loved, that was all that was important. Just being here with him, being loved by him, made me happier than I had ever thought possible. And knowing that we'd created a life together... There were no words to express the amount of joy I felt.

"Thank you," I told him softly.

"For what, baby?"

"For loving me. For giving me a home, a real home. And a family. When you rescued me at the gates that night, you changed my life in so many ways. Before I met you, I wasn't really living. I was just trying to survive day after day. But now. Now my life is pretty perfect."

He cupped my cheek. "I'm the lucky one, sweet girl. You're giving me a second chance, and I'm not going to screw it up. I love you so damn much."

Bull kissed me, and I heard gagging. I snickered as I looked at my dad, who winked at me before giving Bull a disgusted look.

"If you're going to molest my daughter, at least do it where I can't see," my dad said.

"I think that sounds like an excellent idea. Scratch, you know where the clubhouse is. Make yourself scarce."

Bull lifted me into his arms and carried me down the hall to our bedroom. I heard the front door shut and knew my dad wouldn't be back for a while, if at all tonight.

My sexy man lifted my shirt and fell to his knees, pressing a kiss to my belly.

"You're everything I need, Darian, and everything I never knew I needed."

"I think we have the rest of the night to ourselves," I said, running my fingers through his hair. "I'll get naked while you get the handcuffs."

He chuckled and swatted my ass. "I think I created a cock-hungry monster. Don't ever change."

"Never," I promised.

A warm glow filled me as I stared into his eyes. Life had pretty much fucked me over from the time I was born, but somehow, I was exactly where I was supposed to be. In his bed every night and in his arms every morning. And that was precisely how it should be. Bull was the love of my life, and despite our age difference, I knew there was no one more perfect for me.

My hand pressed to my belly. "You're going to have an awesome daddy."

Bull came back over toward me, tossing the handcuffs, lube, and scarf onto the bed. Then he leaned down and placed his face near my belly. "And you have a very naughty mommy. But she's going to love you very much."

I smiled as he rose, looking at me with so much heat.

"Thought you were going to strip," he said.

"I am."

"Then get to it, woman." His hand cracked against my ass. "Just remember what happens when you disobey an order."

I shivered and took my time undressing. He might think that was a threat, but all he did was guarantee that I would misbehave as often as possible, for the rest of our lives. Because if there was anything I loved better than my sweet and tender biker? It was my sexy, dominant badass who demanded to be obeyed.

Who'd have ever thought being bad could be so damn good?

Harley Wylde

Short. Erotic. Sweet.

Harley's other half would probably say those words describe her, but they also describe her books. When Harley is writing, her motto is the hotter the better. Off the charts sex, commanding men, and the women who can't deny them. If you want men who talk dirty, are sexy as hell, and take what they want, then you've come to the right place.

Harley Wylde is the "wilder" side of award-winning author Jessica Coulter Smith. Visit Jessica's website at jessicacoultersmith.com/ or Harley's website at harleywylde.com/. Join her Facebook fan group, Harley's Wyldlings, for book discussions, teasers, and more. For fans of Gay Romance, Harley/Jessica also writes as Dulce Dennison.

Find more books by Harley Wylde at changelingpress.com/harley-wylde-a-196.

Changeling Press E-Books

More Sci-Fi, Fantasy, Paranormal, and BDSM adventures available in E-Book format for immediate download at ChangelingPress.com -- Werewolves, Vampires, Dragons, Shapeshifters and more -- Erotic Tales from the edge of your imagination.

What are E-Books?

E-Books, or Electronic Books, are books designed to be read in digital format -- on your desktop or laptop computer, notebook, tablet, Smart Phone, or any electronic ebook reader.

Where can I get Changeling Press e-Books?

Changeling Press ebooks are available at ChangelingPress.com, Amazon, Barnes and Nobel, Kobo, and iTunes.

ChangelingPress.com

Printed in Great Britain
by Amazon